"How long do you plan to stay today, Murdock?"

"Another hour or so. Then I have to get to work. I have a town to protect."

"I know I feel better knowing you've left *my* house and are out in the community securing our safety."

Wade chuckled and turned back to fixing the window.

Meg smiled as she went into the house. The words she'd just spoken were actually the exact opposite of the way she was beginning to feel about Wade. She'd missed seeing his patrol car in the drive yesterday. And she'd been relieved to find the car by the barn today. As much as she might try to fight it, she was starting to like the man, a dangerous and unwise reaction to a person who was trying to sabotage her dreams for the future. But, darn it, he was just easy to like.

"Keep your mind on your goal, Meggie," she said to herself. "Find the deed and protect your rightful ownership of this house. Remember, Wade Murdock has a good job and a secure future. He'll survive the disappointment."

Dear Reader,

This book is about special places. We all have at least one. It could be a place we've visited all our lives or one we've yet to discover, but it's out there waiting for us to stumble upon its magic. My special place is a rambling old farmhouse in western Kentucky where my aunt and uncle lived and where I spent some of the happiest moments of my life.

It's gone now, this house, passed to other hands, to hearts that I hope will hold it as closely as I still do. In my mind I will always remember the plank wood floors, the old wooden rockers, the upright piano and every Christmas decoration that turned this home into a wonderland each December.

In these pages you will read about such a house and two very different, wounded people who both long to cherish it forever. But only one of them can have it. I hope you enjoy this journey of a man and woman who find their heart's desire, and perhaps a miracle or two, within the walls of a very special place.

I love to hear from readers. Please visit my Web site, www.cynthiathomason.com, or e-mail me at cynthoma@aol.com. My address is P.O. Box 550068, Fort Lauderdale, Florida 33355.

Sincerely,

Cynthia Thomason

Your House or Mine?

Cynthia Thomason

HARLEQUIN®

TORONTO • NEW YORK • LONDON
AMSTERDAM • PARIS • SYDNEY • HAMBURG
STOCKHOLM • ATHENS • TOKYO • MILAN • MADRID
PRAGUE • WARSAW • BUDAPEST • AUCKLAND

ISBN 0-373-71268-5

YOUR HOUSE OR MINE?

www.eHarlequin.com

Printed in U.S.A.

This book is dedicated to my best "Buddy,"
my husband and cherished traveling companion
for the past twenty-six years. Thanks, Walter, for paying
my admission to all those tours of old houses
and never once complaining.

Books by Cynthia Thomason

HARLEQUIN SUPERROMANCE
1120—THE MEN OF THORNE ISLAND
1180—THE HUSBAND SHE NEVER KNEW
1232—THE WOMEN OF BAYBERRY COVE

CHAPTER ONE

MEG HAMILTON REACHED for the telephone with one hand and grabbed a pen and paper with the other. She flinched at the recurring pain in her neck as she once again held the receiver to her ear with her shoulder and said, "Colonial Auction House. Meg speaking."

She tried to be patient with the caller. "Mrs. Winkler, as I told you yesterday, you don't have to call every afternoon to confirm. You have an appointment for tomorrow. Our buyer will be at your home just as I explained to you a week ago when you first contacted us."

She nodded her head several times in tempo with the nervous woman's plaintive voice. "Yes, I promise. My brother Jerry will be coming with a truck and a helper. They'll pick up anything you want to consign to the auction." She blew out a long breath as the caller once again repeated what Meg had just said. "Yes, that's right. Until tomorrow then. Goodbye, Mrs. Winkler."

Meg leaned forward to settle the phone into its cradle. Then she put her elbows on the desk and massaged her temples. It was four o'clock, the end of an especially grueling day. Time to pick up her son at the neighbor's house and go home, if only Jerry would get back from his last call of the day. She was imagining a tall glass of iced tea and her favorite chair when she heard the repetitious beep of the auction house truck as it backed up to the loading door. "Thank goodness."

Moments later Jerry poked his smiling face inside the entrance of their building. "Hi, sis, has it been busy around here?"

Meg could only stare at him. It really was a rhetorical question because he darned well knew the answer. She often thought Jerry got the best of the deal in their business partnership, just as he'd gotten off easy growing up as her kid brother. He drove around in the truck all day making house calls and picking up merchandise for their weekly auctions. She was stuck in the building for eight hours answering the phone, handling drop-in customers, and inputting auction debits and credits on a computer spreadsheet, not to mention acting as the auctioneer.

She didn't even try to hide her fatigue and frustration when she said, "If I have to answer that phone one more time…"

Of course it rang.

"Get that, will you, Meggie?" Jerry said. "I want to bring something from the truck to show you."

She groaned once, picked up the phone, and immediately switched to her professional voice. She politely explained to the caller that a ten-year-old sofa which had coexisted with eight cats probably would not sell at Colonial Auction. She'd just ended the call when Jerry clanked and rattled back into the building.

Meg gaped at the rough-hewn piece of lumber in his right hand. It was about ten inches in diameter and nearly as long as he was tall. In his left hand he held an assortment of chains and hooks and other metal fittings she couldn't identify.

Jerry dragged the contraption to the desk and stood grinning down at her. "Isn't it great?"

"*It* might have been once," she admitted. "But now, maybe a hundred years later, I haven't the faintest idea what *it* is."

"You're wrong about the age. It's more than a hundred years old." Jerry stood the end of his worn log on the office carpet and gave the antique a look of reverence. "This probably went west with the pioneers a hundred and fifty years ago."

Jerry imagined potential heirlooms in every cast-off piece of flotsam sticking out of a garbage can. And he was usually wrong. Meg liked old things too, pretty ones whose value could be verified in a collector's catalogue.

She scrunched up her nose at the worm-eaten log. "You still haven't told me its use," she said. "If, indeed it has, or had one."

"It's a doubletree," he announced, draping the chains over his shoulder and running his palm halfway down the length of the lumber. "See how it's arched in two places…" He jerked his hand away and pulled a splinter out of his little finger with his teeth.

Meg automatically opened a drawer to get the antiseptic ointment and tin of bandages she always kept handy.

"That's so the farmer or wagon driver could fit it over the necks of his team of oxen," Jerry explained. "Then, of course the chains and hooks enabled him to attach the yoke to the tongue of the wagon." He rattled the chains still dangling from his shoulder. "Amazing, isn't it? This thing's as good as new."

Meg handed him a bandage and pointed to the nearest window. "Truly amazing, Jerry. Just this afternoon I was wondering how we were going to bring in our oxen from the south forty along Colonial Boulevard in downtown Orlando. Looks like that problem's solved."

He scowled at her. "Go ahead and make fun, but this is a real antique. And the guy I bought it from…"

The hackles stood up on Meg's neck. "You actually paid money for this?"

"For something this rare? Of course. A hundred and twenty-five bucks—a bargain."

Somehow Meg managed to keep the scream in her head from erupting into what her brother would call another hissy fit. She'd long ago accepted that she was the sensible, mature one, and Jerry, five years her junior, was the charming, unpredictable one—the one she'd helped out of too many jams to remember. Now he was the one who was adored by everybody who came to the auction while she was the one they mostly tolerated. But never was this personality difference more difficult to accept than when money was concerned.

She drummed her fingers on the desktop and spoke calmly. "Jerry, do you remember me telling you this morning that I didn't know how we were going to pay next month's rent? Much less the Yellow Pages ad, workman's comp insurance and a host of other bills."

"Sure I remember, but I think the doubletree will bring at least three hundred at the next auction."

Suddenly Meg had a splitting headache. She could practically feel the veins tightening behind her eyes. And worse, the phone rang for the hundredth time. She tried but couldn't find her professional voice. "Colonial Auction," she half barked into the phone.

The voice that responded was competent and controlled. "Is this Margaret Hamilton?"

"Yes."

"This is Nadine Harkwell, administrator of the Shady Grove Convalescent Center in Mount Esther, Florida."

"Convalescent Center?" Meg repeated. "Is this about my aunt?"

"I'm afraid it is."

Meg's stomach plummeted. Her great-aunt Amelia was elderly, ninety-two on her last birthday. And while her mortality was something everyone in the family would have to face, Meg had never wanted to think about it. Aunt Amelia was a treasure. And she'd seemed in good health and great spirits when she'd traveled by bus to Orlando to spend Christmas with the family. That had only been six months ago.

"What's wrong with my aunt?" she asked. "She's not…?"

"No, Ms. Hamilton," Nadine Harkwell said. "Amelia hasn't passed away. But she fell in her home on Sunday. Broke her hip and bruised some ribs."

She fell four days ago? "Why didn't anyone call me before this?" Meg asked.

"Amelia didn't want us to call until now. I should tell you, though, that she's confused and disoriented. It's no secret to those of us in town," she added in a conspiratorial whisper, "Mrs. Ashford has been suffering from dementia that has worsened considerably in the last few months. I'm afraid that because of this fall, she'll never be herself again."

Meg talked to her aunt at least every other week. She hadn't noticed the woman's mental capacity slipping. But maybe she should have been listening more closely. "What can I do?" she asked. "Can I talk to her?"

"That wouldn't be practical. Amelia probably wouldn't even recognize your voice. But in one of her lucid moments today she asked for you. She wants you to come to Mount Esther. Something about settling her affairs. I can give you more details when you arrive assuming you are able to come."

"Of course I'll come. I'll be there tomorrow."

Something near panic was etched on Jerry's features. *Tomorrow?* he mouthed, having heard only her part of the conversation. *You can't go tomorrow.*

Meg silenced him with a warning look. Leaving the auction in Jerry's hands was just one of the problems she would have to address before leaving for Mount Esther. A minor one really when compared to the welfare of her ten-year-old son who still had a week left in the school year before he'd be out for the summer. What was she going to do about Spencer? Still, she reconfirmed the plans with Nadine. "Tell Aunt Amelia I'll be there tomorrow afternoon. And tell her I love her."

Meg hadn't even hung up the phone when Jerry asked in a voice high-pitched with tension, "You're leaving? How long will you be gone? A day? Two?"

The last thing Meg needed right now was her brother's attempt to make her feel guilty. He would just have to manage the auction without her.

"How nice of you to ask about our aunt, Jerry," she said, using sarcasm to switch the burden of guilt to him. "She fell in her house, suffered a broken hip and other injuries, and isn't coping well mentally." She stood up and removed her purse from the desk drawer. "I'll be sure and tell her you send your regards."

"Oh, fine. I guess it makes you feel better to make me look like the bad guy. I'm not the one leaving town. And of course I care about the old girl, but it's no secret that you were always her favorite."

Meg couldn't argue. Her unflagging sense of responsibility had earned her the title of "favorite" with most of their extended family. Jerry was the one who made everybody laugh. Meg was the one they depended upon.

She walked out of the office and into the section of the auction house where the customers sat. "I have to go home and pack. I don't know how long I'll be gone. Hopefully I'll just miss the Saturday auction, but I'll call tomorrow and give you an update. Aunt Amelia wants me to handle her affairs, but at this point I don't know exactly what that means or if I can accomplish anything with the weekend coming up."

"You can't stay away too long," Jerry pointed out. "Spencer's got school, doesn't he?"

Meg had already come up with a plan for her son. "I'm not taking him. I'll leave him with Mom."

Jerry shook his head. "Not unless you think your ten-year-old kid wants to jump on board a geriatric Greyhound bound for Biloxi for a week of playing the slots." He smiled. "Mom's Golden-Agers are on the move again, this time with pockets full of quarters."

Meg dropped into the nearest chair. "Darn. I forgot."

"No problem. I'll keep the sprout."

Meg gasped. "You?"

Jerry pretended to be offended, maybe actually was

a little. "Meg, we're talking about my favorite nephew here. You know I'll take good care of him. Besides, I am an adult."

"I'm not sure twenty-seven going on fourteen qualifies." Meg regretted her words the moment they'd slipped out of her mouth. How could Jerry ever live up to her expectations if she didn't expect more from him? "Anyway," she said, trying to cover her blunder, "I'm counting on you to run the business."

His previous doubts about taking charge seemed to have faded, and he gave her a smug look. "You manage the whiz kid and the auction, so why shouldn't I? I'll get a couple of my friends to help out temporarily. Look, sis, do you have any other ideas?" Jerry added when she hesitated to trust him with her son. "I've got one big advantage over anyone else you might think of to babysit. I'm here, and I'm offering."

It was a convincing argument. And on short notice, Meg had no other choice. She sighed. "Okay, but you'll stay at my house, so Spence has all his stuff and he's near the school. And you'll drive him there every morning by 7:45 and pick him up at the neighbor's every afternoon?"

Jerry nodded. "Yes, yes, and yes. I'll be there in the morning. Don't worry. My nephew is a chip off the old Hamilton block. He idolizes me."

"That's what worries me. But thanks, Jerry. I really appreciate this."

"No problem."

She headed for the door but stopped before going outside. "One more thing. No parties. And no poker games or gambling of any kind in the house."

Jerry saluted. "Right. I'll make sure the kid knows he'd better not negatively influence me."

Despite the rough day and the bad news from Mount Esther, Meg was smiling when she got in her car.

AT 7:30 THE NEXT MORNING Meg double checked Spencer's backpack to make certain he had the supplies he would need for the day. Once satisfied that the pack was in order, she took a frozen juice box from the refrigerator and tried to stuff it into his nylon lunch sack.

Her son gave her a look that combined exasperation with sympathy. "Mom, will you relax? You already put juice in there."

She looked down and frowned. A brightly colored box was nestled between a baloney sandwich and a bag of chips. "So I did." She took the extra one out and tossed it back into the case of twenty-three others she'd bought the night before at the wholesale club. Then she hurried to her front window and scanned the street with mounting panic. "Where *is* Uncle Jerry?"

"Right here," her brother said two seconds after the back door slammed. He entered the living room and announced, "My car's in the driveway. I must have missed your radar by coming in fast and low." He ruffled Spencer's hair. "Ready to go, kid?"

Spencer slipped his backpack over his shoulders. "Yep, I'm ready."

Meg wrapped her son in a huge hug. They'd never been apart for more than a day or two since Spence had been born. There hadn't even been a problem when Meg divorced Spencer's father two years ago. Dave had walked out without a backward glance and without asking for visitation rights. It was as if Dave Groller had never been married and didn't have a son.

In the beginning, when Spence was born, Dave seemed to enjoy being a father. At least he'd soaked up the attention he got whenever he took their son to the park or wheeled him in the stroller. But that was when Dave had enjoyed being a husband, too. When Spence had grown older, more demanding perhaps, he'd tried every childish trick he could think of to get his father's attention. And then Dave left, and Spence had to live with the fact that his father didn't care about him.

Meg held her son's face between her hands and studied his features. Unlike Meg, whose complexion was coppery and whose hair had the deep auburn highlights of her mother's side, Spencer had inherited the handsome Hamilton traits of his grandfather and his Uncle Jerry—fair, lightly freckled skin, emerald-green eyes, and thick, wheat-colored hair. In appearance, he was a Hamilton through and through, which is one of the reasons Meg reverted to her maiden name when the divorce from Dave was final.

But contrary to his genetic makeup, Spencer had become a bookish sort of boy since his father left them. His beautiful eyes peered through the unbreakable lenses of heavy-duty glasses. And he rarely played outside, even in the near-idyllic sunshine of central Florida. He much preferred his room with its ever-expanding shelves of books and computer games.

"I'll call you every day," she said, at last prying her hands away from his cheeks. "And I'll have my cell phone on all the time so you can reach me."

"Okay."

"You mind your Uncle Jerry."

"I will."

Jerry put his hand on her shoulder in a comforting gesture while glancing at his watch. "It's seven forty-five, sis. I'm trying to keep to the schedule you set up, but you're holding us back."

"I'll be fine, Mom, don't worry," Spencer said.

"I know you will. Go on now."

Meg stood at the door until Jerry backed his car out of the drive. Then she shook off an uncomfortable feeling of emptiness and tried to concentrate on the day ahead. She knew she could trust Jerry to take care of Spencer. He truly loved her son. But the auction—that was another story. She could only pray she had a business to come back to.

She went into her room to retrieve her suitcase. She had almost a five-hour drive ahead of her, and even though every mile was taking her away from Spence, a familiar feeling of anticipation flowed through her now that she was only minutes away from leaving. After a nearly four-year absence, she was going back to Mount Esther, and in a way, it was like going home.

AT ONE O'CLOCK Friday afternoon, Meg exited Interstate 75 onto a two-lane county road about fifteen miles south of the Georgia border. The road twisted and dipped in a westwardly direction over rolling hills. After twenty minutes she had her first glimpse of the Suwannee River through a thickly wooded area of oak and mulberry trees.

She turned off her car air conditioner and rolled down the window. This far north, the humid June heat of Orlando was gone, replaced by a moist cool breeze that rustled the spring blossoms of purple and white trilliums along the side of the road. The rich, pungent smell of damp earth, and the fragrant scent of wildflowers teased the air outside the window.

She rounded a curve that led into an expanse of flat land between the hills and immediately spotted the sign announcing her arrival in Mount Esther. Population 1412, it read. She smiled when she remembered that a member of the town council was appointed every year to change the figure with each birth and death in the close-knit community.

At the traffic light in the center of Mount Esther's business district, she turned right onto a narrow road that led across a single-lane wooden bridge spanning one of the tributaries to the Suwannee. After a mile she reached the turnoff to Aunt Amelia's gracious old Victorian home—the home that Amelia had deeded to Meg several years before.

INTENDING TO DROP off her belongings before heading to Shady Grove, Meg drove up the lane to the house. She frowned as she noticed the large potholes in the sparse gravel. This lack of attention to upkeep wasn't like Amelia. Each spring she ordered truckloads of gravel for the drive so it was neat and resistant to flooding during the rainy season. It also looked as though the trees hadn't been trimmed in ages. The magnificent live oaks dripped with spongy gray moss that bristled against Meg's windshield and cloaked the road in deep shadows.

But soon she cleared the three-hundred-yard drive and had her first look at the house. The green and cream colors she remembered seemed duller now, faded in the harsh Florida sun, but the structure, with its turret and peaks and wraparound porch was still a remarkable example of Queen Anne Victorian. Meg might have simply stopped for a moment and enjoyed the welcome sight had it not been for one detail that was completely out of place.

A police car was parked midway between the house and the barn.

Her heart pounded. Meg considered that she should approach the parked car with caution. After all, if a crime were being committed at this moment, she shouldn't interfere with police procedures. And she certainly didn't want to become a victim herself. But concern for her aunt's home, and basic burning curiosity, got the best of her. She accelerated and pulled alongside the police car.

Mount Esther Sheriff's Department was printed on the driver's door panel. Meg shifted her car into park and peered out the windows to scan the backyard and trail to the barn. Seeing no one, she opened her door and stepped onto the path.

And then she spied a tall man pushing a wheelbarrow out of the barn. There was nothing in his appearance or demeanor to indicate that he was a law enforcement officer. He was dressed in blue jeans, a plaid shirt, and a Yankees baseball cap. He turned the wheelbarrow to guide it around the side of the building.

Realizing that for the moment at least she was the only other person witnessing this activity, Meg hoped she'd catch the attention of the police officer who must be elsewhere on the property. This was her aunt's home—she wasn't about to stand by and let someone take something from the barn.

"Hey, you there. Stop!"

Amazingly the man did what she said. He set down the back supports of the wheelbarrow. Then he stared across the open space at her and said, "Okay."

Still looking around for the police, Meg marched up to him. He truly didn't look all that threatening up close though he stood over six feet. He appeared strong but with a lean, solid strength defined by hard work rather than the sculpted tone of weight training. He took a kerchief from his back pocket, removed his cap and wiped his brow. After stuffing the cloth back into his jeans, he said, "Do you want something?"

Meg put her hands on her hips and tried to make the most of her five feet five inches. "What are you doing?"

He gave her a look that might have been more appropriate if he were indulging a child's question. "Pushing this wheelbarrow around to the back of the property."

She took a step closer. "What's in there?"

His mouth lifted at one corner in a cocky sort of smile. "You don't want to know, ma'am."

"I asked you, didn't I?" She walked near enough to have a look for herself. A healthy whiff of foul air curled up from clumps of damp straw. She wrinkled her nose and hopped back.

The man snickered. "Satisfied? It's good old-fashioned horse manure. I figure it'll be a lot more welcome down by the Suwannee than up here by the house. The wild ferns by the river bank seem to like it."

"Where did you get it?" she asked.

He merely raised his eyebrows while his smile widened.

"You know what I mean," she amended. "There hasn't been a horse here in twenty years."

"There is now."

Meg glanced over her shoulder. No one else had appeared, prompting her to assume that she and this man were the only people around. But she was no longer worried. Obviously this man wasn't stealing from the barn. He was cleaning it. And somehow her Aunt Amelia had neglected to tell her that a horse had taken up residence in Uncle Stewie's old stable.

She folded her arms over her chest and said, "Who are you?"

He held out his hand, glanced down at the dirt, or whatever, that had stuck to his palm and dropped it to his side. "My name's Wade Murdock. I'm the deputy sheriff of Mount Esther. Been here five months now."

That explained the patrol car. "And whose horse is in the barn?" she asked.

"My daughter's. I promised her a horse when we left Brooklyn."

And that explained the man's distinctive northern accent. "Mrs. Ashford allows you to keep the horse in her barn?"

"We worked out a deal," he said and let his gaze wander over the property from where they stood to the back of the house. "For all practical purposes it's my barn anyway. I bought this place, lock, stock and barrel from Mrs. Ashford."

CHAPTER TWO

DEPUTY MURDOCK frowned with concern. "Are you all right, ma'am?"

No, she wasn't all right. He'd just aimed verbal darts at the reality she'd always depended upon. She wanted him to take them back. *I just bought this place lock, stock and barrel,* he'd said. That couldn't be.

He held out his hand, cautiously, as if he might have to grab onto her. Apparently she looked as shaken as she felt. "Stay there," he ordered. "Don't move."

For some reason she obeyed. Maybe she didn't trust her legs to hold her up if she tried to move. Or maybe she stood still because he was a cop. He stepped inside the barn and returned with a galvanized washtub which he upended next to her. "Sit down."

She didn't want to sit, but he obviously thought she should.

He slapped at his pockets, searching for something. "Do you need medical attention? Where's my damn cell phone?"

As if a 911 call would provide an antidote for what he'd just said. "No, I don't need medical attention," she assured him. "I need answers. You can't have bought this property."

He seemed to relax once she started talking. "Why not?"

"Because it's not for sale. Amelia Ashford would never sell this house to anyone."

He scrubbed his hand over the back of his neck. "Well, I'm sorry, but she did. She sold it to me six weeks ago."

Six weeks ago? Impossible. Meg had spoken to her aunt at least twice during that time frame, and Amelia never mentioned anything about it. She snorted her disbelief and sat on the washtub. This was ridiculous. Ashford House had been promised to her when Amelia prepared a Quit Claim Deed four years ago giving the property to Meg.

She surveyed the house and acres that stretched from the out buildings through groves of stately trees to the river. This land, that beautiful, curious, gingerbread house was her safety net, her last resort, the refuge for her and Spencer if all else failed.

Meg stared at Deputy Wade Murdock, a newcomer to Mount Esther, a man who couldn't possibly understand what Ashford House meant to her. She wanted to believe he was lying to her. Unfortunately he didn't look like the sort who would make up this story. He had a strong, proud face, centered by a nose with a subtle crookedness to it, as if he'd defended his principles on more than one occasion. His hair was the deep brown color of a walnut, slightly unkempt and just long enough to be interesting—the outward symbol of a man who avoided fussiness.

And he wasn't likely a con artist or a crook. After all, he was the deputy sheriff of Mount Esther. Surely the man the town appointed to defend the law wouldn't be the one to break it. But there had to be a logical explanation for what he believed to be true and what Meg knew to be fact.

Wade leveled a look at her that was every bit as intense as the one she gave him. "Look," he said, "there's obviously some mix-up here. Why don't we try to get to the bottom of this. Tell me your name and your connection to this property."

Once she told him who she was, he would have to accept that there had been a terrible mistake and they could work to correct it.

"My name is Meg Hamilton," she said. "I live in Orlando...."

He nodded. "You're the niece, the one whose husband—"

"Yes, I'm her niece," she announced, cutting him off. She was acutely aware that while Aunt Amelia may not have told Meg all the details of her life the last few times they'd talked, she'd obviously been confiding personal information to this stranger. Did he also know that Dave had left her and Spence without so much as a forwarding address?

"I was called here yesterday," she continued, "because my aunt fell in her home a few days ago and is convalescing at Shady Grove."

"That makes sense," he said.

"She asked me to come to Mount Esther to help sort out some things."

"So let me get this straight," he said. "You didn't know that your aunt sold her house?"

Meg stood up and faced him squarely. "Frankly, I'm not at all convinced there has been a sale."

"Do you think I'm imagining the contract that she

and I both signed and which is right now sitting in my desk drawer?"

"No, I'm not suggesting that you are making up a contract. Clearly *something* was signed, something that has you believing you own this house. I would like to see the document for myself. Then maybe I can sort this out."

"I'd be happy to show you my contract," he said. "Although your aunt has a copy, and so does Betty Lamb, the real estate agent who handled the transaction. You might feel more comfortable dealing with one of those ladies instead of me."

"I'll certainly ask my aunt," she said. "As soon as I take my suitcase into the house." She half expected him to contest her right to stay here. To his credit, he didn't. Once she'd moved her things in, she would go to Shady Grove and evaluate her aunt's medical condition. And if Amelia were in good spirits, Meg would question her about this supposed contract.

Wade pointed to the rear of the house. "Go in the back way," he said. "I left the door unlocked."

"You have a key?" An alarming thought occurred to her. "You're not living here, are you?"

He smiled. "No, not yet. But I have access to the property. With your aunt's permission, of course." He swatted his ball cap against his thigh, settled it back on his head, and took a few steps toward the wheelbarrow as if he were dismissing her. "Oh, by the way, don't be alarmed by what you see in there. The place may not look exactly as you remember it. Your aunt's been a busy lady the last few weeks."

She matched his smug expression with her most skeptical one. "What is that supposed to mean?"

"You'll see when you get inside." He grasped the handles of the wheelbarrow, but before he turned the corner of the barn, he called back over his shoulder. "Make yourself at home, Meg." And then he smiled. "While you're here I promise to knock before coming in."

BEFORE MEG COULD utter an appropriate comeback, Wade had turned the corner with his Suwannee riverbank fertilizer. Consequently he probably didn't hear when she slammed her car door after retrieving her suitcase and stomped along the old cement patio stones that led to the back door. Maybe Deputy Murdock didn't appreciate the full effect of her frustration, but it made Meg feel better to release it.

His attitude was unnerving. He almost acted as if this dilemma were a laughing matter and that his claim to Ashford House was real. Of course she supposed he believed it was. Meg lugged her bag up three porch steps and twisted the doorknob which was, indeed, unlocked. She'd set Deputy Murdock straight soon enough. Meg knew Ashford House had been deeded to her. She'd seen a copy of the Quit Claim document before it was filed with the attorney. Her name was on it.

"This house guards our souls, Margaret," Aunt Amelia had told her one warm, fragrant night many years ago. "We two are the only ones who feel its pulse and hear it breathe. Not even your Uncle Stewie understands these old walls like you and I do. We are the destiny of Ashford House."

Through the years Meg had explored every nook and cranny of the mansion. She'd daydreamed at the windows of all six bedrooms. She knew about the secret panels in the library, the removable top to the newel post at the base of the front stairway where Uncle Stewie always hid a bag of silver dollars which he passed out to Meg and Jerry when they visited.

She stepped across the threshold into the kitchen and let out a breath. A sense of overwhelming relief washed over her. This was Hattie May's kitchen, just as Meg remembered it with its six-burner stove, mammoth refrigerator, and ten-foot pine scrub table. She could almost picture Hattie May washing vegetables at one of the giant sinks as she spun tales about her ancestors who had been brought to America as slaves.

Don't be alarmed, the deputy had said. *The place may not look as you remember it.* What nonsense, Meg thought. As far as she could tell nothing had changed.

Then she noticed that the pantry door was ajar. Several boxes protruded from the opening, making it impossible to close. Certainly the shelves were not stocked with food as they once used to be. Hattie May passed away a few years after Uncle Stewie's death, and Aunt Amelia, with hired help only a few hours a day, prepared most of her own simple meals herself.

Meg crossed to the door, pulled it open the rest of the way and stood face-to-face with a solid wall of cardboard cartons. "What *is* all this?" she said to the empty room. The boxes she could see had been opened and resealed. She read a few of the shipping labels and discovered with a feeling of relief that each carton had been shipped to Amelia Ashford. At least the deputy hadn't moved his personal possessions into her house! The postmarks were from the past two months. The return addresses were various companies located throughout the United States.

If this collection of cartons was what the deputy meant by alarming, then perhaps he had a point. Determined to get to the bottom of this mystery, Meg went out the back door and stood on the service porch. "Deputy," she shouted. "Deputy Murdock!"

He came around the barn, pushing the wheelbarrow with ease since it had delivered its cargo. "What is it?" he called to her.

"These boxes. What do you know about them?"

Leaving the cart by the barn door, he came halfway to the house. "They're all Mrs. Ashford's," he said.

"I can see that, but what's inside them?"

He shrugged one shoulder. "Amelia's been ordering things. I bring her mail up every day, and she gets stacks of catalogues. Since she's been at Shady Grove I've left an accumulation on the wicker table on the front porch. If you look through the mail, I think you might get some answers."

Meg shook her head. "I can't believe it," she said. "She's filled up the pantry."

Deputy Murdock laughed. "The pantry? Haven't you been in the dining room?"

"No."

He let out a long whistle. "I hope you aren't planning any dinner parties while you're here."

She frowned at him. "Of course not. You're just full of riddles and surprises, aren't you, Deputy?"

"No, ma'am. I deal in facts, and you're about to face some of them right now."

Meg returned to the kitchen and walked cautiously to the dining room. When she pressed on the hinged door that normally provided easy access between the rooms, she discovered that it allowed only enough room for one person to walk through. And when she did, she couldn't believe what she saw. Piled on the floor, the table, all ten Chippendale chairs were more boxes. Dozens and dozens of them. All sizes and shapes.

She sidestepped down a narrow path that wound between two columns of cartons until she was in the middle of the room where her aunt had once hosted friends and family and which now resembled a warehouse. She scanned a wall of corrugated cardboard while she ran her hands along the dusty exteriors of the boxes. Then, she absently noted Wade Murdock's voice coming from the doorway to the kitchen. "It's a little overwhelming, I guess. I suppose eventually we'll have to figure out what to do with all this stuff."

WADE FOLLOWED HER through the dining room to the formal parlor in the front of the house. She hadn't asked him to. In fact, she probably wasn't even aware that he was so close. But it was the least he could do, stand guard over her while she faced the evidence of her aunt's eccentricity. She peered warily around the door frame into the parlor as if she expected to see additional boxes and was steeling herself to deal with even more chaos. She released a long sigh when she saw a mere half-dozen cartons sitting on the desk and an end table. They were the ones he'd carried in today. As long as Meg didn't look too closely at the details of the parlor that had fallen into disrepair, she would be comforted to find this room at least familiar.

"As far as I know," he said, "all the boxes are confined to these downstairs rooms. Although I haven't been on the upper floors since I first saw the house and made an offer on it."

Startled at the sound of his voice, she spun around and laid her hand across her chest as if she were sending a message to her heart to keep beating. Then she stared at him with wide, vivid blue eyes and shook her head. "How long has it been like this?"

"Roughly since Mrs. Ashford came into some money."

Her eyes rounded. "What do you mean?"

He had to smile, since he knew the source of the unexpected income. He knew, too, as most everyone in Mount Esther did, that Amelia Ashford had suffered financial difficulties recently. Like many elderly folks, she'd watched her savings dwindle. "It was my money," he said. "I gave her a deposit on the property when we signed the contract."

Meg's eyebrows arched with the unspoken question.

"Twenty thousand dollars," he told her.

Her gaze darted to the entrance to the dining room and she groaned. "You don't think…? All that money?" She read the label on a long, narrow box. "This is from a company called Star Search." She tore the plastic envelope from the top, removed an invoice and read the particulars. As if expecting Wade to validate what she read, she held the paper out to him. "There's a telescope inside. And it cost five hundred and forty dollars."

He studied the invoice, adding that Mrs. Ashford had paid with her bank debit card. "For that amount of money, it's no doubt a fine instrument."

Meg let out a bark of laughter. "And this one," she said, reading the label from a box on the end table. "It's from a toy company called Furry Friends." She raised the box and shook it, creating a soft, rustling sound. "My aunt bought a stuffed animal?"

Wade shrugged.

"Where did you say you'd put her mail?"

He went out to the porch and returned with the stack of catalogues he'd brought from the mailbox in the last few days. He handed them to Meg, and she sank into the nearest chair and thumbed through them. When she looked up at Wade, her eyes reflected shock and confusion. "Did you know that my aunt was spending all this money?"

"I knew she was receiving deliveries, yes." He glanced over his shoulder toward the dining room. "It's a little hard to ignore."

Meg's voice rose a notch. "Why didn't anyone stop her?"

"Stop her? For what reason? There isn't a law in this state against spending money."

"But didn't you find this behavior suspicious?"

"I've only known your aunt a few months. I wasn't qualified to judge her behavior. As I saw it, a ninety-two-year-old woman suddenly had extra cash and she spent it as she wanted to. I knew where the money came from since I gave it to her myself, so there was no need to investigate her windfall and what she did with it. But it might comfort you to know that the bank manager of the Mount Esther Savings and Loan did find your aunt's habits suspicious. He strongly suggested that she quit using her credit card when the charges became abnormally high. That's when she resorted to using her debit card."

Wade hadn't been inside the house in over two weeks

since he'd been doing repairs on the outside and in the barn. When he'd come in today he'd been shocked at the accumulation of deliveries.

Meg stared at the glossy catalogues on her lap as if they were written in a foreign language. And then she tossed them to the floor, stood up, and looked at Wade. "Why wasn't I called?" she asked. "You obviously know about me, Deputy. My phone number's in my aunt's address book. Didn't you think I should know my aunt was spending her money so foolishly?"

The hairs on his neck bristled. Was this woman actually expecting him to defend himself further? "You think I should have called you? Mrs. Ashford told me that she has two nieces. One of them, the one she talks about a lot…" He jerked his thumb toward a photograph on the wall. It showed Meg in her high school graduation gown. "…is you I assume since I've seen your pictures hanging all over this house. And I know you haven't been to see your aunt in quite a while. The other one…" He picked up a photo from a bookshelf. "…a woman who lives in Chicago, hasn't been to Mount Esther in years."

He leveled his sternest gaze on her. "Besides, this really wasn't my business. I simply observed a sweet old woman spending her own money."

Meg scowled. "So, you stood by and watched as this *sweet old woman's* mind slowly but certainly failed her without doing anything about it."

"What would you have wanted me to do? As I saw it, Amelia Ashford was having the time of her life."

What happened next completely unnerved him. Meg's features slowly changed from righteous anger to a sort of chilling understanding. "Wait a minute," she said. "Perhaps you had something to gain by ignoring my aunt's unusual behavior."

He backed up a step. "What do you mean by that?"

She gestured to the packages. "You'll excuse me for saying so, Deputy, but I can't help thinking that this wild spending was a sign of my aunt's vulnerability and an open invitation for you to con her out of this house."

Anger flared inside him. "That's ridiculous. I didn't even express an interest in buying this place until after I made the deal to board my daughter's horse. And then I only mentioned it as a sort of remote possibility. But Mrs. Ashford was more than willing to get an offer on this old place. She welcomed my interest, encouraged it. And another thing…your aunt didn't start her spending spree until after she sold me her house. I didn't observe her buying so much as a sewing needle before she accepted my offer. So much for your theory about me watching her odd behavior with some sort of sinister intent."

She didn't seem to have a reasonable counterargument, so she sank back down in the chair and stared at the cartons around her. Then she looked up at him, some of the fire back in her eyes. "You won't get this house, Deputy," she finally said. "You are going to find that the contract you signed with Amelia Ashford is worthless."

"I hardly think so."

She leaned forward, fixed him with an unblinking gaze. "You'd better be ready to accept disappointment," she stated defiantly. "Four years ago, Amelia deeded this house to me."

Okay, she'd finally presented an argument that could pose a problem. Had Betty Lamb overlooked something? Still, he couldn't resist pointing out the obvious. "Then why didn't that little detail show up when my Realtor did a title search?"

"I intend to find out," she said. "It has always been my aunt's wish that I would get Ashford House when she dies, and she prepared the deed to insure that would happen."

For a moment, the cold grip of panic coiled in Wade's gut. He'd given Amelia Ashford twenty thousand dollars, every penny he'd saved while working fifteen years for the New York City Police Department. There was no way he would stand by and watch the savings he'd scrounged from hauling in thugs and criminals squandered on the contents of boxes in an old woman's dining room without getting what he'd paid for.

He drew a deep breath to steady his nerves and stared hard at Meg. "It appears we both have documents we need to inspect," he said.

"That's fine with me." Meg stood up and walked around him toward the kitchen. "I'm going to take my suitcase upstairs now, and then I'm going to see my aunt. Perhaps she can explain what's been going on here."

She disappeared into the dining room and he could visualize her threading her way back through columns of boxes that reached higher than her head. And, strangely, a bout of conscience, or more accurately, pity, washed over him. Meg Hamilton was obviously going to fight for Ashford House just as vehemently as he was.

There was something about this place. Wade had felt its spirit the first time he came in the door. And his connection to the house had grown once he'd decided to buy it. Now, it was as if he'd been destined to find this old place and make it his. He sensed that after two and a half years of grieving over a senseless tragedy, he could finally put down roots again in this quirky old mansion.

CHAPTER THREE

MEG WAS THINKING about Ashford House as she drove back to Mount Esther, turned at the traffic light, and headed to the Shady Grove Convalescent Center. She also thought about Deputy Wade Murdock. While he'd been adamant about defending his claim to the property, she had to admit that he had treated her decently, especially considering that she'd accused him of taking advantage of her aunt's confused state. Plus, the announcement that Ashford House had been deeded to her must have been a shock. Twenty thousand dollars was a lot of money to invest in property that was never going to be his.

She chewed on the end of one nail as she scanned the side of the road for a sign that identified the drive to the nursing home. She wondered about what sort of contract the deputy had and if it was truly valid. It couldn't be. She had legally owned Ashford House for four years. A man can't just move into town and make a deal on a piece of property that has been given to someone else.

In spite of this controversy, Meg did feel some compassion for the deputy. He was obviously a family man. He'd mentioned his daughter, and Meg supposed he had a wife and perhaps other children who depended on him.

And now he would have to disappoint them when he explained about the house. This whole mess really was unfortunate, and certainly not a problem Meg had ever thought she would have to deal with. Just as she never thought she would pull into her aunt's drive and find a good-looking lawman carting manure from the barn.

She shook her head to dispel the very clear image of Wade Murdock standing so close behind her in the parlor of Ashford House. When she considered Wade's appearance, which she shouldn't, since he obviously had a family, she had to admit that Murdock had a certain appealing quality, in what she imagined was a down-to-earth, working man, New York sort of way.

Shady Grove Convalescent Center, five hundred yards ahead.

Meg slowed when she saw the sign and snapped on her blinker, putting Wade Murdock out of her mind. The gracious, solidly constructed two-story structure sat amid leafy mulberry and flowering sweetbay trees. An expansive green lawn displayed a riot of pink-and-white periwinkles clustered around wrought-iron benches. Shady Grove was a picture of pastoral serenity.

Meg parked in front of the entrance and went inside. A pleasant young woman offered assistance and gave Meg directions to Amelia's room. She walked down a long hallway with doors on either side. Each room had a window with the curtains drawn to let in the sunshine. Some patients appeared to have personal belongings in their rooms, a favorite chair, a painting, something that reminded them of home. Most of the occupants seemed confined to bed, confirming what Meg had thought when she saw a sign identifying her aunt's wing as "continual care."

When she neared Amelia's room, Meg heard a distinctive voice coming from a television. "Come on down. You're the next contestant on *The Price is Right*."

She held a deep breath, stepped inside and looked at the thin, white-haired woman lying in the bed. A smile broke on her face as she recognized the ravaged but still familiar features of her beloved aunt. Amelia seemed to have aged a decade in the last few months.

Meg followed her aunt's gaze to the TV screen where a young, dark-haired Bob Barker welcomed his latest participant. She recognized the logo of the Game Show Network in the corner of the screen and realized Amelia was watching a repeat of a previous *Price is Right* broadcast. She came to the side of the bed and spoke softly, "Aunt Amelia?"

Her aunt glanced briefly at her with pale gray eyes that seemed to have lost the spark of enchantment that always twinkled in their depths. She pointed at the television. "Did I order a set of those?"

Meg looked back at the screen where an announcer was describing a set of golf clubs. Taken aback by the ambiguous greeting, she said, "Are you asking me if you ordered golf equipment?" She thought of all the boxes in the dining room and knew some of them were large enough to hold a set.

"If I haven't, I will. I've always wanted some."

Realizing the futility of asking for further explanation, Meg searched her aunt's face for some sign that the old woman had recognized her. Her eyes remained cool and remote. Disappointed, Meg gripped the railing of the bed and leaned over the thin form that barely made a ripple beneath the sheets. "Aunt Amelia, it's me, Margaret."

Amelia smiled, though not at Meg. "Oh, look. That woman's got to give the price of an electric blender. I should be on that show. I just bought one, and it cost twenty-nine ninety-five."

Bob Barker flipped a card over and revealed a price of fourteen dollars for the blender, probably an accurate amount for an appliance that was sold twenty-some years ago when the show was first taped. Amelia clasped her hands under her chin. "See, I told you."

Meg took Amelia's hand, thinking the gesture would divert the woman's attention from the television. "I'm here, Aunt Amelia," she said. "Remember me? Margaret."

Her aunt's attention to the program didn't waver. "If you're going to stay, sit down and watch."

Meg obeyed. She sat in an upholstered armchair by the bed and remained silent through the Showcase Showdown. Once a winner was proclaimed, she asked if she could turn off the television.

"Go ahead. I don't like *The Joker's Wild*."

Grateful for the silence, Meg tried to reach her aunt again. "It's so good to see you, Aunt Amelia," she said.

Amelia's head swivelled slowly and she finally gave Meg her attention. "It's good to see you, too. You told me your name, didn't you? I should have written it down. I tend to forget now and then." She leaned over and took a notepad and pencil from her nightstand. "That's why I write things down." She smiled at Meg. "Now, what is your name again, dear?"

Meg wiped at a tear that slid down her cheek. "My name is Margaret Hamilton. I'm your niece."

Amelia repeated the words as she wrote Meg's name down. She stared intensely at the page before narrowing her eyes and squinting at Meg as if she were trying to pull a distant memory from the faulty recesses of her once sharp mind.

Meg swallowed, trying to ease the burning in her throat. Of all the receptions she'd imagined during her drive to Mount Esther, she'd never expected that her aunt would have totally forgotten her existence. After all, hadn't Nadine Harkwell said that Amelia had asked for her to come?

As she watched her aunt's face, hoping for a spark of recognition, Meg longed for the chance to go back just a few years, back to when she and Amelia sat on the front porch swing talking for hours about things that mattered to girls, young and old. Back then, they'd been best friends, not distant strangers. But now, the blank look in her aunt's eyes was almost too much to bear.

Meg patted Amelia's hand and started to rise. And then a small miracle made her believe that somewhere beneath the muddled thinking, a vibrant, mischievous Amelia Ashford still thrived. Amelia turned her hand over in Meg's and threaded their fingers together. "Margaret," she whispered. "My darling Meggie. You've come. I knew you would."

Meg laughed through a choking sob, leaned over and kissed her aunt's cheek. "That's right. I'm here. What do you want me to do?"

"We need to talk, Margaret. There is much that needs to be done and I'm afraid there's too little time." Amelia's eyes fluttered and closed. "But I must rest now. Just a wee nap."

She was sound asleep when the nurse came in to

check her. Meg introduced herself. "Did she recognize you?" the nurse asked as she held two fingers against Amelia's wrist and checked her pulse.

"Yes," Meg said. "After a while at least."

"Good. She has lucid moments, and during those times you're all she talks about."

"How is she, really?"

The nurse inhaled deeply, indicating her response was not going to be good news. "She's like many elderly people. They are able to maintain their mental capacity as long as their health is strong. But once they suffer a physical injury, it's as though their systems shut down." The nurse jotted something on Amelia's chart and smiled down at her patient. "But she's a dear old soul. We're all quite fond of her."

"How long will she sleep?" Meg asked.

"Not long. She catnaps all day."

The nurse was right. After a few minutes, Amelia wakened. She looked around the room and reached for the television remote on a cord dangling from the bed. Before she turned the set on, she regarded Meg with the same distant look she'd had earlier. "Hello. Did you bring my supper?"

Meg smiled. "No, but I'll see that you get it soon."

"Thank you." Amelia turned on the set and tuned Meg out. Meg smoothed her palm along the wisps of snow-white hair on her aunt's forehead, whispered good-night and left the room. Tomorrow she would try again.

NORMALLY MEG DIDN'T talk on her cell phone while she was operating a car, but when she left Shady Grove, her desire to connect with her son was greater than her code of responsible driving. Besides, she'd only passed two cars in the mile she'd traveled back toward town. She pressed the speed dial to her home phone number.

"Hey, sis," Jerry said. "How's it going up there?"

Meg covered her disappointment that Spencer hadn't answered with a cheerful greeting to her brother. "Hi, Jerry. Truthfully, it's been quite a day."

"I'll bet. How's Aunt Amelia doing?"

"She's quite frail. And not thinking all that clearly." That was an understatement. "How's Spence? Did you remember to pick him up at the neighbor's?"

"Nope. Completely forgot. Good thing the kid stole a car and drove himself home."

Meg sighed, hating herself just a little. Of course Jerry wouldn't forget to pick up Spence. She was going to have to quit treating her brother as if he were the ten-year-old and show more confidence in him. "I'm sorry, Jerry. I never should have suggested that you might forget."

"No, probably not, but I know you, so the assumption was expected…and forgiven."

She heard her son's voice in the background. "Hey, Uncle Jerry, can I have another hot dog?"

"Hot dogs?" Meg said. "You're having hot dogs for dinner? I left a turkey meat loaf in the refrigerator."

"No offense, Meggie, but isn't that an oxymoron using *turkey* and *meat* together in the same sentence?"

Meg could picture her brother's teasing grin.

"Besides, Spence and I are bonding," he continued. "You need guy food to do that—good old-fashioned frankfurters." Before Meg could respond, Jerry said, "Hey, kid, back off on the Easy Cheese."

She rolled her eyes and decided it was best to adopt the philosophy that a short-term lack of nutrition probably never killed anyone.

"So you had a bad day?" Jerry said.

"Not the best. A few surprises, not the least of which was the presence of a man at the house when I got there."

Jerry hooted. "Aunt Amelia has a boyfriend?"

"No, you idiot. This was a much younger man, the deputy sheriff of Mount Esther by the way. He's probably not much older than I am."

Jerry laughed again. "So *you* found a boyfriend? Fast work, and it's about time. Two years is long enough to go dateless."

"Why do I bother talking to you?"

"Because I'm the only one you know who talks about nothing of any importance, and it's a nice change of pace."

"Maybe you're right. Anyway, the deputy claims Amelia sold Ashford House to him a few weeks ago."

"Whoa! No way. The house is yours, isn't it?"

"Yes, at least I think so." She hated the edge of doubt in her answer and quickly amended her statement. "Of course it is. This is obviously just a big mistake. All I have to do is find the deed, and…"

"Right," Jerry said. "You'll straighten it out, I know you will." Typical of Jerry, he changed the subject before he might actually be called upon to give advice or listen to someone else's problems. "Speaking of boyfriends…"

"Which we weren't, really."

"Well, no, but a girl came in today. Real cute. I'd call her definite girlfriend potential for your baby brother."

"What did she want?"

"She has a business proposition. I'll tell you about it tomorrow. The brainiac is reaching for the phone."

The words *business proposition* immediately translated into *harebrained scheme* in Meg's mind. "Jerry, don't you let a pretty face—"

"Hi, Mom!"

Tension ebbed from Meg's shoulders at the sound of her son's voice, and she relegated the solving of another problem to tomorrow's already crowded list. "Hi, honey, how are you?" she asked. "Tell me all about school today."

MEG BLEW A KISS into the phone and disconnected the call as she drove up the path to Ashford House. The sun was setting, sculpting the old home in rose-gold shadows that transformed the faded paint with a renewed glow. In contrast, the skeletal shadows cast by the tallest tree branches swayed across the roof peaks and porch eaves. Meg had never spent even one night alone in the house, and suddenly that didn't seem like the most appealing idea. And then she saw two cars parked in the driveway. One of them belonged to Wade Murdock, and Meg's apprehension eased.

She pulled to the back and parked. The deputy acknowledged her arrival with a brief wave and returned to tightening the girth on the saddle of a chestnut horse. A young girl walked under the animal's neck and stared at Meg's car.

Meg stepped out of the car and watched the exchange between Wade and the girl. He pointed in Meg's direction and appeared to be explaining her presence. The girl chewed on her bottom lip and nodded a couple of times. Meg wondered if the deputy was describing her to his child as the wicked witch who'd come to ruin their dreams of home ownership.

Sensing movement to her right, Meg's attention was captured by an elderly man who stood up from the washtub where she had sat earlier. He approached the two by the horse. If this was a delegation of Murdocks intent on challenging her right to be at Ashford House, then Meg was sorely outnumbered.

She walked to the threesome prepared to defend her position. "You still here?" she said unnecessarily to Wade.

"Actually I'm back," he answered. "I left for a while to check the traffic out on the highway and just returned so my daughter could ride while we still have some daylight." Noticing that the girl had her foot in the stirrup and was staring at him expectantly, he hoisted her into the saddle. "Jenny, this is Miss Hamilton," he said once she'd wiggled into position on the horse.

The girl swept her long black hair over one shoulder and peered down at Meg with eyes that Meg now noticed were as dark and haunting as her father's. "Hi."

Still uncertain how she'd been portrayed to the Murdock family, Meg said simply, "Nice to meet you."

"And this is my father, Roone Murdock," Wade said, indicating the man who stood with his back slightly bent and one elbow on the horse's rump. The elderly man extended his free hand and she shook it.

"We'll be out of your hair in a half hour or so," Wade said. "Just as soon as Jenny has a quick ride and we get Lady Jay put back in her stall for the night."

Jenny stared hard at Meg and then shot a glance at the house. "How long you planning to stay?" she asked.

Sensing that Jenny was fishing for a response of only a few days, Meg shook her head. "I don't know. I'm here to take care of my aunt, Mrs. Ashford. She's…"

"Yeah, I know all about her," the girl said. "I know that you—"

Wade distracted his daughter by handing her the reins. "Go on now, Jen. Just down to the river and back and into the side yard." Roone moved aside and Wade patted the horse's backside sending the animal off at a slow walk. "Nothing too fast or too fancy, you hear me?" When horse and rider had moved away, he said to Meg, "She doesn't know the whole story, just an abbreviated one."

Meg frowned. "I guess that makes two of us."

He smiled, showing a line of mostly even white teeth with a slightly crooked one in front which gave him an air of comfortable imperfection. "Yeah, I suppose there are a few details missing at this point."

Roone Murdock headed toward the corner of the barn. "I'll keep my eye on her," he said to his son.

"Thanks, Pop." He bent to retrieve a curry brush from the ground and addressed Meg when he stood again. "So, how's Mrs. Ashford today?"

"Confused about things, but okay, I guess."

"Did she know you?"

"After a while but only for a minute or two. I wasn't able to ask her about the house…."

"I wouldn't expect you to if Mrs. Ashford isn't in a state to handle a lot of questions. From what I can tell, she has her lucid moments, and you can talk to her then."

Meg tried to analyze the deputy's tone. He didn't seem worried about what she would discover when she was finally able to ask Amelia about the supposed sale of the house. In fact, he was almost confident.

"I was in the kitchen a few minutes ago," he continued. "There aren't many supplies in the cupboards. Mrs. Ashford's maid came in yesterday and took most of the food so it wouldn't spoil. If I'd known you were coming…"

Was he actually concerned about what she would eat? Funny, she hadn't thought of food until now, and suddenly she realized that she was starved. "I'll be fine," she said without conviction.

He gave her a little smile that said she wasn't fooling him. "We live in a rental place about a half mile from here. I think we've got a pot of spaghetti on the stove. I have to go out on patrol later and I could drop off a plate."

"No, that won't be necessary," Meg said. "You have to feed your family and I'm sure your wife wouldn't appreciate—"

"I don't have a wife," he said, taking a couple of steps toward the barn. As he went through the opening, he called over his shoulder. "It's just a plate of spaghetti and I'll be out anyway. I'll bring it by."

He disappeared into the barn and Meg stared at the shadows that had swallowed him up. "Well, thanks, then," she hollered back and headed toward the house and all its uninhabited twelve rooms. Not only did she not have any answers, now she had even more questions.

CHAPTER FOUR

WADE TOOK HIS beige uniform shirt out of the dryer, examined it for wrinkles, and slipped his arms into the sleeves. He was buttoning the front as he came from the garage into the kitchen.

Roone looked up from the sink where he was standing a clean plate in the dish drainer. "How late you gonna be tonight?" he asked.

"Midnight or so I imagine, assuming there are no emergencies. I'll sweep the businesses along Center Street a couple of times and probably nab a few speeders on the county road." He caught his daughter's eye as she dried a plate and stacked it in the cupboard. "If it's like every other Friday night, the high school boys will try to turn Route 21 into a drag strip."

Jenny spun around and glared at him. "Oh, great. I can just see my popularity soaring in this podunk town." Under her breath she added, "Everybody already hates me as it is."

Wade tucked the shirt into his trousers and buckled his belt. "I don't think anybody hates you, and besides you're only thirteen. You're not even in high school yet." Quietly, he said, "Thank God."

She took the next plate from the drainer. "So what am I supposed to do tonight?"

"How about homework?"

She rolled her eyes. "Dad, it's Friday."

Having expected that reaction, he chuckled. "Maybe Gramps will take you to the Video Market to rent a movie." He gave his father a pleading look.

"Sure, why not?" Roone said. "I think there's a Rambo flick I haven't seen yet."

Jenny groaned and Wade winked at his father. "Too bad, Pop. I think you're stuck with Brad Pitt or Tom Cruise."

"Puh-leeze," Jenny moaned. "They're so old!"

"Sorry, pumpkin. I guess I missed a couple of issues of *Teen Idol*," Wade said and then checked the snap on his holster. While he'd never have considered patrolling the streets of Manhattan without a weapon, he hated carrying one in Mount Esther. He thought the image of deadly force was inappropriate in the quiet community, but the sheriff had told him that first day on the job that small towns weren't exempt from crime. He emphasized his motto that a smart cop was a prepared cop. So Wade sported a Smith and Wesson 40 caliber automatic, though in six months, he'd never had the safety off unless it was to test the weapon at a firing range.

Ready to go, Wade picked up a plate of spaghetti from the table. "Okay you guys, behave yourselves. And Jen, tomorrow we'll take Lady Jay to the equestrian park. Sound good?"

"Yeah, I guess so…" She never finished her sentence because she burst into a fit of laughter which was obviously aimed at her father. "Are you sure you want to go out like that, Dad?"

"Like what?"

She circled around him and pulled something off the back of his shirt trailing a crackle of static electricity. When he turned around, he saw a tank top in her hands that didn't look like it would fit a Barbie doll. It was a postage-stamp-sized piece of white jersey with shoulder straps the size of pencils. Across the front was the image of Lady Liberty with sparkling paint on her torch. "Tell me that's a costume for one of your dolls," he said.

She gave him one of those looks teenagers use when they are talking to clueless antiquarians. "Geez, Dad. We donated my dolls to that kids' charity in Brooklyn, remember? I don't play with dolls anymore."

"More's the pity," he said and then hesitated as he tried to erase an image from his mind that would make any father's blood flow cold. "Then…you actually wear that thing yourself?"

She stretched the top against her chest where her small breasts barely made an impression in the jersey. Still, the fabric was flimsy enough to interest an adolescent boy's imagination. "Of course I wear it," she said. "Just not around you or Gramps." She sighed dramatically. "I guess I goofed when I put it in the washer with your uniform."

"Oh, yeah. You're busted."

"Dad…"

"Tomorrow, Jen. Make some time for me to take a tour of your closet."

She put a fist on her hip and gave him a pinched-lip, how-dare-you look of a woman filled with righteous indignation. "You can be so ridiculous."

"So I've been told. But heck, you're stuck with me."

He went to the door. When another disturbing thought occurred to him, he stopped, looked at the spaghetti, and then narrowed his eyes at his father. "You didn't put any Tabasco in Meg's sauce, did you?"

Roone hung the dish rag over the sink divider and stared at his son. "No, but I thought about it. I still don't know why you're being so neighborly to a woman who's determined to pull our house out from under us."

Wade thought they'd put this discussion to bed earlier, but he should have known better. Feisty old Irishmen live to hold a grudge. "For one thing, I'm not jumping to any conclusions about Meg Hamilton's motives or her plans." He stared down at the plate in his hand. "For another, I ate your spaghetti myself tonight, and I think serving her up a plateful ought to send enough of a message that she's in for the fight of her life."

"You're a funny man, Murdock," his father called as Wade made his escape out the door. "But you ask her to show you that deed. Until we see that document in black and white, everything she says is just her blowing smoke."

Wade waved toward the back door where his dad was silhouetted against the kitchen lights. "Will do, Pop." He set the plate on the floor of his patrol car, backed out of the drive and headed toward Ashford House. His dad was ornery, but he was also right.

MEG LOOKED DOWN at the mess she'd created in the middle of the parlor and released a long groan of frustration. She'd opened every drawer in every end table, desk, and cabinet and pulled out a mountain of paperwork chronicling her aunt's life. She'd scrutinized each scrap and found receipts dating back to the 1940s, warranties from companies that had long since gone out of business, and phone numbers that consisted of only four numbers on note paper that had yellowed with age. But she hadn't found the deed prepared just four years ago.

She stepped carefully among the debris of her aunt's past, hoping that maybe this time she'd see the legal document she'd missed on first inspection. "There has to be a copy here somewhere."

Disappointed, she sat heavily in a frayed old wing chair and grimaced at the chaos of paper that marked a fitting end to a demoralizing day. Besides the fruitless result of her investigation, she'd discovered after a brief tour through the rooms, that Ashford House was in need of numerous repairs. The wainscoting was rotted and mildewed. The wallpaper was dry and peeling. And the windows—Meg decided that nothing short of a miracle kept the cracked and scratched panes in the frames.

At least the frantic search for the deed during the last two hours had kept her from reflecting on the fragile state of the home's security and the fact that she was completely alone in the rambling old house. She tried to push the creaks and moans of the ancient framework to a far corner of her mind, but realized that the eerie sounds would probably translate to a sleepless night.

"Damn. Where *is* that deed?" she said, "and why didn't I request a final copy for my own records when it was prepared?" She had a copy of the original document somewhere in her house in Orlando, but it was an unsigned facsimile Amelia had sent to her so she could check the wording for accuracy. Without Amelia's signature, it was worthless.

In spite of the run-down state of Ashford House, Meg wanted it now more than ever. This place was like a member of her family, one she could count on when others had disappointed her. She couldn't give up on it or toss it aside just because its hair had turned gray or its old bones were brittle.

She stood up and went to a front window. Beyond the limited sphere of the porch light, the yard and surrounding acreage were fading into the bleakness of a moonless night. The trees already seemed like ghostly specters in the descending darkness. Meg told herself that in time Ashford House would feel like home again.

She started to turn away from the window when she noticed headlights twinkling through the shrubbery lining the driveway. Someone was approaching the house. Moments later, the Mount Esther patrol car pulled in front of the house and Wade Murdock got out. He had a plate in his hand.

Meg's stomach tightened into a knot as she stared at the litter on the parlor floor. She'd become so involved in the search for the deed that she'd forgotten the deputy had promised to bring her supper. She certainly couldn't let him see that she'd been rummaging through the house like the desperate woman she was. Absolutely not. She had to show that she had the same strength of conviction as he did. She raced to the front entrance as he rapped lightly. Opening the door just a crack, she said, "Oh, hi."

He held the plate out to her. "I told you I'd bring some spaghetti."

She nodded, took the plate, and set it on a foyer table. "Yes, yes, you did."

"You might want to nuke it a little in the microwave. I think Mrs. Ashford has one."

"Oh, she has one, all right. The control pad looks like the instrument panel of a 747."

"I guess that's one of the things she bought in the last few weeks," Wade said.

"No doubt. Well, thanks for the spaghetti. I'll give you the plate back tomorrow." She started to close the door.

"You're welcome," Wade said. Instead of leaving, he raised up on his toes and peered over her shoulder.

"Is something wrong?" Meg asked.

"No. I was just wondering if you'd gone through any of the boxes."

Meg maintained a narrow opening in the doorway. "Not yet, but I've seen evidence of Aunt Amelia's shopping all over the house. She's decorated one of the bedrooms upstairs in a jungle motif complete with a fake fur Zebra-striped comforter on the mattress. Somehow it doesn't seem like her taste, but I suppose there's a lot about my aunt that I don't know anymore."

As if determined to chat, Wade leaned against the jamb preventing Meg from shutting the door. "I suppose you've noticed that the house needs a little fixing up," he said.

Wade Murdock was an expert at understatement.

"I promised to do some of that work for Mrs. Ashford," he continued. "But lately I've been concentrating my efforts on the barn. It needs a lot of attention, too."

"I haven't been inside the barn," Meg admitted. She shifted from one foot to the other. Did Wade intend to chat half the night away? If he did, Meg wasn't sure how she felt about that. She definitely didn't want him to see the clutter in the parlor, but it was kind of nice having a lawman on the property to offset some of her fears. Still, Meg couldn't forget that she and this particular lawman had a huge, three-story Queen Anne obstacle sitting between them.

After a few moments of silence, Wade finally said, "I guess I'll be going then."

"Okay. Thanks again."

He stepped down from the veranda and walked away. Meg was about to close the door at last, but suddenly the subtle creaks of Ashford House were snuffed out by a tremendous crash originating somewhere in an upstairs room.

Meg flung the door wide, ran onto the porch, and screamed, "Deputy Murdock!"

He was already tearing back to the house. He rushed by Meg and burst through the open door. "Stay here," he ordered as he took the stairs two at a time.

Meg watched him until he disappeared upstairs. Then, her heart pounding, she clutched her arms under her breasts and tried to obey the deputy's instructions. It was no use. She chose the more appealing protection of Wade's presence over the blackness of the landscape around the house. She darted inside and followed him up the stairs.

He snapped his attention to her while his back was flattened against the wall outside the bedroom where Meg had slept as a child and where she'd put her suitcase earlier. The room still had a comfortable, cozy appearance, but that was before Wade stood outside the threshold with a weapon in his hand.

Wade waved her back with the barrel of his pistol.

She interpreted the look he gave her to mean he wasn't pleased that she'd ignored his orders. Her breath coming in short gasps, she crouched down in the door frame of an adjoining room and watched as Wade slowly slid along the wall toward the open door. Oddly, a beam of light sliced across the threshold and into the hallway.

Pivoting with one giant step into the open doorway, Wade pointed his weapon with two hands and announced his presence. "Police," he said with a resounding and authoritative tone. And then he dropped the weapon to his side and expelled a long breath.

Meg scurried up behind him and tried to see over his shoulder. "What is it?"

"The lamp fell from the nightstand," he said. "I'm afraid it's shattered."

That explained the strange spear of light. "It must have been the wind," Meg said, remembering that she'd opened the window a few hours ago.

Wade secured his weapon in his holster as he moved into the room. "Maybe. But unfortunately the lamp isn't the only casualty."

Meg understood what he meant as she followed him inside. She covered her mouth with her hand and whispered, "Oh, no."

Wade scooped up a lifeless bird from the floor. And then he poked his fist through the corner of the window screen revealing how the bird had gotten inside.

"The poor thing," Meg said. "I didn't notice that tear earlier when I opened the window."

Wade looked around the room and then down at the bird. "Just as I thought," he said. "This is definitely the work of Mr. Cuddles."

Meg gaped at him. "The bird has…*had*…a name?"

"Not the bird. The cat."

"Cat? What cat?"

Wade pointed over Meg's bed to the floor on the other side of the room. There, peering up at both of them with piercing golden eyes was a long-haired champagne-colored feline, whose insolent expression clearly indicated that he was not happy about two humans invading his space.

"My aunt never had a cat," Meg said.

"She does now. I forgot to tell you. She bought Mr. Cuddles from a private breeder over in Lake City a few weeks ago."

Meg closed her eyes and counted to ten. "Don't tell me…with your money?"

"I suppose so. He's a purebred Persian. Anyway, either the maid or I have been feeding Cuddles since Mrs. Ashford's accident, but with all the commotion earlier, I forgot, so the ingenious fellow went into the trees to do a little grocery shopping." He regarded the casualty of Mr. Cuddles's appetite still in his hand. "This poor bird was intended as supper. I guess Cuddles misjudged his entrance into the bedroom and knocked the lamp over which in turn scared the sparrow right out of his jaws."

Meg had never been a cat lover and was even less so now that she realized she would have Killer Cuddles to take care of until arrangements could be made for his adoption. Her sympathy definitely lay with the poor mangled sparrow. She glared at the cat. "I hope you'll eat spaghetti, Cuddles, because you're not getting so much as one bite of this poor bird."

She caught Wade's smile out of the corner of her eye. He folded his long fingers over the bird and headed for the door. "I'll show you where the cat food is," he said, "and then I'll do something with the victim."

"Thanks." Meg started to follow him out the door but Cuddles strutted in front of her, his head high and the end of his tail twitching with an arrogant indifference to her presence. She trailed the cat down the rear staircase and into the kitchen.

Meg didn't know what Wade would do with the dead bird once he went out the back door. But she was glad she had the job of feeding Mr. Cuddles to occupy her mind. The cat attacked his bowl of food with relish, including the special cat treats she spread on the floor next to his bowl. If she had to endure days in the house with only this sullen cat for company, she was determined to do her best to make friends with him.

After a few minutes Wade returned. He pulled out a chair for Meg and said, "Now you. Sit. I'll go get the spaghetti."

He came back with the plate, set it in the microwave, and deftly pressed a few buttons on the control pad. When he set the food in front of her, Meg realized her mouth was watering. She twirled a few strands around her fork and took a healthy bite. "This is good."

"I'll tell Pop you said so." Wade stood watching her for a few moments as if he was uncertain if he should stay or go. Finally he opened a drawer, withdrew some masking tape and said, "I'll fix that screen upstairs tomorrow. For tonight you might want to patch up the hole with this."

She took the roll of tape. "Okay, thanks. But, under

the circumstances, if you don't want to fix the screen, I'll understand."

His mouth twitched upward in a strange sort of grin. "What circumstances are you talking about?"

Was he pretending ignorance of their obvious dilemma? She felt her face flush. "Well, I'm sure you've been repairing things around here because you thought the house was yours…"

He shrugged a shoulder. "I still do believe it. I bought this house."

A spark of anger flared inside her. "Look, Deputy Murdock…"

"Wade."

"Fine, Wade. I told you. My aunt gave the house to me. I plan to live here someday, and any repairs that need to be done are my responsibility. I don't want you to put any more effort into a property that will one day be mine."

"I'll take my chances," he said. "Besides, fixing this old place has sort of become a hobby. A labor of love you might say."

"But you're wasting your time…and money."

"I don't see it that way." He leaned back against the counter and appraised her with cool, confident eyes. "And if you don't mind an honest observation, I don't think you're that sure of your claim."

She dropped her spaghetti-laden fork. "What? I've been sure of my claim to Ashford House for years, Deputy."

"Wade."

"Whatever. Why would you think such a thing?"

"Because I just went through the parlor to pick up the plate of spaghetti."

"And?"

"And I saw that mess on the floor. You've been looking for something, Meg. Rather frantically, it seems to me."

"What I've been doing is none of your business."

"You didn't find it, did you?"

"Find what?"

"The deed."

She picked up her fork and began twirling spaghetti as if her life depended on curling the strands into a concise, compact roll. "I don't want to talk about this with you. I don't think we should talk about it."

"That's funny. When I've got twenty thousand dollars invested in something, I don't consider it a taboo subject."

She raised the fork and peered at him over the top of the pasta that had immediately begun to unravel. "Don't you have some crimes to solve? Aren't there cats to get out of trees?"

"That's the fire department. Besides, I've already had one cat caper tonight. But, yeah, I've got to go." He crossed the kitchen and pressed one hand on the swinging door to the dining room. "Just one more thing…"

She whirled around in her chair. "What now?"

"When I went through the parlor, I noticed you did find the contract of sale."

Right. The contract had been in the lap drawer of Amelia's desk. "You're quite a snoop, aren't you?"

"Training. When you're part of a two-man law enforcement team in a hotbed of crime like Mount Esther, you don't leave any stone unturned." He smiled as he pushed the door as far as it would go. "And it helped that you left the contract on top of everything else on the desk…like maybe you'd been reading it."

She crossed her legs and began pumping the right one up and down. "Okay, I may have looked it over, and I'm glad I did…"

"Me, too."

"…because it's only a lease-option agreement. You haven't actually bought the house."

He took a step back into the kitchen and let the door close. "It's a binding contract, Meg. I've paid Mrs. Ashford a down payment and I've been giving her rent on the barn. It's a done deal."

Meg didn't know enough about real estate contracts to rebut his argument, but she did know that four years ago, Amelia had prepared a clear deed with her name on it—if only she could find it. "I wouldn't be so sure, Deputy," she blustered.

"We'll see," he said. "Anyway, you've seen mine. Now it's time for me to see yours. Then maybe we'll figure out what to do about this mess."

She listened to his footsteps recede through the house. "I'll find the deed, Deputy," she called out. "And I'll be only too happy to show it to you."

His voice carried from the parlor. "It's Wade, Meg, for the third time. And you know where to find me."

CHAPTER FIVE

A RINGING TELEPHONE jolted Wade from a dream of an auburn-haired woman, her full lips tugging down into a frown, sitting in Mrs. Ashford's parlor in the middle of a pile of papers. He turned over in bed and opened one eye to see the digital clock on his nightstand. 6:36. Great. He'd had a whopping five hours sleep and lost the end to a fantasy whose possibilities were far more exciting than his reality.

In the darkness, he fumbled for the portable, grabbed it off its cradle, and croaked, "Deputy Murdock. If this is anything short of murder, call back in two hours."

The voice that answered was familiar, and irritating. "Wade, this is Harvey Crockett at the Quick Mart. You'd better get over here right away. Newton Bonner just ran out on his gas bill and left me holding a twenty-dollar tab."

"Oh, geez, Harvey," Wade grumbled. "Can't it wait till the sun's up? Newton isn't going anywhere."

"How do you know that? He peeled away from the pump like a bat outta hell. He could be halfway to the county line by now—on my tank of gas."

Wade pictured eighty-eight-year-old Newton Bonner and doubted the man could peel a banana, but it didn't pay to argue with a citizen he was hired to protect. He swung his feet to the floor and arched his back to stretch his muscles into service. "I'll drive on over to Newton's place and check it out, Harvey. Call you when I know something."

"I'm gonna have to make folks pay before they pump from now on, Wade. I don't give credit here, and I can't cover the cash drawer myself…"

Wade held the phone away from his ear and stood up. "Harvey, do you want to keep me on the phone listening to you, or do you want me to go after Newton?"

"You get that old buzzard, Wade. He can't get away with this."

Wade pressed the disconnect button and returned the phone to his nightstand. He was thankful tomorrow was Sheriff Hollinger's day to answer the calls.

A DOZEN PEACOCKS and three times that many chickens scattered in advance of the patrol car as Wade pulled on-to Newton Bonner's property. Wade didn't know much about peacocks, but he'd heard that old Newton had made a living for more than fifty years selling their colorful quills to novelty shops and the birds to petting zoos. Now that he was retired, Newton still kept a few birds around his place because he claimed they were good company. Since the old guy had never married, Wade supposed that a family of fowl would be preferable at this point in the man's life to living, breathing, arguing people. The birds appeared content as well, Wade observed. The property wasn't even fenced, and Wade had never been called out on a rampaging peacock emergency.

Newton emerged from a shed and began scattering

pellets of feed on the ground. The birds forgot about
Wade and, with their colorful tail feathers spread, beat
an awkward path to the goodies. When he saw Wade,
Newton and his entourage crossed the yard to meet him.

"Morning, Deputy," Newton said. "What brings you
out here?"

Mindful of his clean uniform, Wade swatted a couple of curious hens away from his pants leg. "You know
why I'm here, Newton," he said. "You're not so old that
you forgot what you did not more than half an hour ago."

Newton ground the stub of an unfiltered cigarette into the dirt. "That damn Harvey Crockett. Did he call you
out this early in the morning to run me down?"

"Yes, he did, and he had a right to. You stole twenty
dollars' worth of gasoline."

Newton removed a wide-brimmed felt hat and ran
long, gnarled fingers through white hair that hadn't seen
a barber in quite a long time. "I woulda' gone back
there in a day or two to pay up," he said.

"That's not the way it works, Newton, and you
know it."

"I left my wallet at home. I remembered it when I
was already halfway to the feed store. What was I supposed to do? If I'd a' passed on by the Quick Mart, I'd
a' run out of gas before I hit the county road."

"You forgot your wallet?" Wade repeated.

Obviously thinking he'd brought Wade over to his
way of thinking, Newton nodded his head vigorously.
"That's right. Left it on the kitchen table."

Wade scowled at the old man. "Then you were driving without your license, too?"

A spiderweb of veins turned pink under Newton's

thin skin. "Hell, no, Wade," the man lied. He patted his shirt pocket. "I always put my license right here, and I had it with me."

"So where do you keep your twenty-dollar bills?" Wade asked him. "You bring me one now and maybe I'll overlook a charge of petty larceny this time."

Newton grinned with the half dozen teeth still in his mouth and trotted off to his house. He returned a minute later with a crisp twenty-dollar bill, one of the newly minted ones. Wade bet that the sly old fella had a trunk full of them hidden away somewhere.

"You're a fair man, Deputy," Newton said.

Wade tucked the bill into his pocket. "Maybe, but I'm also a man who's running out of patience. The next time you do this, I'm writing you up."

Newton bent over and scooped a fat hen from the ground at his feet. "Here, take this home for dinner. It's my treat."

Imagining Jenny's reaction at witnessing the decapitation of what would later appear on her plate, Wade politely refused. "Some other time, Newton."

The old man walked Wade back to his patrol car. "So how's everything going with the Ashford place?" he asked. "Are you thinking that you bit off more than you can chew?"

Wade shook his head. "Nope. Not yet. I'm pleased as I can be with that house. Working on it has brought me and my dad closer than we've been in years." He scanned the clear blue sky above him. "And this climate has done wonders for his pleurisy. I think another winter in New York might have killed him. Now I believe he'll go on forever."

"You started working up in the attic yet?"

"No. That'll be the last job I tackle," Wade said.

"You been up there, though, haven't you?"

"Sure. When I bought the place from Mrs. Ashford I took a quick look around the third floor. All I saw was some worn-out furniture, a mess of cobwebs and a couple of critters. It's a small space, so…"

Newton cackled. "A small space, you say?"

"Yeah. Besides the turret which opens onto all three floors, the actual attic can't be more than twelve feet square."

They'd reached the patrol car, but Newton was obviously not done talking. "Guess you didn't see the mural then."

Wade thought back to that day several weeks ago. He'd seen some ratty old picture frames leaning against a wall, but nothing the size of a mural. "I didn't see anything as big as that."

"You missed the best part then. I remember when Stewie Ashford built that place and hired a guy to paint a picture the size of a church door in the attic. There were some high times up there once that mural was finished. Why, a fella could stand in the turret and see a car pull into the drive all the way from the county road. I was there once when I was just a youngster, not more than seventeen, I'd say. Stewie let me come up there anyways. He didn't pay any mind to county laws."

Wade crossed his arms over his chest and leaned against the hood of his car. "What are you talking about, Newton?"

A wide grin creased the old man's face. "Guess I've said too much already. You go on back up there, Wade, and look for the mural. That's all I'm saying. I won't be the one to blacken a dead man's memory, or for that matter, start up rumors that'd vex his sweet widow."

Wade had heard other such vague references to Stewart Ashford's reputation, all from the few old-timers who still remembered the town's most famous patriarch. He didn't know exactly what shenanigans Stewart participated in way back when, but he'd surmised that maybe the guy stood a little to the left of the law. Well, more power to him. The old days were long gone. The house would soon belong to Wade, if Meg Hamilton didn't pose a stumbling block. What did Wade care if Stewart Ashford operated a shell game more than half a century ago.

He walked around to the driver's side door and raised a finger at Newton before getting inside the car. "You pay your bills from now on, Newton. I mean it."

The old fella stroked the back of the hen whose life had been spared. "You betcha', Deputy."

Wade headed back toward the Quick Mart to pay Newton's debt. But he wasn't thinking a whole lot about what he would say to appease Harvey Crockett. Mostly he was thinking about the idea of a mural existing in that tiny little attic room of Ashford House.

AT EIGHT O'CLOCK Saturday morning, Meg was already on her way to Shady Grove. She was determined to meet with her aunt when Amelia might be most alert. Besides, the antics of Mr. Cuddles and the heart-thumping police work of Wade Murdock had kept her tossing and turning most of the night. She wasn't sorry to be leaving last night's escapades behind her to deal with today's problems.

Giving herself time for a second cup of coffee, Meg pulled into the parking lot of the Quick Mart and headed straight for the brewing machine. She'd just stirred sugar and cream into her cup when the door to the convenience store opened. "Oh, great," she said under her breath when she realized who had entered. "Just who I need to see this morning."

Wade stopped at the counter and slid a sum of money toward the clerk. The two men maintained an animated conversation until Wade finally threw his hands in the air and accused the clerk of being unreasonable. "He's an old man, Harvey," Wade said.

"He's slippery as an eel," the clerk responded, "and I'm holding you responsible if there's any more trouble."

Wade strode away from the counter. "Fine. How's the coffee this morning? Still taste like motor oil?" When he saw Meg, he tossed a final comment over his shoulder. "Don't answer that, Harvey. There's someone here who'll give me an honest opinion." He set a paper cup under the dispenser. "So, Miss Meg Hamilton, what do you think?"

She leaned against the condiment counter and nodded toward a case with clear plastic doors. "The coffee's fine, but since you're a policeman, I figure you won't be satisfied until you grab one of those donuts."

"Ah… another misconception that you civilians have about us cops." He dumped three envelopes of sugar into his coffee and stirred vigorously. Then, despite his statement, he opened a door, took out a chocolate-covered Bavarian Cream and took a huge bite which he followed with a smug grin. "But, heck, who am I to destroy a legend?"

Meg shook her head.

"So how's Mr. Cuddles this morning?" Wade asked after sucking a dab of filling from his index finger. It was a gesture Meg found oddly disturbing.

"He's like all males, I guess," she said. "He left the house early to find a poor creature in the yard that he could lord his authority over."

Wade raised that finger to make a point. "Yeah, but he made you notice him, and that's what counts." He wiped his hands with a napkin and tossed the paper into the trash bin. "By the way, I'll be at the house later after I do rounds. I'll fix the window screen before I get started in the barn."

"If you want to," Meg said with an aloofness that disguised her very strong desire to have the window secure.

"Oh, I do," Wade said. "If for no other reason than I need to establish my superiority over Mr. Cuddles."

Meg headed for the cash register to pay for her coffee. "I guess I'll see you later then."

Wade tossed a couple of bills on the counter and followed her outside. "Say, Meg, before you go, can you answer a question for me?"

"Depends on the question."

"It's about your Uncle Stewart."

Meg's interest was immediately piqued. Even though he'd died when she was only twelve, she remembered her Uncle Stewie vividly. He was so handsome sitting astride his prized Arabian mare and cantering gracefully around the property. And he was completely unpredictable in his antics. Like her brother Jerry, he made everyone laugh. "What about him?" she said.

"What did he do for a living?"

"He was an entrepreneur."

Wade's lips twitched as if he were trying to hide a smile. "That's a little vague, isn't it?"

Meg had never thought so. Even when she hadn't understood what the word meant, she'd always believed that it described her uncle perfectly. "Maybe, but that's what Aunt Amelia always called him."

"So that's how he made all his money, as an entrepreneur?"

"I suppose so. Plus his parents had a little money. His father was a cattleman on Florida's west coast. Stewie dabbled in land development in this area, and I heard that he got in on the ground floor of a couple of profitable local businesses." She shrugged. "I think my uncle was lucky to be in the right places at the right times."

"Lucky, eh? I wonder if any of that Ashford luck rubbed off on you."

"What do you mean?"

He lowered his sunglasses and peered at her with those interesting dark brown eyes. "Did you find the deed?"

We're back to that again. "You seem awfully worried about that document, Wade, and you should be. I'll definitely find it because it definitely exists." She got in her car. "And when I do, you'll be the first to know." She shut the door but rolled down her window. "But since you brought up our little predicament, I'll tell you about an idea I had."

"I'm listening."

"I'm going to go through the boxes this afternoon with the idea of returning everything to the catalogue companies. My intention is to give you back the twenty thousand dollars."

He twirled the sunglasses while giving her a bland stare. "I don't want it back."

"But that's the perfect solution."

"Not to me it isn't."

As if there weren't a hundred houses to buy within a thirty-mile radius of hers! And to think Wade had called the store clerk unreasonable. "Look, Wade, I read the entire lease-option contract last night."

"Good."

"You only promised to pay a pittance of what the house and property are worth."

"You call ninety-eight thousand dollars a 'pittance'?"

"I certainly do. In Orlando…"

He tapped the insignia on his shirt sleeve. "This is Mount Esther. That's what I like about this little town. The cost of living is quite reasonable, especially to a transplant who's used to New York prices."

"But even in Mount Esther a twelve-room house, a six-stall barn, and all that land—"

"—in good condition would be worth about one hundred and fifty thousand," he interrupted. He put on his glasses and folded his arms across his chest. "I've already put a couple of thousand into the house, borrowed from the Mount Esther Savings and Loan, and you can see that a complete renovation will cost much more."

He'd borrowed money against *her* house? Meg gripped the steering wheel to control her temper. "If Ashford House is costing you so dearly, why not cut your losses, take the twenty thousand and go buy something that's livable right now?"

"Don't want to. Ashford House is perfect for my family. It's a dream we can work on together."

It's my dream, too, damn it, Meg thought. My dream first.

"And besides," he continued, "I don't think you'll get more than a small percentage of the twenty thousand back. Most of the items have been unpacked and put to use in the house. And I've read some of the labels on the boxes. They say a full refund is available within seven days. That time limit has elapsed. And since most of the purchases were made without the security of a credit card…"

"Enough." Meg rolled her window up and jerked the gearshift into reverse.

Wade waved at her as she backed out of the parking space. "See you later, Meg," he hollered.

She veered onto the road but resisted the urge to stomp on the gas pedal. With her luck, Murdock would race after her, lights flashing and siren blaring, just for the pleasure of giving her a ticket.

AS SHE APPROACHED the door to Amelia's room in Shady Grove, Meg was immediately aware of a change in the environment. It was quiet. Yesterday she'd heard her aunt's television well in advance of reaching her door. Today she heard nothing. At the threshold she looked down upon an empty bed, stripped of sheets.

Meg stood rooted in the doorway. "Oh, my God, no…"

A worker came up behind her, touched her lightly on her shoulder. "Can I help you, ma'am?"

Meg whirled around and stared into the young woman's face. "My aunt. She's gone. What happened?"

The woman held up a stack of linens. "It's not what you think. I'm just changing the sheets. Miz Ashford's down the hall in the gathering room."

Meg felt limp with relief. She held on to the arm of a chair until she caught her breath. "Of course. I shouldn't have jumped to conclusions."

The woman set the sheets on a dresser, took the top one and flipped it open over the bed. The scent of bleach trailed in the wake of the fluttering cotton. "Five doors down," she said. "You'll find Miz Ashford."

"Thank you." As she walked down the hall, Meg was able to think logically again. Of course Amelia wouldn't spend every waking hour in bed. The staff would encourage her to mingle with other patients, at the same time giving the employees opportunity to keep the rooms maintained.

At the door to the gathering room, Meg recognized the voice of Gene Rayburn coming from a big-screen television. Amelia was seated in a wheelchair several feet from the set. She was propped up with pillows and a thick floral throw covered her knees. She was, as yesterday, enraptured by the television show.

Meg looked at the screen and watched celebrities give answers on *Match Game*. She pulled a chair close to her aunt and sat down. "Good morning, Aunt Amelia," she said.

Amelia glanced over and smiled. "Margaret, you've come back. I told them you would."

Grateful that Amelia knew who she was this morning, Meg said, "Of course I came."

Amelia returned her attention to the screen. "That Charles Nelson Reilly. He's a funny one."

"Yes, he is," Meg agreed. "We need to talk about what you want me to do while I'm here, why you called me to Mount Esther."

Her eyes focused straight ahead, Amelia said, "I fell, you know. They say I broke something."

"Yes, I know. Are you in pain?"

"Not much."

"I'm glad of that. Now, what can I do?"

"Sell it all, dear, every last stitch."

Meg tried to pin down the vague instructions. "Sell what, exactly, Aunt Amelia?"

"Everything in the house. All of it. I don't need any of it anymore." She waved her free hand with a gesture of authority. "Auction it all off." She leveled a sharp gaze on Meg. "You still do that sort of thing, don't you?"

"Yes, I do. I'm licensed to hold an auction anywhere in the state of Florida."

"Good. Then get busy. Take your commission and give the rest of the money to Gloria."

"To Gloria?" Amelia wanted the profits from the sale of the contents of her home to go to Meg's cousin?

"Yes, it's what I decided. What I told Jude Smothers."

The mention of the Ashford family lawyer brought a flood of memories to Meg's mind, and she knew Amelia was in control of her faculties for at least this moment. "That's right," she said. "You left the contents of the house to Gloria in your will."

A lot had changed since Meg and Gloria were kids spending their summers at Ashford House. Gloria had moved far away to Chicago while Meg had stayed close by. Gloria never called Amelia, and she hadn't been to see their aunt in years. Still, Meg would honor her aunt's wishes if that's what Amelia wanted.

"*Blank* in a row…" Amelia said, echoing Gene Rayburn's instructions to the celebrity panel and capturing

Meg's attention once more. "Oh, my, that is difficult. What will Charles Nelson Reilly say?"

Meg sensed that her aunt's delicate hold on reality was fading. She gently squeezed her hand. "Aunt Amelia, think about this. Why should I give the money to Gloria now? You should keep the profits…"

"No use for it," she stated simply. "Give it to Gloria."

"But if I sell everything, then the house will be empty when you go home."

"Ducks…ducks in a row. Bottles…bottles in a row." Amelia was mumbling. "I won't ever go back there," she finally said, and Meg knew she believed it. Oddly, she didn't seem sad.

"But you might," Meg said. "You might get better…"

Amelia stared hard at Meg. "No, dear, I won't," she stated with uncompromising defiance. "Besides, I like it here. They have cable." Her face wrinkled in concentration as she returned her attention to the screen. "Pretty maids in a row."

Meg prayed that her aunt would stay focused for a few more seconds while she pressed for the information she desperately needed. "But the house, Aunt Amelia… do you remember what is to become of the house?"

"Ashford House will stand long after I have gone."

"That's right. But who will own it? Do you remember making out a Quit Claim Deed?"

Amelia's eyes clouded with uncertainty. She was slipping into that place that comforted her. An enigmatic smile curved her lips. "Hello, miss," she said to Meg. "Will you bring me some tea?"

Meg rose. "Yes, dear, of course." On her way out,

Meg stopped in the dining room and asked that a cup of tea be sent to Amelia Ashford in the gathering room.

IN THE PARKING LOT, Meg sat in her car and punched the number of the auction house into her cell phone. Her brother answered, and Meg explained what had just taken place with their aunt.

"You're kidding?" he said. "She wants you to auction off everything in the house?"

"That's right. It's going to be a huge job. I'll have to make a list of everything she owns, advertise the sale in the local papers, contact dealers in the area—"

"Has she got anything worth money in that place?" Jerry interrupted.

"I guess we'll find out. Her furniture is old, mostly from the thirties and forties, but it's been well cared for. I don't suppose her things qualify as antiques, but their age certainly puts them in the collectible category, and they're sought after by people who want Deco pieces. Plus she's got tons of small items, knickknacks that will probably sell well."

"So what's she going to do with the money in a nursing home?"

"That's the odd part," Meg said. "She told me to take our twenty per cent commission and give the rest to Gloria as she stated in her will."

"Gloria? No way. I'll bet she hasn't been to see the old gal more than five times in the last fifteen years."

"Which makes her only slightly less attentive than you, Jerry. But obviously Aunt Amelia doesn't hold a grudge. I remember the generous sum of money she gave you when she sold Uncle Stewie's tools."

"Oh, right. I wish I still had it."

Meg smiled. She was certain Jerry didn't have anything left of the paycheck he got two days ago, much less that windfall from Amelia. "Anyway," she said, "when Amelia made out her will, I'm sure she was recalling the fun times we all had together when we were kids. I'm not surprised she left something to Gloria."

"That's good news, Meggie," Jerry said. "If she remembers leaving the contents of the house to Gloria, then she must remember giving you the house."

Meg blew out a long breath and started her car. "I was hoping she would, but she didn't, not yet anyway. But it's a start."

"So the deputy still thinks he's buying Ashford House?"

"Yes, he definitely does."

"Well, just get a copy of the Quit Claim Deed and shove it in his face. That should convince him."

"I would, but I can't find a copy anywhere in the house."

"So look somewhere else. A safety deposit box. Her lawyer's office. You'll find it."

Imagine. Jerry actually coming up with a positive suggestion. "Of course. I will. Thanks, Jer."

"Oh, gotta go. That girl I told you about yesterday— the good-looking one—she just came in the door. I'll put the sprout on the line."

"No, wait! Forget about the girl for a minute. I haven't asked you about the auction. Are you set up? Did you call in the newspaper ad? Did you clean the furniture so it looks presentable?"

These jobs were generally Meg's responsibilities,

not that Jerry wasn't capable of handling them. But, typically, Meg had never insisted that he take charge of day-to-day auction chores. She regretted that now.

She'd lost him. She knew it when Jerry's voice sounded distant, as if he were holding the phone far from his ear. "Hi there," he said. "Be right with you. Hey, Spence, buddy, come take the phone, will you?"

The next voice Meg heard was her son's. And the distant charming drawl her brother used when he was trying to impress the heck out of someone.

CHAPTER SIX

HIS ATTENTION GLUED on the petite blonde who'd just come in the door, Jerry walked briskly up the center aisle of the auction house. He intercepted his visitor near the platform where merchandise for that night's sale was set up. "Hey, Mary Beth, isn't it?"

Of course he darned well knew her name. He'd been singing it in his mind since the day before. But he didn't want to appear overanxious.

She rewarded him with a quick smile. "Oh, you remembered."

He leaned against the platform. "Sure. There are some names and faces that a guy just can't forget." *So much for playing it cool.*

She twirled a strand of strawberry-blond hair with her index finger. "You're sweet."

Before he openly drooled, Jerry switched the conversation to a business topic. "Did you bring samples of that merchandise you told me about yesterday?" he asked.

"Sure did. I've got lots of pieces in my van outside. You want to have a look?"

"You bet. Just a sec." Jerry shouted into the office, "Hey, Spence, I'm going into the parking lot for a minute. Be right back."

As they walked toward the door, Mary Beth looked into the office as well. "What a cute little boy," she said. "Is he yours?"

Jerry almost laughed out loud. "Mine? Hell… I mean heck no. I'm just—"

"I love children," she interrupted. "Look at those glasses and that curly hair. He's adorable."

"Yeah, he's adorable all right." Noticing that Mary Beth's expression became blissfully maternal, Jerry added, "The kid and I—we're practically inseparable."

"But you're not related?"

"Oh, we are. I'm his uncle, but I guess you could say I'm more like a father to him. I've been watching him since his mother left…"

"His mother left him?"

Mary Beth appeared ready to jump to the aid of two men in distress. Picturing an interesting benefit to Mary Beth's obvious nurturing instincts, Jerry decided on an evasive explanation that wasn't exactly a lie. "It's a long story."

Spencer looked over at them and Jerry waved.

"You must be doing a wonderful job with him. He looks happy."

"He is, most of the time," Jerry said. "It's not easy assuming the role of a single parent these days." *At least that's what Meggie tells me.*

He should have stopped right there, but the sympathetic interest in Mary Beth's violet eyes was irresistible. "I think the kid misses a woman's touch, though," he said. "I'm the rough and tumble type. I play football, go to baseball games, eat cheeseburgers for breakfast. Those kinds of activities are okay for my nephew I guess, but I'm learning to look deep into my emotional side, for his sake."

Mary Beth gave him an approving smile. "Not many men would do that. I admire you."

"Thanks. I suppose I'm just naturally a caring type of guy." He took her elbow and led her to the door before Spencer could get off the phone and begin repeating everything his mother had just said. "Okay, then, let's have a look at what you brought."

They went outside to a van marked Good Samaritan Charity. Mary Beth unlocked the loading door in back and stepped aside so Jerry could see the cargo.

He stared at sealed cartons of household appliances, electronics and computer equipment. "Wow. This is some great stuff." He gave her a casual sort of grin. "It's not hot, is it?"

"Oh, no," she quickly assured him. "Our charity would never accept merchandise like that. It's mostly just returned items."

"Is any of it damaged?"

"None of it. The man who gave it to us said they get factory overruns, close-outs, and, like I said, unopened customer returns. He just wants to make a little money for his time and effort, so he asked us if we'd consider consigning the merchandise to a local auction for a fifty-fifty split. We get a lot of stuff donated, and this deal sounded fair."

As he unloaded boxes onto the blacktop so he could see farther into the van, Jerry was mentally adding up what each item might bring at auction. The amount was pleasantly staggering. "What would our deal be?" he asked Mary Beth.

"I don't know what you consider fair, but I think if Góod Samaritan Charity gets half, we should split that amount with you for selling it. In other words, Colonial Auction Company would get twenty-five percent, and we'd take twenty-five." She looked up at Jerry with long-lashed, trusting eyes. "What do you think?"

"Ah…sure. I think that's okay. Is there any more where this came from?"

"A ton," she said. "Mr. Horton, who brought me this first load, said that depending on how well these items did, he'd bring me as much as I can handle."

Good clean merchandise week after week without worrying about scrounging for things to sell… It was a dream come true, especially with his sister out of town for an indeterminate time. Jerry jumped at the opportunity to impress Meg with his business sense and to put Colonial Auction in the black by simply unloading a van once or twice a week. "Your contact will be satisfied," he said. "And I'll handle all of this you can bring me."

"Great. Let's take it inside."

They spent the next half hour carrying boxes into the auction hall. When the van was empty, Jerry set Spencer down with a notepad and pencil and had him catalogue the items on an auction consignment form as each one was unpacked and set on the platform. This delegation of authority served two purposes. It kept Spence busy so he wouldn't talk about the phone call from his mother, and it insured that the list would be spelled correctly.

"That's it," Jerry said when the job was finished. He'd set up five complete computer systems, six game consoles that made Spencer's mouth water, several microwave ovens, three thirty-two inch televisions, two dozen expensive watches, and over thirty name-brand kitchen appliances and electronic organizers. Easily several thousand dollars' worth of goodies, even by auction standards.

Jerry was darned proud of himself. He'd show Meg that she could leave the auction in his hands without worrying. And when he looked at Mary Beth Watson, he felt even better.

"I guess that's it then," she said as she dusted her hands on floral pants. "What time does the auction start tonight?"

"Six-thirty," he told her.

"I'll be here." She sat down beside Spencer. "Thanks for all your help. Will you be here tonight?"

A second pair of Hamilton eyes looked at Mary Beth with adoration. "I don't know what else Uncle Jerry's going to do with me, so I suppose I will," he said.

"Good. See you later." She picked up her purse and headed for the door. Jerry sat next to Spencer and both men watched out the window until Mary Beth had climbed into the van.

"She's pretty," Spencer said.

"You're right about that," Jerry said. "I'm just glad she's too old for you."

Spencer tapped his sneakers on the cement floor and appeared thoughtful. "Maybe now, but in fifteen or twenty years…"

"Heck with that," Jerry said. "In fifteen years I plan to have had three kids with that woman and season tickets to Disney World." He turned in his chair and gave his nephew an earnest stare. "But in order to facilitate this marriage proposal I'm planning to make, there's one little thing you've got to know about your condition."

Spence pushed his glasses to the bridge of his nose. "My condition? What are you talking about?"

"Mary Beth sort of thinks your mother ran out on you, and I'm raising you for the time being. I think it's in my best interest to let her believe that for just a little while."

"So you're lying to her."

"I haven't lied. I'm just taking advantage of a potentially beneficial misunderstanding. I'll set her straight once she's nuts about me. All you've got to do is act like you're kind of sad, but eternally grateful to me. Can you do that?"

Spencer was silent for several seconds, prompting Jerry to think the kid might actually turn down his request. "Okay," Spence said at last. "I can do that. Besides, sometimes I am sad, so that won't be acting."

Jerry, you stupid jerk. The poor kid was depressed too much of the time and had been since his worthless father walked out on him without sending so much as a birthday card since. He ruffled Spencer's hair and smiled at him. "Thanks a lot, Spence. I promise to make it up to you." And Jerry meant it. A ten-year-old kid ought to be happy, not mooning his life away over a name-only father who didn't deserve a second thought or worrying about a mother who was scared to take a chance on life again.

DURING THE RIDE BACK to Ashford House, Meg thought about Colonial Auction and the mess her brother might get them in. Once she arrived at the house, though, she didn't have time to think about anything but sorting through the boxes taking up a good portion of Amelia's first floor. Once the cartons were unpacked, she could begin seriously setting up for the auction of her aunt's belongings.

Five minutes into the job, she discovered that Wade Murdock's warning was true. The large majority of Amelia's purchases had been in her possession too long to be returned for a refund. Meg resigned herself to selling these new items along with the old things in Amelia's house, and giving the proceeds to Gloria.

As she opened each carton, Meg used a kitchen knife to tear down the boxes and stack the folded cardboard in one expanding heap in a corner of the room. She decided not to open some of the boxes—the ones that contained many small parts. She would sell the deluxe barbecue grill unopened as well as the ten-speed bicycle and nine foot pre-lit Christmas tree. As she unwrapped the more manageable items, she set them on the dining room table, and with each unveiling, she became more and more amazed at the directions her aunt's thinking must have taken in the weeks after she acquired Wade's money.

She was dismantling a box which contained a mink hat from Asia when she heard someone at the back door.

"Hi! Is anyone home?"

She recognized the young voice and hurried into the kitchen. "Hello, Jenny," she said to Wade's daughter. "What can I do for you?"

The girl's face reflected misery. "I have to use the bathroom."

Meg held the screen door open and Jenny came inside. "There's one by the library, but you can't get into the hallway from the dining room. You have to go through the parlor…"

"I know where it is." The girl ran by Meg and disappeared through the kitchen door. A few minutes later she returned. "Whew. I should have gone at home, but Gramps was in a big hurry to drop me off and get to the grocery." She took a set of keys from her jeans pocket and jangled them in the air. "Usually I let myself in, but I sort of forgot about you being here until I saw the back door open."

How many keys to Ashford House are floating around this community? Meg wondered. "Are you here by yourself then?" she asked the girl.

"Yeah, but my dad's meeting me here with the sheriff's department pickup truck and horse trailer. We're supposed to be taking Lady Jay to the equestrian park today." She frowned. "If he doesn't take too long fixing your window."

Meg opened the refrigerator and offered Jenny one of the sodas she'd bought on the way back from Shady Grove. The girl took it, popped the tab and sat at the table.

"I'm sure he'll be able to fix the window quickly," Meg said, noticing that Jenny hadn't said thank you for either bathroom privileges or the soda. "Besides it wouldn't matter to me if he didn't fix it until you came back from the park."

Jenny snorted. "You don't know Dad. If he says he's gonna do something, he does it. And he's always fixing stuff around here. It's like he's suddenly become that guy on TV."

Meg thought a moment. "Bob Vila?"

"Yep, him."

Meg could easily picture Wade on television describing the joys of home improvement. "I suppose he likes the work."

"Oh, yeah." Jenny looked around the kitchen with a disapproving gaze. "If you want my opinion, this place gives me the creeps. You can have it back."

Back? I haven't given it up yet. Meg sat opposite the girl at the long table. "Why do you say that? What's so creepy about Ashford House?"

"All these musty old rooms. And everything creaks. The power goes out all the time. The plumbing is awful. I had to flush twice." She took a big swallow of her Coke. "I wouldn't be surprised if the house is haunted with the ghost of that Stewart guy."

Meg smiled. "I don't think the house is haunted. And even if it were, if the ghost were my Uncle Stewie, we'd only have a lot more fun around here."

"Right. It would be a riot." Jenny placed her elbows on the table and leaned forward to give Meg an intense stare. "Do you think there are secret passageways in the house or locked rooms that haven't been discovered yet? That might be sort of cool."

"No, I don't think so. When I was your age, I explored every inch of this house. I did find a secret cubbyhole or two, but that's about it."

"Really? I'll have to look for them when we finally move in this place for good."

Meg didn't want to think about that possibility and was glad when Jenny brought up another topic.

"So how's Mrs. Ashford today?" the girl asked.

"All right I guess."

"Did she tell you she sold this place to my dad?"

"No. It never came up."

"Sheesh. If it weren't for Lady Jay, I'd have made my dad move into one of those model homes in Esther

Landings out of town. They have high-speed computer hookups even in the kitchen."

Somehow Meg couldn't picture Wade Murdock giving in to a teenager's demand on which house to buy. Not when he professed to be so much in love with this one. "I can see that you really like your horse," she said to keep the conversation going.

"Lady Jay's the greatest. I told my dad that I'd be depressed for sure if he hadn't gotten her for me."

Meg had studied a bit about childhood depression, and she knew it was a serious problem. But she figured if Jenny Murdock were threatening to become depressed, then she was actually far from it. She suspected the girl had an arsenal of complaints that she used as weapons against her father.

"Hey, there. What are you girls up to?"

Jenny and Meg stared at the back door. Wade stood on the steps, his fist raised to knock. For emphasis, and probably because he'd promised, he tapped lightly on the door frame.

"You don't have to knock when I can plainly see you," Meg said.

He came inside with a roll of screen tucked under his arm and a small tool box swinging from his hand. Mr. Cuddles padded in behind him and went to his bowl which Meg now kept filled all the time. Wade strode to Jenny and placed a quick kiss on the top of her head. "You ready to go, cowgirl?"

She gave him a look of exasperation. "I don't ride Western, Dad. It's English, remember?"

He grinned. "Yeah, I remember. Just pulling your ultrasensitive chain."

"Like you always do."

He switched his gaze to Meg while he spoke to his daughter. "Jen, you don't mind if we put off going to the park for just a few minutes, do you? I promised Miss Hamilton…"

"It's first names, Wade," Meg said smartly. "I thought we decided that, so we might as well extend the privilege to your daughter."

"Okay. I told Meg that I'd…"

Jenny sighed dramatically. "…fix her screen, I know."

"Right. You wait here and finish your soda. I'll be quick."

Jenny slumped down in her chair as if she fully expected to spend the next five hours waiting for her father. Mr. Cuddles abandoned his bowl, jumped up on the table and strutted in front of her. When Jenny actually petted the arrogant cat, Meg held back from swatting him off the place she ate her meals. Sometimes the wisest move is to let two stubborn creatures face off in their own way.

Wade walked around the table and stopped by Meg's chair. "Will you come with me?" he asked.

She shot him a questioning look, but he just nodded toward the door. "I guess so."

They went into the dining room where Wade stopped and surveyed the progress Meg had made that morning. "Wow, look at all this stuff. Who would have thought that Mrs. Ashford had all these interests."

Meg frowned. "I know she wasn't thinking clearly when she ordered some of these things, but you're right. She had a wide range of tastes I never knew about, even if they aren't exactly typical of a woman her age."

"So what are you going to do with all this?"

Meg hesitated a moment and then realized she might as well tell Wade about the auction. "I guess you should know. I'm an auctioneer, and this morning at Shady Grove Aunt Amelia asked me to dispose of everything in the house at a public sale. It could get a little hectic around here for a while."

Far from distressed at the idea of a large crowd wandering over the grounds, Wade seemed almost glad. At least relieved. "That's a great idea. I was wondering what I was going to do with all of Mrs. Ashford's…" He paused as if aware that any further comment related to his claim on the property would only irritate Meg. Then he pointed to the entrance to the parlor. "I guess we should go on upstairs."

They went into the foyer where the wide staircase led to the upper floors. Wade followed Meg up, but took her elbow to prevent her from veering toward the bedroom with the broken screen. "Wait a minute. There's something on the third floor I want to see. Do you mind?"

"You want to go to the attic? No, I guess I don't mind, but there's nothing up there but a small storage room and some old junk. At least that's all that was there the last time I looked."

Wade set down the equipment to fix the window and led the way to a door at the end of the upstairs hall. "How long ago was that?" he asked.

"Oh, gee…" Meg had to think. "I don't remember being in the attic in the last fifteen years. Maybe longer." She recalled what Jenny had said a few minutes before and decided that the attic really could give someone the creeps. "But if you want to go…"

He was already halfway up the steps, so Meg followed behind him wondering what in the world he was looking for. And wondering why she'd agreed to go to the dark attic alone with him in the first place.

WADE NOTICED two things about the narrow third-floor staircase that he hadn't seen the only other time he'd been to the attic. One was the musty smell. He doubted that the door to the stairs had been opened very often in the last couple of decades. The other was that the stairway had once been quite elegant. The walls had been papered with a flocked covering whose golden scroll design had mutated to a dingy brown. Every few feet, ornate electric candle sconces, now pitted and dull, suggested that the passage had been lit with a subtle flickering glow—an odd extravagance for a little-used entry to a small attic room.

At the top of the stairs Wade turned the glass knob which wiggled in its setting just as he remembered it from his quick inspection a few weeks ago. As before, he had to use his shoulder to loosen the warped door from the frame.

"I wonder when someone was last up here," Meg said when she could see into the room.

"It was probably me when I was thinking about making an offer on the house," Wade answered.

"Then why do you want to come back today?"

"I didn't look around much that time," he said. "Today I'm following a hunch, or more accurately, a clue." He stepped inside the small room and, guided by sunlight from one dormer window and the grimy panes in the turret, he searched for a lamp.

Meg crossed the threshold and stood with her arms wrapped around her waist as if she were making a tight circle of her body to avoid contact with the dusty cast-offs surrounding her. "What are you looking for?"

"I'm not sure," he said, picking up a small table lamp from the floor. "But I think I'll know it when I see it."

He plugged the cord into an outlet by the door and turned the switch. The lamp crackled menacingly for a second and then maintained a steady, weak light. And a furry creature with four legs jumped from a dresser by the window, scurried across the sill and darted out a hole in the glass to the second-floor roof.

Meg gulped back a squeal. Wade rushed to the window to get a look. "It's only a squirrel," he said, watching the little animal run across the gutters. He brushed acorns and assorted nuts from the top of the chest onto the floor. "He's obviously found a good place for a pantry up here." Seeing Meg's expression, Wade added, "I'll cover that little hole later."

"All I can think about now is that one squirrel probably isn't the only nonhuman who's taken up residence here."

Wade dusted his hands and examined the open rafters which were veiled with cobwebs. "That's a good bet. I imagine this room could use a thorough fumigation."

Her gaze followed his and she shivered. "Okay. Which one of us wants to pay for that?"

He smiled. "It's one of the joys of home ownership, even if that ownership is still in question. But I have a few bucks left from the loan, so I'll call someone to come out."

"Thanks." She took a couple of steps into the room.

"I suppose I'll have to sell everything up here when I have the auction."

"Makes sense."

She ran a finger over the top of an old parlor table which wobbled on spindly legs. Leaving an imprint in the layers of dust, she added, "I don't look forward to getting these items downstairs for the sale."

"The auction's going to be a big job."

"Tell me about it. And I have to get it done in as short a time as possible and get back to Orlando, assuming I can leave Aunt Amelia." She lifted the lid on a dome-top trunk that contained musty clothes. "So, if you're done investigating up here, I'd better get back to work."

"Actually I haven't even started." He went to a corner of the room and began searching along the wall.

"If you'll give me a hint, I can look, too," Meg said.

"A painting. I'm looking for a large painting," he said as his inspection was blocked by a bed standing on end and covered by an old blanket.

Meg rifled through a stack of frames against another wall. "What does the painting look like?"

And then he saw it. Hovering above his head but just below the rafter where the bed stood was a nude cherub with wings on its back and a bunch of grapes in one chubby hand. Wade slid the mattress out of the way and followed the lines of the painting downward. It was a scene of pastoral debauchery. Trees heavy with flowering limbs hung over a meadow populated with buxom, naked women and half-clothed suitors vying for their attention with gifts of wine and cheese and fat loaves of bread. A trio of the mischievous cherubs, obviously male, fluttered overhead, their bright gazes focused on the passion about to explode on the leafy carpet of grass.

Examining the painting from various angles, Wade said, "Ah... Meg, maybe you ought to take a look at this."

"Oh, you found the painting?" After resting the frames against the wall again, she came up beside him and stared at the mural. Her breath hitched and then sputtered, almost as if she were stifling a burst of laughter. "Oh, my God," she finally said, "how did *that* get here?"

"Amazing, isn't it?"

"Amazing? It's bizarre... it's indescribable..." She angled her head to the side. "It's disturbing."

Wade rubbed his chin with his thumb and forefinger. "Some would call it art," he said, pretending to appreciate the work's inner beauty.

"Surely my Uncle Stewie didn't buy that painting. And my sweet Aunt Amelia never knew that it was up here!"

"I'll bet she did," he said. "Just this morning I found someone else in town who knows of its existence."

She slapped at his arm. "You didn't! Who?"

"An old farmer on the outskirts of town. He almost dared me to come up here and look for it."

Meg blinked hard, took another peek at the mural, and finally settled a stern gaze on Wade. "Why is it here? And more importantly, we have to get rid of it."

Acting on a hunch, Wade began tapping the surface of the painting. "I think you've asked a vital question, Meg," he said. "Why *is* this here?"

"What are you doing?"

It was just as he'd thought. There was a lot more to the Ashford House attic than just a small storage room. Why hadn't he suspected this possibility before now?

From the home's exterior, it was obvious that the third floor should have been a much larger area than indicated by this simple space. "Before we get rid of it," he said, "I think we should look behind it, at what this mural might be hiding."

Wade took out his pocket knife, opened the blade and inserted it into a narrow crack where the panel met the wall. Then he wiggled the knife back and forth, up and down the painting until finally the huge mural loosened. Flecks of old paint and rotted wood rained down on them as the panel gave way. Meg spit wood chips from her mouth and fluffed dust motes out of her hair. But she stepped right up next to Wade and lent her support until together they had freed the panel and tugged it from the wall. They laid it facedown on the floor and looked into a space more than twice the size of the storage room.

Wade took Meg's hand and stepped inside. "Will you look at this?"

The only light came from a second window which Wade realized now was visible from the outside of the house. When he'd first looked in the attic, he'd never wondered about the existence of that other dormer.

"What is all this stuff?" Meg asked.

It was hard to tell what the hulking objects were. One huge table stood against a wall while several smaller ones in half-moon shapes were scattered about the room. An assortment of stools and padded chairs and other oddly fashioned pieces sat haphazardly in no particular order.

A pall of dust hung over everything, shrouding each piece in a thick layer of what looked like smoke-gray powder. Cobwebs, some nearly reaching the floor, drift-ed from ancient chandeliers. As Meg and Wade walked farther into the room, old floorboards creaked, causing vibrations like tiny earthquakes. The elaborate crystals above their heads tried to tinkle like they once had but the sound was muffled by the intricate weaves of count-less spiders.

And then, as Wade's eyes adjusted to the dim light, it all made sense. The mysterious objects took form and shape. Old Stewie Ashford hadn't run a simple shell game out of his twelve-room mansion. He'd once op-erated a fully equipped casino with craps and blackjack tables, a roulette wheel and slot machines. And a racy painting as the primary decoration.

Wade swiped at dust coating the craps table and un-covered chip trays still loaded with booty. Of course the chips weren't worth anything now, their value being in direct relation to Stewie's ability to bankroll his gam-ing enterprise. From the looks of the objects in this room, Wade suspected that the operation had been aban-doned hastily, perhaps when the authority to govern such activities had switched to law enforcers who re-fused to look the other way.

Wade refrained from further exploration of the room when he realized that Meg was gripping his arm with both hands as if they'd stepped into quick-sand instead of Stewie Ashford's questionable histo-ry.

"Good grief," she said. "Is this room what I think it is?" He disengaged his arm and wrapped it around her shoulders, offering the support he sensed she needed.

She swallowed with an audible gulp. "If this were a

Dickens novel, I'd say the title should be *Miss Havisham goes to Las Vegas.*"

Wade laughed at the reference to a book he'd been forced to read in the ninth grade. The image of Miss Havisham came back to him, and he could definitely picture the abandoned bride's wedding cake sitting in the middle of all this decay.

"I think we may have just found out how your entrepreneur uncle made some of his money," Wade said. Unfortunately it wasn't the only alarming discovery Wade had just made. With Meg Hamilton pressed against his body, shivering ever so slightly, he'd discovered that it felt awfully good to have a woman in his arms again. So, he asked a question which he could just as logically have directed at himself. "Are you okay?"

CHAPTER SEVEN

SOMEWHERE IN THE back of her mind, Meg knew Wade had just asked her a question, but her body was overwhelmed by long-buried sensations, and she couldn't remember what it was. She turned in his arms, stared into warm chocolate eyes and murmured, "Did you say something?"

"I just asked..." He paused as if he, too, couldn't remember.

Responding to the subtle pressure of his fingers flexing against her arm, she leaned naturally into him, welcoming the comfort of a strong hand. She was trembling, not so much from shock anymore as from a galloping case of nerves. She hadn't been this close to a man since David left, since long before actually. And she didn't know what to do. Or how to act. Or, even worse, how to feel.

His face lowered even closer. Her heart thundered when she felt his breath caress her cheek, when she heard his voice rumble across the small space that separated her lips from his.

"I asked if you were okay," he said.

She blinked several times. "I...I don't know. I didn't expect to see anything like that painting. I never knew about this room or that my uncle…" She stopped rambling when she realized he wasn't listening. His focus was on her mouth, but he didn't seem to hear the words coming out of it. Wade Murdock was milliseconds away from kissing her, and she hadn't done a thing to let him know he shouldn't. And worse, she was absolutely terrified. "You're not going to…?" She stopped herself from saying the words because speaking them out loud might cause it to happen.

"To what? Kiss you?"

Good heavens. He knew that she knew. She nodded.

"Frankly, I was thinking about it. It seems like a good idea."

She shook her head in a succession of frantic little motions. "Well, don't think about it."

"Why not?"

"Because you hardly know me. And because this house…it stands between us like this giant…thing!"

He glanced down at the juncture where their bodies met, his gaze fanning a sudden warmth where her breasts brushed against his chest. "Meg, I've been hearing about you for weeks. I've been looking at your pictures. Sorry, but I do know you well enough. And I don't see anything standing between us right now except for too damn much thinking." With his free hand he brushed away a wispy filament that had fallen from the ceiling onto her hair. "And maybe a bit of Stewart Ashford's illegal dust." He cupped her chin and tipped her face to his.

She raised her hand to his shirtfront, intending to push him away. But her traitorous fist bunched around flannel and she held on.

He lowered his mouth. "I don't see that any of those things should keep us from doing this."

She closed her eyes to savor the brush of his lips, like a breeze on a petal, the first promise of a kiss.

"Dad! Where are you?"

Meg jumped back, out of Wade's reach. "Oh, my God."

He leaned against the wall and covered his eyes with the back of his hand. "Up here, Jen. We got sidetracked."

Did we ever! When the backs of her knees hit the seat of a chair, Meg melted into it. Dust rose around her, and she waved her hand briskly in front of her face, an effort to cool feverish skin as much as to disperse the air.

"You're in the attic?" Jenny called.

"Yeah. I'll be down in a minute."

Footsteps sounded on the staircase. "Never mind. I'm coming up. I want to see the attic."

Meg stood and went through the door to the storage room. "Do you think Jenny should see this?" she asked Wade, pointing to the mural.

Wade followed her out. "Since it's sitting here with all the subtlety of a whale in a bathtub, I don't see how we can hide it." Wade's mouth tilted into a sort of scowl. "Unfortunately, I've become aware lately that my daughter already *knows* about the subject matter."

Meg figured Jen had probably seen worse, considering some music videos today. But she hurried through the doorway and quickly descended the stairs to where Jenny stood with a perplexed look on her face.

"What's going on up there?" the girl asked.

"Nothing," Meg answered.

"That's not the way I saw it," Wade growled from behind her.

"I was just showing your father..." Meg shot him a look over her shoulder. "...where a squirrel had gotten in the attic through a broken window."

Jenny drooped against the faded gold wallpaper. "Oh, great. Now he's got to fix that, too?"

"No, no," Meg assured her. "You two go on to the park. It can wait."

Once in the second-floor hallway, Wade retrieved his toolbox and roll of screen. "I'll just take care of the job in the bedroom before we go."

Meg waved him toward the stairs. "Don't be silly. You can do it some other time. The tape I put on the screen last night worked quite well."

"Are you sure?" He gave her a half smile that defied interpretation and added, "You probably don't know this about me, but I hate to start something and then leave it unfinished."

Heat rose to her cheeks. "Some things are best left unfinished."

He studied her features for a moment and then said, "Okay. We'll let it go for now."

She stood at the top of the stairs and watched them go down to the foyer. When they'd disappeared through the house, Meg sat on the top step and leaned against the banister post. She released a breath and thought, *What is wrong with you, Meg? It's not as if you don't already have enough problems in your life—and certainly enough with this man!*

Still she couldn't erase the memory of that almost kiss. She put a fingertip to her mouth and lightly rubbed her lip in a fruitless attempt to recreate the featherlike feeling of Wade's mouth on hers. What would it have become? Would it have been a kiss to remember? It didn't help to wonder, because Meg had to think of it as no more than a shooting star—something to be experienced once and then tucked into the farthest corner of her mind.

DECKED OUT IN riding gear and a velvet helmet, Jenny cantered past Wade. Her eyes darted briefly from the dressage course to her father's face to see if he was paying attention to her ride.

Concentrate, man, he said to himself. Forget about what just happened in the attic and think about the constructive comments you're going to give your daughter after she finishes the course.

As if I know anything about English riding, he thought. *Keep your heels down, your eyes straight ahead, your back straight.* He could tell Jenny that much. Her trainer was being paid to fill in more information.

If Jenny hadn't called up the stairs, Wade would definitely have intensified that kiss with Meg. He'd been thinking about doing just that since he'd burst into the house to save her from Mr. Cuddles last night. As it turned out, Meg didn't need saving at all, but it made him feel like something of a hero at the time. And after what happened to his wife back in Brooklyn, Wade needed to feel he still had some hero potential. Despite Meg's outwardly confident demeanor, and her obvious frustration over his claim to the house, he sensed that she needed someone on her side.

He leaned on the fence rail and forced his gaze to follow his daughter's progress around the oval track. But his mind refused to leave the Ashford attic. If he'd really and truly kissed Meg, it would have been the first time in over two years since he'd kissed a woman, and more than twenty years since he'd kissed anyone other than his wife. He wondered for a split second if a man got out of practice at that sort of thing.

"Hell, no," he said out loud, "though when you got the urge to start the juices flowing again, you might have picked a woman who didn't present quite so many complications to your life."

Yeah, hooking up with Meg Hamilton in any way would be a mistake. A smart man wouldn't have anything to do with a woman whose appearance in Mount Esther was creating a major roadblock to his future. And Wade was a smart man, most of the time.

And so, when he went back to Ashford House that afternoon he told himself he should be relieved to discover that Meg wasn't home. He let himself into the house, went up to her bedroom, and fixed the screen in the broken window just as quickly as he could.

And it was probably a good thing that the next day was Mount Esther's once-a-month Festival in the Square. With half the population of the county converging downtown to eat strawberries and listen to live country music, he knew he'd be on duty all day without any time to tend to his chores at Ashford House. And then Monday he'd head straight for his real estate agent's office and try to get one mess straightened out. At least the mess about who had the better claim to his house.

MEG WOKE EARLY on Sunday morning to a steady humming in her ears. She opened her eyes and found herself face-to-face with Mr. Cuddles, who had apparently decided her warm body deserved an enthusiastic purr. She pulled her hand out from under the blanket and stroked the cat's head. "At least you're good for something," she said, reflecting on how she'd searched the house the day before for a simple wind-up alarm clock. Amelia must have thrown out all the sensible clocks when she ordered the space-aged model that sat by Meg's bed with its digital numbers still blinking 12:00.

She was dressed and ready to tackle auction preparations by seven-thirty. Unfortunately her heart wasn't in the project. Neither were her thoughts which kept returning to the attic again and again. It didn't help that the newly repaired window in her bedroom reminded her that Wade had been in that very room sometime late in the day on Saturday when she was at Shady Grove.

Aware she was procrastinating, Meg took a cup of coffee to the parlor and sat by a front window that looked over the driveway to the house. "I would have figured Wade Murdock for an early riser," she said aloud. "And I would have thought that knowing another window needed fixing would have sent him scurrying over here with the sunrise."

Berating herself for giving in to a totally unproductive interest in Wade's activities, Meg went to the dining room and picked up the clipboard she'd left on the table the night before. She thumbed through the blank consignment forms she'd prepared on her aunt's old manual typewriter and began listing items to be sold. After a few minutes she went into the kitchen and looked out a window that faced the barn. No patrol car. No man with a wheelbarrow. "You don't suppose he purposely waited until I was gone yesterday to fix the bedroom window?" she asked Mr. Cuddles who had jumped on the counter.

It didn't seem like something Wade would do. So far, he'd displayed the most irritating confidence, even knowing that their dilemma could cost him twenty thousand dollars. Surely he wouldn't avoid her now just because he'd nearly made a mistake and kissed her. Meg confided once more in the cat. "Whatever his reason for not coming here today, it's just as well. I have plenty to do without dealing with him."

By ten o'clock Meg had removed items from her aunt's china cabinet and listed each dainty knickknack on a consignment form. She'd only stopped once in the middle of making her inventory to go to the veranda and water the sadly neglected flowers in all twelve hanging baskets. Of course while she was nurturing the plants, her attention kept wandering to the traffic passing on the little used county road. There were more cars than usual this morning. And not one of them was an official sheriff's vehicle.

Putting off the auction preparations once more, she walked to the mailbox at the end of the path and took out Saturday's delivery which consisted of more catalogues and the weekend edition of the *Mount Esther Tattler*. Meg unfolded the thin paper and immediately noticed a banner headline notifying residents of a strawberry festival to be held in town that day. Wade must be working at the festival.

Satisfied at last that she'd come up with a logical explanation for Wade's absence, Meg decided to call her house in Orlando to get details of last night's auction from Jerry.

He answered on the first ring, his voice alert and animated. When he realized his sister was the caller, his enthusiasm deflated and he spoke in a whisper. "It was a good auction. Everything went well," he told her. "I'll call you later with the details."

"Where's Spencer?" she asked.

"He's here. I'll have him call you back."

"No. Put him on. I want to talk to him."

Jerry hesitated, then said, "Well, okay. Just a minute." He put the receiver down and Meg could hear his footsteps on the kitchen floor. Then in a conspiratorial voice which Meg was certain Jerry didn't intend for her to hear, he said, "Hey, Spence, there's a woman on the phone for you. I think it's your teacher."

Meg's instincts went on full alert. Jerry was up to something—again.

"Uh…hello?"

"Spence, it's Mom."

"Oh, hi."

"What's going on?"

"You know. The usual. How's everything up there?"

"Fine. Why did Jerry say your teacher was on the phone?"

Spencer chuckled, a sound that came across as forced. "He was fooling around. Can I call you back? It's really not a good time…"

Anger was replacing Meg's previous alarm. "Sorry, but it *is* a good time for me. I know something's going on. I can hear voices in the background. Who is Uncle Jerry talking to?"

She had to struggle to hear Spencer's next words. It sounded as if he'd cupped his hand around his mouth and the telephone. "He's talking to a girl. Uncle Jerry and I are kind of playing this game. We met this lady named Mary Beth, and she kind of believes that he's taking care of me."

"He *is* taking care of you…isn't he?"

"Oh, yeah, sure. He's doing a great job. But this girl thinks my mom sort of left me for good, and he's…"

Meg's grip tightened painfully around the telephone. "What?"

"Don't worry," Spence said. "It's all okay. See, this girl is really hot… I mean she's really nice. She likes me, and she likes Uncle Jerry."

Meg collapsed into a kitchen chair. "Put Jerry on the phone!"

"He's sort of busy. I can have him call you back."

"Now, Spencer!"

Her son hollered, "Uncle Jer, my ah, teacher, wants to talk to you."

"I'll take it in the bedroom. Hang up out there for me, buddy."

A minute later he picked up. "Now, Meggie, don't blow a cork—"

"What the hell is going on?"

"I met this girl. I told you about her, remember? She consigned a bunch of stuff to the auction and we made a great profit on it."

"I don't care about profits now, Jerry. I want to know why you told her that Spencer doesn't have a mother."

"I didn't tell her that. I said he has a mother, but that you sort of ran out on him."

"Are you insane?"

"No, no. Relax. I'm going to tell her the truth. She

saw Spence in the auction hall and thought he was this adorable little kid. She loves kids. She just assumed I was his guardian. I never told her I was."

"You just let her believe it?"

"It's not all bad. It makes me look good. And it's good for the auction. And I'm going to tell her the truth. Maybe today after we get back from Disney World."

"You're going to Disney World with her?"

"We're taking Spence. He's all excited. Mary Beth is the sweetest, most generous…you'd really like her. She runs this charity…."

"I may have to kill you, Jerry."

He laughed, but at least it was a nervous little rattle, as if he were truly considering that the threat was real.

"If anything happens to my son…"

"It won't. The kid's having the time of his life."

"Sure he is. Telling a lie that his other parent has run out on him must be boosting his self-esteem to new heights."

"I thought about that, but he's okay with this—really. I'll call you as soon as we get back from Disney. You'll see that everything's okay. And when you hear how much money we made last night you'll thank me."

"No, I won't thank you, because I'm never speaking to you again."

"Even that doubletree brought two hundred and fifty."

"Call the minute you get home, Jerry. I mean it. And put Spencer back on the phone."

Meg managed to get her temper under control by the time her son returned. "Honey, I'm coming to get you next Sunday when school's out. I'm bringing you back up here with me for a while. But, tell the truth, do you want me to come before that? Because I'll leave right now, and—"

"No, Mom, don't do that. We're going to Disney World."

She smiled in spite of the torture techniques she was imagining for her brother. "So I heard. But Spencer, I'm a little worried. I don't like Jerry telling that woman that your mother left you."

"Mom, I know you didn't do that. I know you wouldn't. We're going to have lots of fun today. Mary Beth is really neat."

And she wants to comfort my motherless son! Still, it was Disney World, and Spencer was a ten-year-old boy, one who desperately needed fun in his life. But did he have to get it this way? "Okay, Spence," she finally said, "I won't spoil your day. I know you're smart enough to know that sometimes Uncle Jerry gets a little carried away."

"Thanks, Mom. I'll call you when we get back."

"Fine." She was ready to end the conversation, but added one more warning. "Spence, you know it's never right to lie. Uncle Jerry is setting a very bad example…."

"I know, Mom. I've got to go, okay?"

"Okay. I love you."

"Same here. Bye."

Meg dropped the phone to the kitchen table and buried her face in her hands. Men! What was wrong with them? First Dave couldn't stick around long enough to see his son through grade school. Uncle Stewie, whom she always idolized, turned out to be some sort of crook with a penchant for Rubenesque erotic art. Jerry has gone off the deep end with her son as a life raft. And even Wade Murdock, who right now was probably keeping Mount Esther safe from strawberry thieves, doesn't show up when she expected him to.

Meg stomped into the parlor and took one more look out the window. She couldn't stay in this house any longer. She'd go to Shady Grove and visit Amelia. Maybe this time her aunt would remember deeding the house to her supposedly favorite niece. Meg grabbed her keys and slammed the front door. She wasn't waiting for Wade Murdock to show up, and she definitely wasn't going into town to eat strawberries!

MEG'S PLAN TO DRIVE to Shady Grove didn't take into account that her route took her directly past the park in the center of Mount Esther's business district. From two blocks away, she noticed throngs of people strolling in front of the shops where merchants had set up sidewalk sales to attract browsers.

As Meg approached the square, someone pulled out of a parking space in front of Nancy Lou's Curiosity Shop, leaving a sought-after spot. Meg swung her car into it, telling herself that Aunt Amelia would probably love a strawberry shortcake.

She stepped out of the car and crossed the street, intending to stop at the first colorful concession stand and order a mound of pound cake covered in ripe berries and cream. But the first person she noticed wasn't a salesperson. It was Wade Murdock.

He was standing next to the sheriff's department horse trailer, and he had his fist securely wrapped around the short reins of a huge horse in full western regalia. He was surrounded by a group of children who patted the patient horse and raised their hands to ask questions. And equally as eager were their mothers who seemed more interested in Mount Esther's handsome deputy sheriff than they were in his horse. Wade explained the various parts of the animal's body and its decorative leather gear.

"Oh, for heaven's sake," Meg said to herself as she pulled a baseball cap low over her forehead, stared straight ahead at the nearest strawberry booth and walked briskly away from the horse trailer.

"Say there," Wade called. "Miss Hamilton."

She stopped, whirled around and was caught in the curious stares of a dozen citizens.

"Would you like to meet Deputy Dare, the town's fastest and strongest law enforcement officer?"

"Thanks, but some other time, Deputy Murdock," she said. "I just stopped for a serving of strawberries."

"Okay then. By the way, have you discovered any more nuts in your attic?"

A few children tittered. Meg's face flushed. "No. I think the ones left by the squirrel and the spirit of my uncle Stewie were the only ones."

He tipped his hat. "Good to hear. I'll see you tomorrow."

Meg flipped him a little wave and headed toward a red and white awning fluttering in the breeze. But she wasn't thinking about strawberries, or nuts, or even about the unreliability of men in general. She was thinking about tomorrow.

THIRTY MINUTES LATER, when Meg handed Amelia a serving of strawberries, she was still thinking about Wade. She found the cord for the remote control and turned down the volume on *The Newlywed Game*. Amelia delicately wiped a dab of whipped cream from her chin and said, "It's a repeat anyway."

"Aunt Amelia," Meg began, "do you know the deputy sheriff, Wade Murdock?"

Amelia hadn't yet acknowledged Meg, so getting a sensible answer seemed like a long shot.

"Oh my, yes," she said. "What a nice young man. In my day we would have called him a dreamboat."

Encouraged, Meg continued. "What else do you know about him?"

Amelia concentrated. "Let me see. Oh, yes, his wife died, and he takes care of a daughter and his father."

Amazingly reliable information. Meg became more hopeful. "Anything else?"

"Yes, indeed," Amelia said. "I sold him my house."

Meg muffled a groan. This was definitely not what she wanted to hear, but maybe she could take it as a sign that Amelia was remembering something that might prove helpful. She draped her arms over the bed rail and asked, "Do you know who I am, Aunt Amelia?"

Amelia stabbed her plastic fork into a large, tempting berry. "Of course I do. You're the young lady who brought me this delicious strawberry shortcake."

CHAPTER EIGHT

BY NINE O'CLOCK Monday morning Wade had written up a fender-bender out on the highway, issued three speeding tickets, and released a raccoon from the garbage pail of a hysterical woman who lived on the outskirts of Mount Esther. After all that he felt he deserved a second cup of coffee even if it meant facing Harvey Crockett at the Quick Mart.

He paid for the coffee, left the patrol car in the store parking lot and walked a block to his real estate agent's office. Betty Lamb heard his voice when he asked the receptionist if she was in and came out of her office immediately.

"Why, Wade Murdock, my absolute favorite public servant…"

She took his hand and planted a quick kiss on his cheek. Wade often wondered if Betty, at least ten years older than he and divorced, hid a deeper meaning in her always enthusiastic greetings. But probably not. She fit the image of Miss Perky Personality, but then wasn't that part of the arsenal of traits necessary to be a successful agent? Betty wasn't a member of the Million Dollar Sales Club for nothing.

"Hi, Betty," he said. "I was wondering if you had a minute?"

"For you, darlin', I have as many minutes as it takes." She tucked her hand into the crook of his arm and winked at the receptionist. "No calls, Melanie."

"So what's up, Wade?" she said after seeing him settled comfortably in a chair across the desk. "That look on your face says problem."

He took a sip of his coffee. "I think maybe there is one, Betty. Have you heard that Amelia Ashford's niece is in town?"

"Old news, hon. Margaret something-or-other, isn't it?"

"Yeah. She goes by Meg. Meg Hamilton."

"Rumor has it that Mrs. Ashford has decided to sell everything in your place at auction with her niece conducting the sale." Betty leaned back in her chair and crossed her legs. "Imagine. A lady auctioneer. That ought to be interesting."

"I don't know about that," Wade said, wondering if Betty's comment was intended as disparaging. "She seems competent. And I'm sure she personally cares about what each item could bring. She wants to do the best job she can for her aunt."

"I suppose," Betty admitted. "I heard that Miss Hamilton used to spend a good deal of time at Ashford House, some years ago, that is."

"That's true, and that's the crux of the problem." Wade leaned forward and set his coffee cup on the desk. "It seems that Miss Hamilton had planned to spend a great deal more time at her aunt's house in the future."

"What do you mean?"

"She says her aunt made out a Quit Claim Deed a few

years ago that gives Ashford House and all its surrounding property to her."

The smile faded from Betty Lamb's face. "A deed? I'm not acquainted with any such document concerning that property." She picked up a pencil and began tapping it on the desktop. "Have you seen this deed?"

"No, and apparently neither has Meg…ah, Miss Hamilton. She hasn't seen it recently anyway. But she's living in Ashford House and actively looking for it."

"But so far no deed has surfaced?"

"So far. But why would she lie about its existence?"

Betty clucked her tongue as if amazed by the simple naivete of men. "Oh, honey, why indeed? Maybe to get her hands on ninety-eight thousand dollars?"

"No, I don't think so. She doesn't seem interested in the money. She truly wants to live in the house someday."

Betty's perfectly shaped eyebrows arched in surprise. "In that old place? I understand that Miss Hamilton is divorced. A woman alone couldn't possibly expect to fix that old monstrosity into a livable condition." Then, realizing how her words must have sounded, she amended her statement. "Not nearly so well as a big strong man with an eye for the possibilities could."

Wade knew when he was being played, and he felt his patience slip. "At any rate, Betty, where do I stand on this thing?"

"My first thought is, if there's no deed, there's no problem. And I didn't uncover one when I did a search on the property."

"But I believe that a deed did, or does, exist. If not in Mrs. Ashford's house, then somewhere."

Betty chewed on the pencil eraser. "I've got an idea."

She picked up her phone and pressed a couple of numbers and a speaker button. In a moment another agent answered from his office down the hall. "Hi, Milt," Betty said. "Do you happen to know who handled legal affairs for Amelia and Stewart Ashford?"

Milton Joyner's voice boomed over the speaker. "Jude Smothers. He was the attorney for almost all the old-timers in town, until he died over three years ago."

"Do you know what happened to all his files?"

"Sure do. Everything was lost in the rains of 2002. The river rose and flooded every business on Center Street. That's why we have the embankment today. Jude's files had been stored in the Save-It-Safe storage facility behind the post office. As I recall, every last scrap was ruined."

Betty appeared almost jubilant when she disconnected. "Now, then, Wade, as I said before. No deed, no problem. But if you're still worried, then I'd suggest that you exercise your contractual right to purchase immediately. Miss Hamilton and her aunt will have to be out of the house within thirty days. You close on the property, take possession, and *voilà*, case closed."

Pretty cut and dried, Wade thought. The only problem was that he'd promised Mrs. Ashford when they signed the contract that he wouldn't force her to leave her home. Plus it gave him time to scrape more money together before signing a mortgage. That pledge had only been an oral agreement, but Wade wasn't about to back down on his word to the old lady. He reminded Betty of the agreement now.

"Look, hon," Betty said, "Mrs. Ashford isn't ever coming back to that house. You know that. I know that, and so does everybody at Shady Grove. So you can put your conscience to rest on that one. I'll dig out the contract this afternoon, make the necessary adjustments, and have it ready for you to sign. Then we'll notify Miss Hamilton that she has thirty days to hold her little auction and get out."

"I don't think we need to hurry on this, Betty," Wade said. "Even though we're taking a chance that the deed might appear."

"Unlikely," she said. "There's no evidence that it was ever filed. But you should sign the Right to Purchase Agreement just in case. In the meantime, be nice and polite to Miss Hamilton. Here in the South we have a saying about catching more flies with honey. If Meg likes you, if she sees your country-boy charm, she'll be less likely to want to see you lose the property."

Wade almost laughed out loud. He was about as country as Rudy Giuliani. "So I should be nice and polite," he said, "and just not mention that I want to throw her out of the house."

Betty smiled. "Something like that. Let her have her sale and go back home with the profits from that. Eventually she'll probably stand to gain some of the money from the sale of the property anyway. I don't think Mrs. Ashford has many close relatives. Believe me, when that city girl lives in Ashford House for a while, she'll be happy to relinquish it to you and go home to the twenty-first century."

She stood up, effectively dismissing Wade. "You just be the sweet small-town deputy you can be, and I'll do the legal work to make sure this works out in your favor."

Wade left, but he wasn't nearly as confident as Betty.

He'd sure feel a heck of a lot better if he knew for certain that there wasn't a copy of that deed lying around someplace.

THE MOUNT ESTHER Savings and Loan inspired confidence the minute a customer walked in the door. Meg noticed the dark paneling on the walls, the subdued wildlife prints hanging in eye-appealing groupings and the dark blue Colonial-style furniture with amply padded seats. She walked up to the receptionist and asked to see the bank manager. After sitting in one of the plush chairs for ten minutes, she was greeted by a portly middle-aged man in a conservative gray suit decorated with a plain etched lapel tag which said Horace Acres.

"What can I do for you, Miss Hamilton?" the man asked.

Meg explained her need to gain access to Amelia Ashford's safe-deposit box. "I'm fairly certain I signed an authorization slip when I was here a few years ago," she said. "And I found this…." She produced a small white envelope with a tiny key inside. "I think it's the key to the box."

"Certainly looks like one of our keys," Mr. Acres said. He led her to the vault where he consulted a file of index records. "Your signature should be in here if Mrs. Ashford authorized you." After a minute of searching, he pulled out a three-by-five card. "Yep, here it is with your name plain as day."

He gave Meg a clipboard with a list of the morning's activities attached. "If you'll just sign here, I can check the signature to see if it's a match." He smiled again. "Not that I expect otherwise, of course."

Once the paperwork was complete, Mr. Acres gave Meg the safe-deposit drawer and ushered her into a private room with a table and one chair. When he left, Meg closed the door and stared at the box before releasing the metal clasp. "The deed has to be here," she said as she lifted the lid. *After all, what else are security boxes for if not important papers and family records?*

Recipes? A certificate of authenticity for a Mickey Mantle baseball? A high-school class ring with the initials SHA on the inside? Meg searched frantically, taking papers out of the box and spreading them on the table. When she reached the bottom layer and the yellowed copies of birth certificates, social security information, and marriage license, she was certain she would find the deed. She had proof that Amelia Adele Levenger had been born. She'd held a job during the Great Depression. And she'd married Stewart Hall Ashford. But there was no evidence that she'd ever made out a deed.

Meg took a few items and slipped them into her pockets. When she handed the drawer back to Mr. Acres, she asked if he could direct her to the law office of Jude Smothers. Surely he would have an original copy of the deed, and this problem would be solved. Unfortunately the banker gave her the discouraging news that Jude Smothers was resting in peace in the Presbyterian cemetery, and his records had been destroyed in a flood.

This can't be happening, Meg thought as she drove back to Ashford House. She'd always relied on the fact that Ashford House would be there for her and Spence. Driving almost as if she were on auto-pilot, Meg continued down the county road, thinking, planning, searching for a solution. A copy of the deed had to be somewhere. Someone had to know where it was.

When she pulled into the drive she was reminded once more of the urgency to find the document. Wade's car was parked near the barn. She scanned the yard looking for him and finally noticed clouds of dust sailing out the open dormer window of the attic. Wade's face appeared next when he leaned over the second-story roof to get a breath of fresh air.

Fighting the unexpected reaction the sight of the deputy had produced inside her, Meg climbed out of the car and strode to the veranda. "You're getting your dust all over my flowers!" she yelled up to him.

"Yeah? Well, you've got spiders all over my blackjack table!" He stuck a broom out the window and pulled dust bunnies from the bristles. "I've got to get this area cleaned out so the fumigation guy can come in. Do you want to help me?"

Meg wasn't about to go up in the attic with him again. "Sure," she said, "if you'll help me sort through two drawers of hankies, three dozen handbags, and a linen chest filled with tablecloths and napkins."

"I don't think so," he said, pulling the broom back inside and ducking behind it.

"Wait a minute," Meg said.

His face appeared again.

"I saw you coming out of River Real Estate this morning."

"Oh yeah? Was that when you were on your way to the bank?"

Good grief! Was there ever a town with a more efficient grapevine than Mount Esther? "Did you meet with your agent and decide to tear up your worthless lease option contract?"

He laughed. "No, sorry. Did you find anything of interest in Mrs. Ashford's safe-deposit box?"

Nothing was sacred in this tiny burg. "Yes, I did as a matter of fact," she shouted up to him.

"But it wasn't the deed, was it?"

Oh, how she wished she could tell him she had the document in her purse at this moment. "I'll find it! In the meantime I'm going in the house to look for a signed Mickey Mantle baseball to match the certificate I brought home from the bank."

"Oh, cool," he said. "I guess I'll have to bid on that at the auction. I am a Yankees fan you know." He leaned far out the window. "Can I come back later tonight when I'm off duty to see the ball?"

"Absolutely not. Once I'm finished working here I'm going to Shady Grove. It's family night. The residents and relatives are having a potluck dinner followed by a variety show featuring kids from the middle school."

She caught the teasing edge to his voice when he said, "Does that mean you're cooking something?"

She stuck her hand in her pocket and felt the index cards she'd stuffed there earlier in lieu of a deed. "I've got a recipe or two I thought I'd try."

"I'll tell the paramedics to be on the alert for a call from Shady Grove around dinnertime."

"Very funny, Murdock. How long do you plan to stay today?"

"Another hour or so. Then I have to shower off spiderwebs and get to work. I can't devote all my time to your little eight-legged pets, Miss Hamilton. There is a town to protect."

"Of course. I know I feel better knowing you've left my house and are out in the community securing our safety."

He chuckled and leaned back from the window. "Don't concern yourself with amenities, Meg. I'll let myself out."

She was smiling when she went into the house. The words she'd just spoken were actually the exact opposite of the way she was beginning to feel about Wade. She missed seeing his patrol car in the drive yesterday or knowing he would soon be on the premises. And she'd been relieved to find the car by the barn today. As much as she might try to fight it, she was starting to like the man, a dangerous and unwise reaction to a person who was trying to sabotage her dreams for the future. But, darn it, he was just easy to like.

"Keep your mind on your goal, Meggie," she said to herself. "Find the deed and protect your rightful ownership of this house. Remember, Wade Murdock has a good job and a secure future. He'll survive the disappointment."

She stood in the middle of the parlor and looked around at all the familiar objects her aunt had acquired over the years, things Meg had admired since she was a little girl. In a short while, all of them would be gone, but the house would remain. Her bulwark against life's disappointments, her comfort in the storms of an uncertain future.

Meg walked into the dining room, picked up the clipboard and tried to concentrate on the painstaking task of making sense of the minutiae of her aunt's life. She worked steadily for an hour until she heard the front screen door open and close. She imagined Wade striding down the porch steps and getting into his car. She didn't resume working until she heard the patrol car heading down the drive. "Come on, Meg," she said to herself as she entered another of Amelia's possessions on her inventory sheet. "Quit thinking about Wade and the darned kiss that never was!"

SOMETIMES AMELIA RECOGNIZED Meg. Sometimes she didn't. But since Meg was at Shady Grove so often, the two women were forging a bond that was based on their relationship today. Amelia seemed to find comfort in the visits, even if she didn't always remember their past. And Meg experienced a renewed connection with the woman who needed her now more than ever.

After family night festivities, Meg wheeled her aunt back to her room. "Did you enjoy the evening?" she asked as she helped Amelia into bed.

"Oh, my, yes. It was lovely."

Meg handed her the TV remote. "Would you like to watch a game show?"

Amelia shook her head. "Not now. I think we should talk a minute about how plans for the auction are going." She reached for Meg's hand, and closed her own around it. "Have I told you how grateful I am that you came to handle things for me?"

Meg pulled up a chair and sat next to the bed. For the moment at least she was Meggie, talking to Amelia, and she was thankful. "I'm happy to do it, you know that, Aunt Amelia."

"You are so dear to me, Meggie. Tell me, are you happy in your life?"

"Of course. Jerry and I have the auction in Orlando and it's doing well." Meg could only hope that was true. She'd spoken to Spencer after school, but she still hadn't spoken to Jerry.

"And that darling boy of yours?"

"He's fine. Growing up and getting smarter every day."

"That's good." Her grip on Meg's hand loosened, a sign that she was growing weary. "Don't sell the family photos, Meggie. Bring some of them here. I want them around me for a while."

"Of course."

Knowing that she might have only seconds before her aunt fell asleep, Meg leaned over the bed and tried to command Amelia's fading attention. "Aunt Amelia, I'd like to talk to you about Jude Smothers."

Amelia nodded. "Jude was my lawyer."

"That's right. He prepared a document for you called a Quit Claim Deed. Do you remember that?"

"Oh, my. I think Jude died."

"I know. And his records were lost. But I was thinking that you must have a copy of the deed, and I'd like to see it."

Amelia's eyelids fluttered toward sleep. "I must have a copy somewhere. I wonder what I did with it."

"In the deed you made a decision to give Ashford House to me."

The delicate skin between her aunt's eyes furrowed. "Oh, I don't think so. I sold the house to that deputy. He paid me twenty thousand dollars for it."

Meg had to smile, though she'd been hoping for a different response from her aunt. "Actually, the deputy paid you ninety-eight thousand dollars. You received twenty thousand as a down payment."

Amelia's face reflected more confusion, and Meg regretted burdening her with trying to recall facts. But she was desperate for her aunt to remember one more detail. "About the house, Aunt Amelia, do you remember giving Ashford House to me?"

"My niece, Margaret Hamilton, loves Ashford House," she said as if talking to a stranger. "She and I are the souls of that old place."

"Yes!" Meg said. "That's right. I do love Ashford House. Do you remember…"

Amelia's eyes closed and Meg had to lean closer to hear her mumbled words. "Ninety-eight thousand? My. I need to see my catalogues. There are things I would like to have…."

Meg placed her aunt's hand on her chest and drew up the blanket. There would be no more conversation tonight.

MEG'S HOPES OF Amelia ever remembering the deed were fading. How could she go into a court of law, if this issue ever went that far, with only her word against Wade Murdock's contract? Any judge would decide in the deputy's favor. There must be something she could do. If she tore the house apart board by board, she might find the deed and gain some satisfaction. But she would destroy the one thing she wanted most.

Still pondering the problem, she pulled into the drive to Ashford House. It was late, after ten o'clock, and she was thankful she'd had the foresight to leave the porch lights on. Then Meg had an idea.

Gloria! It was as if a bulb went on in Meg's head. Of course. Gloria must know that their aunt intended for her to receive the profits from the contents of the house. She might also know of the deed prepared four years ago. If so, Meg wouldn't have to defend her claim all alone. It was a long shot, but Gloria could be the answer to her prayers.

Meg drove to the front entrance. She had intended to call Gloria anyway to inform her of the auction plans, but Meg decided to phone her cousin right away. It was a moment before she realized that Ashford House now sat like a dark Gothic monster amidst its sentinels of twisting, black-as-pitch trees. "What happened to the porch lights?" she said as she angled her car so the headlights shone on the veranda.

She remembered Jenny telling her that the power often went out. Perhaps that's all this was. She dug through her purse until her hand closed around her cell phone and then she got out and walked to the house. Once on the porch she listened for any sound that wasn't part of the chorus of moans that regularly emanated from the old place.

She slipped the key into the front lock but never turned it because the door swung wide with just the pressure of her hand on the knob. She peered across the threshold into the foyer. Nothing was as she had left it. Debris littered the hallway floor, the contents of drawers still yawning open from the hall stand. A lamp was overturned on the foyer table. Even the finial from the front newel post, her Uncle Stewart's favorite hiding place, had been removed and sat on the maple floor.

Meg's hand covered her mouth, trapping a scream.

"Oh, my God." The car's headlamps weren't strong enough for her to see through the doorway and into the parlor, but Meg's instincts warned her that the same chaos existed in that room, perhaps in all the rooms.

Blood surged through her veins and drummed in her head. For a moment she couldn't move, even though she knew someone might still be in the house. And then, her initial fear mutated into a burning anger. How could someone so brazenly break into Amelia's house?

She stood immobilized by shock and fury, though somewhere in her head a rational voice told her that the inability to act often proved fatal to victims of similar invasions. She might have remained rooted to the threshold indefinitely had not a creature streaked by her, emitting a high-pitched wail of alarm and whipping a furry tail against her leg.

"Mr. Cuddles," she cried, scooping the terrified cat into her arms. She ran with him to her car and tossed him ahead of her into the passenger seat. Only when she closed and locked the doors did she punch the three keys on her cell phone which would connect her to the police. She responded to a woman's kindly, calm voice. "This is Meg Hamilton at Ashford House. There's been a break-in."

CHAPTER NINE

HAVING JUST CHECKED the security locks on the back doors of Mount Esther's Center Street businesses, Wade fished his keys out of his pocket and headed out of the alley to his patrol car. When his cell phone rang, he stopped, took it out of its belt pouch and said, "Wade Murdock."

"Wade, it's Bert."

Wade continued his leisurely progress around the buildings. Mount Esther's sheriff often called at the end of the evening shift to assure himself that all was running smoothly in his town. "How ya' doing, Bert? Everything's okay downtown...."

"Well, that's not the case out of town. I just got a call from county dispatch. Your house has been broken into."

Wade's pace ratcheted into a sprint. "What? I just spoke to Pop. He said..."

"Not your rental. The Ashford place. Somebody broke in there."

Meg! "Who called dispatch?"

"The lady who's staying out there. Miz Ashford's niece."

Wade slid into the driver's seat and started the engine. "Is she at the house now?" he asked while backing out of his spot. "Are the intruders still on the property?"

"She's there, but it's not known at this time if she's alone. I'm on my way out there myself, but I thought you'd want to know."

Wade was already headed in the direction of Ashford House, lights flashing. "Absolutely. I'll meet you there."

WADE REACHED the property before the sheriff. He pulled behind Meg's vehicle, heaved a breath of relief when he saw her inside, and got out of his car. She did the same and stood waiting for him, her eyes round and glassy in the headlights of the patrol car. She was trembling. He wrapped his hands around her arms. "Are you all right?"

"Yes, I'm okay. I'd just come back from Shady Grove, and..." Her voice broke on a sob. "Wade, somebody's been in the house!"

She leaned against him and he put his arms around her. Over the top of her head, he scanned the property, looking for any signs that the perpetrators could still be in the vicinity. He'd already determined that unless they'd hidden transportation somewhere in the yard, or, more logically, out on the county road, there was no evidence of a getaway vehicle. The burglars must have hit and run before Meg got home.

He held her a little away from his body and looked down into her face. She was pale, shaken, but she seemed to be in control. "You didn't go in the house, did you?"

She shook her head. "When I saw that the porch lights were off, I thought the power was out, so I went to the front door. That's when I saw that the foyer had been vandalized. I ran back to the car to call 911."

He gave her what he hoped was a reassuring smile.

"You did the right thing, Meg. Coming out to the car was smart. In fact, I'm going to suggest that you get back in it now and lock the doors."

Her hand covered his where it remained on her arm and she stared at up at him with wide, glistening eyes. "Are you going inside alone?"

Was it his imagination, or was that fear he saw in her eyes? It was kind of nice to think that a woman cared about his well-being again. It had been a long time. He brushed a knuckle down her cheek. "It's what I do, Meg. And I do it pretty well. Now get back in the car. Sheriff Hollinger will be here in a minute to provide backup."

She slid into the car and gathered Mr. Cuddles in her lap.

"I see you haven't been completely alone," Wade said.

She ran a hand down the cat's back. "No. I picked up a hitchhiker on my frantic run to the driveway."

He closed the door and pointed to the lock button. She pressed it and he went toward the house. For the second time during his employment in Mount Esther, his gun was drawn.

MEG STARTED SHIVERING all over again. She squeezed Mr. Cuddles tightly to her chest and nuzzled her nose into the cat's neck. She watched Wade stalk cautiously to the veranda and approach the front door.

She said a silent prayer that he would be all right, that the vandals had left, that the sheriff would arrive before Wade stepped over the threshold and that she wouldn't jump out of her skin.

Another pair of flashing lights appeared in her rear-view mirror, and she spun around to watch the approach of the second car. Sheriff Hollinger pulled alongside Wade's vehicle, and he stepped onto the driveway. Hollinger was a big man in both height and weight, obviously years older than Wade but still a formidable presence. Meg darted a glance at the house as the sheriff strode to the side of her car. Wade had disappeared inside. She rolled down her window.

"I'm Sheriff Hollinger. You okay, ma'am?" he said, his southern accent smooth and slow as the ripples in the Suwannee on a hot summer's day—and the exact opposite of the trip-hammer beat of her heart.

"He's inside," she said. "Wade went inside."

Hollinger patted her shoulder. "It's gonna be all right. I'm goin' right in behind him. You stay here."

The sheriff drew his weapon and headed toward the house, his posture bent nearly double as if reducing his towering frame might make him less noticeable to the intruders. He took nearly twice as long to reach the porch as Wade had, and with each plodding step, Meg grew more anxious. Hurry up! she screamed in her mind.

And then Wade came through the door and stood on the veranda. The two men spoke, nodding their heads. Sheriff Hollinger went down the steps and around to the back of the house, and Wade entered through the front door again. If the sheriff intended to check the rear of the property and come in the back way, she assumed Wade had unlocked the door.

Within moments, lights appeared throughout the first floor of the house. Soon after, the upstairs lights came on, and Meg saw Wade moving about in her bedroom. He came to the window, and assuming she was watching, he gave her a thumbs-up sign.

Next the attic was illuminated, probably with the meager little boudoir lamp they'd used on Saturday. But it was enough to provide a glow in both dormers as Wade's body moved eerily behind the windows of Stewie's ghostly casino. He moved to the turret, and with a powerful flashlight shining in the trees and on the ground, he scanned the property in all directions from that third-floor vantage point.

Soon, both men returned to the porch. Sheriff Hollinger waited while Wade walked across the yard and opened Meg's car door. She stared up at him, suddenly aware that her relief went far beyond concern for the well-being of Mount Esther's deputy. It was *Wade's* safety that truly mattered to her, and the revelation was as unsettling as it was comforting.

"Whoever broke in is gone now," he told Meg. "But it's a mess in there. Maybe you should wait...."

She'd already set Mr. Cuddles on the ground and was climbing out of the car.

Wade stepped out of her way and scratched the back of his neck. "Okay, well, I can see that waiting is not part of your game plan."

Focusing her concern on Ashford House, Meg strode toward the porch. "How bad?"

He followed her. "At first glance I don't think any of the furniture is broken. Only you can tell if something's missing."

They passed Sheriff Hollinger on the steps. "I'm getting the kit from my car," he said, and when he urged Meg not to touch anything, she assumed he was referring to a fingerprint kit.

"How did they get in?" she asked, entering the foyer which looked much worse in the light. Papers were strewn everywhere, and Amelia's precious knickknacks lay scattered on the floor, many reduced to bits of broken china.

"Back door lock was busted," Wade said.

She entered the parlor and literally had to make herself breathe. Drawers were overturned, the contents covering chairs and tables. Cabinet doors swung open on their hinges since the treasures they protected had been tossed onto the carpets. Even the sofa cushions sat askew on the cheerful chintz frame.

Wade followed Meg through the rest of the first-floor rooms where the damage was similarly disastrous. The second floor was the same. Whether the vandals found what they were looking for, Meg had no way of knowing.

In her bedroom, Meg stood gaping at her personal belongings flung on the floor around the upended mattress and box springs, her toiletries, clothing, even her underwear. She felt sick. Tears threatened at the backs of her eyes. Her throat constricted. She clutched her hand around her neck and walked toward the window and the fresh breeze it offered.

With a handkerchief he found on the floor, Wade picked up a few bottles by their lids and set them back on the dresser, a kind but futile attempt to put Meg's world in order again. Then he stood beside her at the window that looked over the dark landscape. In contrast to the chaos inside, the lush trees and shrubs of the grounds were serene and calm, unaffected by the invasion.

Wade put his arm around Meg's shoulder. "I'm so sorry, Meg. I can't imagine why anyone would do this."

She let his strength support her and savored the temporary security of his hold. "Do you think this was an act against Amelia, or me?"

"Hard to say. In a town like this, where everybody knows everyone else, it doesn't seem likely that this was a random act." He moved his hand up and down her arm while he continued staring out the window. "But Amelia has lived here all her life. I don't know why anyone would do this to her."

"That's exactly what I'm thinking." Now that her anger had faded, Meg fought an overwhelming exhaustion. But for the first time since returning from Shady Grove, she wasn't afraid. The warmth of Wade's body against hers made her limbs weak. She relaxed and drew a couple of slow, easy breaths. But she knew her unease would return when Wade and Sheriff Hollinger left the house. "I suppose I have to consider that this vandalism was directed at me," she said.

"Don't jump to conclusions," Wade advised. "Who in Mount Esther knows you well enough to inflict this kind of damage to the property?"

She didn't have an answer.

"Hey, Wade!" Sheriff Hollinger called from the first floor. "Everything okay up there?"

He gave Meg's shoulder an extra little squeeze. "We're fine. Be right down."

Meg stepped away from him and went to the bedroom door. "Do you think he's found anything?"

"Hope so. If not, we'll keep looking." He turned around and surveyed the room once more. "I'll come back up in a while and set that mattress back onto the frame again."

She managed to smile. "Thanks, but I can't imagine that I'll be getting any sleep tonight."

Sheriff Hollinger was waiting at the base of the stairs with the fingerprint kit.

"Get anything good?" Wade asked.

"No. Looks like our boy was wearing gloves."

"What makes you think there was only one of them?"

Sheriff Hollinger took another look around the room. "I don't, really. From the looks of this place, it seems more likely that a small army came in that back door." He addressed his next question to Meg. "Do you think anything's been stolen?"

Knowing where Amelia kept her most valuable treasures, Meg went into the dining room to check the built-in china cupboard. The doors were open, revealing the Ashford silver. All the pieces of sterling, the candlesticks, punch bowl, flatware, and other items were still in the cupboard, though they had been slid along the shelves and knocked over. "If anyone knew what was in this house, they would have taken these things," she said. "And as far as I can tell nothing is missing."

Wade rubbed his index finger over his upper lip. "It's not a robbery, then. Strange. What other motive could the perpetrators have for breaking in?"

"I think we've got to consider that it was a robbery," Sheriff Hollinger said. "But who knows if the burglars found what they were looking for."

"What would that be?" Wade asked.

Meg sat down on a chair and stared up at him. "All I can tell you is that if they were looking for the Quit Claim Deed, I can vouch for the fact that it's not in this house."

His lips curled up at the corners. "Glad to see you've kept your sense of humor, Hamilton," he said.

Not privy to the joke, Hollinger continued with his theory. "No, I don't think our guys were lookin' for a deed. They came in search of cold, hard cash. Old money."

Wade and Meg both stared at him. "What?"

The sheriff pulled up a dining room chair and sat opposite Meg. "My guess is, the rumors I've been hearing for years are true. At least there are people in Mount Esther who believe they are."

Meg glanced at Wade and saw the same confusion she felt reflected in his eyes. "Rumors? What rumors?"

"That there's a small fortune hidden in this house."

"Oh, Sheriff, I don't think so," Meg said. "I've been told that my aunt lived frugally." She stole a glimpse at Wade to see if he was paying attention. He was. "At least until she got Deputy Murdock's money."

"Maybe so," Hollinger admitted, "but it's possible she didn't know about the other money. Or maybe she forgot about it. I've only been in this town twenty years. I came here right after old Stewart died. But I remember hearin' whispers every now and then, from the old-timers especially, about how Stewie had hid a bundle of cash in this place."

Wade's expression indicated that this revelation was as new to him as it was to her. "Where would my uncle have gotten a large sum of money?" she asked. "I was always led to believe that he squandered his wealth on…well, various enterprises." *Some of which I now know were illegal.*

Hollinger chuckled. "Where'd he get it? I can't say for sure, but folks tell of Stewart Ashford gettin' his hands dirty in all sorts of ways. I heard he sold Suwannee spring water during the Depression as an elixir of hope. One story has it that he sold bottom land a few miles down river to northern investors who came down to find their property flooded every rainy season." Hollinger raised his eyes to the ceiling as though he were trying to see through the floorboards overhead. "Some say he even ran a gambling parlor in here."

Wade stared off in the distance, his lips pursed as if holding back a verbal reaction to the sheriff's explanation.

"And you think the profits from those ventures are hidden in the house?" Meg asked.

"Could be," the sheriff said. "Folks say that Stewart never trusted banks."

"But that was a long time ago," Meg added. "Uncle Stewie's been dead over twenty years."

"I don't know anything for sure," Hollinger said. "But there are a few people around here who believe it." He scrutinized the mess the intruders had left of Ashford House one more time. "And I've got to give it credence. I think our vandals might have been lookin' to get their hands on some of that cash."

Wade raised his hands in question. "But why now, Bert? If what you say is true, that money's been here for over twenty years. Why did they pick tonight to break in and look for it?"

"'Cause Miz Ashford's in the nursing home," he explained. "We've got basically good folks in Mount Esther. Nobody'd come here while she was livin' in the place. It wouldn't be the thing to do."

Wade squeezed his eyes shut while he took a deep breath. Unfortunately the calming gesture didn't remove the frustration from his features. "But it's okay for those *good folks* to rob Miss Hamilton?"

"I'm not sayin' it's right," the sheriff amended. "I'm just sayin' it's the way our citizens think. Miss Hamilton is an outsider. It could be that the money's suddenly fair game now that Miz Ashford isn't comin' home."

He stood up and walked back to the parlor. Wade and Meg followed him from the dining room.

"'Course all this is merely speculation on my part," Hollinger said as he bent down to retrieve his fingerprint kit. "This could have just as easy been the work of a couple of teenagers lookin' for a bottle of booze."

Finding a sudden need to restore her world, Meg asked if she could touch things in the room. Receiving the sheriff's okay, she picked up a drawer, set it on top of the desk and began scooping papers from the floor and depositing them inside. When that drawer was full, she started on another. Wade and the sheriff went upstairs to check for prints and any clues they might have missed. When they returned, Hollinger emitted an audible yawn, announced it was midnight, and there wasn't much more to be done till morning.

Wade passed a sympathetic gaze to Meg. "What do you want to do? I can secure the back door, but surely you don't want to stay here by yourself."

Hollinger quickly agreed. "Oh, no, ma'am. If these fellas tonight were lookin' for money, they might come back."

Meg hadn't given serious thought to her living arrangements until now. What *was* she going to do? "I can't leave the house unprotected," she said. "And besides, there isn't even a hotel in town."

Sheriff Hollinger hunched one shoulder in a casual

shrug. "That's an easy solution," he said. "Wade, you bought this place from Miz Ashford, right?"

Wade looked at Meg and then acknowledged the sheriff's statement with a little nod.

"Well, then, move in. The sooner the better."

Wade and Meg stared at each other.

"With her?" Wade said.

"With him?" Meg said.

Hollinger responded with a deep-down belly laugh. "It's not as if there aren't enough bedrooms in this danged old place. If you two aren't exactly kissin' neighbors, and I've heard you aren't, then spread out."

Meg's head spun. She leaned against the desk. "Oh, Sheriff, I'm not sure that's a good idea."

Hollinger headed for the door but stopped and gave one last piece of advice to Meg. "Miss Hamilton, if you want to hold your auction and expect to have anything left to sell, you'd better listen to me." His next warning was for Wade. "And son, if you want to protect your investment, you'd best go pack a suitcase. I don't see any other answer to this problem." He walked out the door. "Good night now."

LEAVING MEG STANDING in numb silence, Wade followed the sheriff out the door. He caught up with Hollinger at the bottom of the steps and walked with him to his car. "About that suggestion you made," Wade said. "I don't think Miss Hamilton is going to go for it. You saw her reaction. I don't know if you've heard what's going on between us…"

Hollinger chuckled. "Just rumors. Something about deciding who owns this house. But with what went on here tonight, I don't think either one of you should be worryin' about who's gonna end up with Ashford House. It makes more sense to concentrate your efforts on keeping this ol' monster in one piece so at least one of you gets to live here."

Wade had to acknowledge the wisdom of the sheriff's words in his own mind, but he wasn't at all sure that Meg would. "Do you have any ideas about who did this tonight?" he asked.

Bert opened his car door and leaned an elbow on the roof. "My guess is that it was a couple of the young punks from town, maybe with a few too many beers in them. They probably heard the stories about Stewart Ashford stashin' money somewhere in these walls a long time ago. Probably heard it from their granddads who passed the tales down the generations. But this is a tough case, Wade. We might never catch the boys responsible."

"Do you think they'll strike again?"

"If they found the money, then no." Bert leaned down and slid into his car. "Guess we could keep our eyes open for anybody spendin' a little crazy in the next few days, though."

Wade didn't hold out much hope. Recently that description could fit Mrs. Ashford herself.

Bert gripped the steering wheel and stared at the house. "The problem is, this house is too good a target. She sits back from the road so there'd likely never be any witnesses to a break-in. And whoever wants to try it again doesn't even have to come up the drive. They can just leave their car along the county road in some bushes to make a getaway easy." He popped a toothpick into the corner of his mouth. "Nope, the only solution I can see is for you to move in. Tomorrow morning I'll start spreading the word that the deputy sheriff is livin' in Ashford House. That, and the sight of your patrol car in the drive is the best way I know of to protect this house and Miss Hamilton's chances for a good auction."

He started the engine. "But you two do what you want. If you don't move in, then you and I will do what we can as a two-man department, but it might not be enough. Now I'm goin' home. I still have a report to fill out."

He shut the door, turned the car around and headed down the drive. Wade walked back to the house and noticed that Meg had come outside and was sitting on the top porch step. He sat down beside her and waited for her to express her opposition to Bert's plan.

"That was quite a suggestion from Sheriff Hollinger, wasn't it?" she said, sitting up straight. "Imagine, you and I sharing this house."

He sat back and narrowed his eyes, pretending to be shocked. "What? You don't think that's a good idea?"

Her jaw dropped and she gave him an incredulous stare. "Well, no, of course not."

"Funny. I was just about to ask you if Mrs. Ashford had a new toothbrush anywhere inside."

"You can't be serious. You and I hardly know each other."

"So you've mentioned once before." He looked out over the front lawn and let a small grin precede his words. "I'm thinking we can change that." He spared her a quick glance. "In fact, I thought we'd already made some significant strides in that direction."

She huffed a little bit, a series of slightly frustrated sounds, but she didn't show the indignation he might have expected from her. "This is a small town, Wade. What will people say?"

"Not much, considering I'll be moving in with Pop and Jenny."

"Oh. How do you think Jenny will like that?"

"Since she'll be about fifty yards from her horse, I don't see a problem. And to tell you the truth, I think she'll welcome some female companionship. She's at that age where she believes nobody understands her."

Meg smiled. "She's a teenager. No one *does* understand her."

"So, we're agreed? This is the plan?"

Meg's eyes held a hint of teasing when she said, "Just one more thing. Are you going to hit me with some obscure law about possession being nine-tenths of the law or some such nonsense?"

He placed one booted foot on a higher step and draped his arm over his knee. "Hey, that's not a bad idea."

"Right. And then I'd never get rid of you."

Far from taking offense, Wade was glad that Meg could laugh after the night's ordeal. "Look," he said. "It's up to you. I'll admit I'm a little worried about something like this happening again, and frankly, once I start working on the house, I'm not too crazy about the idea that somebody might come in and destroy my efforts. But you're the one who's staying here, so it's got to be your decision." He looked over his shoulder and into the foyer where debris still littered the floor. "Do you really want to stay here by yourself?"

She stared at him a good long time before releasing a huge sigh and dropping her forehead onto the heel of her hand. "Oh, why did this have to happen?"

"Because your uncle was a crafty old buzzard while he lived who left a Paul-Bunyan-heap of folklore behind when he died."

"So, even Uncle Stewie...he's just like all the others."

She'd spoken so softly he had to lean in to hear her. "What's that?"

"Nothing." She waved off his question even though she proceeded to answer it. "This may come as a surprise to you, Wade, but I've never been able to rely a whole lot on the men in my life."

He cupped a hand around her arm. "This may come as a surprise to *you*, Meg, but some men actually are reliable." When her lips turned up in the slightest suggestion of a smile, he added, "I'm not going to steal your house, Meg, if legally it is yours. But I am going to own it if the law says it's mine. No games, no gimmicks, no cons." He squeezed her arm, a gesture that was as intimate as it was protective. "But right now, I just want to keep what's mine, or yours, from being destroyed, and maybe keep you safe while you're staying here, too."

He reached in his pocket and took out his cell phone. "Now, I've got to call Pop. He always waits up for me when I've got night duty, but it's nearly one o'clock, and I'm testing his endurance. Do I tell him I'll be home in a couple of minutes, or do I say I'll see him in the morning?"

She leaned against the post of the railing and looked at him, her eyes luminous in the porch light. For a moment he considered that tears might be shimmering in her eyes. But then she blinked hard and ran her fingertips over her cheekbones. "I don't want to stay here alone," she said on a trembling rush of air.

He punched the button to his home. "Hey, Pop, we

had a little problem tonight. I'm going to be out all night." In answer to his father's question he said, "No, nothing too serious. I'll give you the details in the morning. You'll see that Jen gets on the bus? Thanks."

He disconnected, turned to Meg and said, "Now, where's that toothbrush?"

AFTER PUTTING MEG'S BED BACK on the frame, Wade announced that he'd sleep on the parlor sofa just in case there was trouble during the night. They cleaned up enough debris to make him comfortable, and then Meg brought him a pillow and blanket and a tray with a snack.

"If you're not careful, you'll end up spoiling me," he teased after consuming half a bowl of chowder.

"I think it's the other way around," Meg said. "You're the one bunking on the sofa." She fluffed his pillow, a small gesture meant to convey at least a little of her gratitude. "I really appreciate this, Wade," she added. "I know I wouldn't sleep all night if you hadn't offered to stay."

"Hey, don't mention it. We're both concerned about protecting what will eventually belong to one of us."

That was true, but deep down Meg knew Wade was protecting her as well, and it felt good, this being able to depend on a man—to know she wasn't facing her fear alone.

He stretched his back muscles and sank onto the sofa. Meg knew he had to be tired. She was, and she hadn't put her life on the line. "Anyway, thanks again," she said and turned toward the stairs.

"Sleep well, Meg," he said softly. "And if you're worried that you'll find me in a state of indiscretion in the morning, don't be. I'll wait to sleep in my skivvies until I get a bedroom."

He pulled his boot off and wiggled his toes inside his sock. "I don't suppose the sight of my naked foot will have any effect on you."

She smiled. "No, I don't think so."

He chuckled and slipped off the sock. "Darn. That's what I thought you'd say."

Meg was still smiling minutes later when she crawled into bed.

CHAPTER TEN

THE NEXT MORNING, Meg came into the dining room with two tall glasses of lemonade. She set hers down on the buffet and waited as Roone Murdock swept bits of broken glass into a dustpan. Once he'd emptied the trash into a garbage can, she said, "Excuse me, Mr. Murdock, I brought you something to cool off."

He stood the broom against the side of the dining table and accepted the drink. "Call me Roone. It is mighty hot today. This'll hit the spot."

Meg surveyed the nearly clean floor with an appreciative gaze. Wade's father may not stand as straight and tall as some men his age, but any physical limitations weren't evident in his efforts this morning. He'd done more in the last two hours than she could have done in twice that time. The dining room was almost back to pre-break-in condition. Now only the auction chaos prevailed along with Amelia's odd purchases.

"I can't tell you how grateful I am for your help," Meg said. "When Wade left for work this morning and told me you were coming over, I was quite relieved." Deciding Roone would appreciate an honest admission, she added, "I wasn't looking forward to being in the house alone. I'm sure in a day or two, when the shock of what happened has passed..."

Roone waved off her explanation. "No need for thanks. It's not easy getting over what went on here last night. Besides, I can't abide a mess, and sorry to say, this place can use more than one pair of hands to put it back together."

She smiled. "You're right about that."

"Imagine somebody thinking there's a fortune hidden in this house." He gestured toward the china cupboard where Amelia's silver still lay in disarray. "If you ask me, there's the fortune. Your burglars walked out on antique pieces which must be worth a bundle." With a chuckle he lifted the lid on one of the packing boxes and picked up a porcelain statue of a dragon with shiny gold teeth. "And they passed up a unique item like this."

Meg laughed at both the gaudy decoration and Roone's sarcasm. "I know what you mean. Whoever broke in here must not be the art connoisseur my Aunt Amelia is." Assuming Wade had told Roone about Stewart Ashford's eccentricities she said, "I suppose money could be hidden somewhere. This house has an interesting history and because of that, it now has a certain appeal to members of the community, as we found out last night."

Roone glanced up at the cracked ceiling plaster. "I guess it has an appeal to my son, too. I've put some sweat into this house, but Wade has put both sweat and cash."

"Yes, I know he has."

Roone set down his empty glass and picked up the broom. "When I'm done here, I'll start on the rooms upstairs."

Meg didn't know if Roone disapproved of the sheriff's suggestion that they all live together, but she sensed maybe he did. Or that he would if he suspected Wade had moved in for any reason other than to protect the property.

Once Roone had begun sweeping again, he said, "So, do you have any idea how this predicament is going to work out?"

Meg wasn't certain if he was referring to the ownership of Ashford House or their current living arrangements. Luckily, Roone cleared up any misinterpretation by continuing.

"For some reason, Wade really wanted this place the minute he saw it." He bent over and scooped up more pieces of ceramic glass. "I'll say one thing for Wade. When he says he's going to make changes in his life, he's not kidding."

Meg began putting Amelia's silver back in order in the china cupboard. "You mean when he left Brooklyn?"

"Yep. One day he was reading an employment ad in a police publication, and the next he announced he'd filled out a job application for Mount Esther, Florida."

Meg dusted the top of a teakettle. "That must have been a big step for him."

"It was. But he said he had to start over, get out of Brooklyn."

When the sweeping stopped, Meg looked over her shoulder. Roone was leaning on the broom handle and shaking his head. His brown eyes reflected a profound sadness. "Maybe Wade took a liking to this place because he'd never lived in a real house before. He and his wife lived in an old brownstone flat only three blocks from the fast-food joint where it happened."

"Where what happened?" Meg asked.

"Wade went inside to pick up an order. Brenda waited outside with Jenny since the place was crowded. It was a Friday night. A car went by with a bunch of punks inside. Two of them had guns. They both fired. The kid standing next to Brenda was killed. He was the target. Brenda was killed, too. She took a stray bullet straight into her heart."

Meg grasped the top of a cupboard door and held on. She felt as if the floor were collapsing beneath her. "My God..."

"I give Wade credit, though. He stuck it out two more years until the punks were caught, tried and sentenced. Said he had to see it through to the end."

Meg couldn't even imagine the horror of sitting through the trial of anyone who had perpetrated such an unconscionable act. Didn't Wade want to forget he was a cop and seek revenge in his own way? And how did he explain such a senseless act of violence to his daughter?

And yet, just two days ago, Wade had stood in the town center with a horse and answered questions from curious, giggling children. Wade Murdock was a nice guy, a seemingly normal man. Who knew he'd suffered something so devastating it would drive most normal men over the edge.

Sometime in the last moments, Roone had resumed sweeping again, though Meg hadn't noticed until he spoke. "Yep, Wade set his sights on this place practically when we first got here. He's worked on it nearly every day since making the deal to buy it and to lease the property to board Jenny's horse. This house has become something of a mission to my son, as if it's the glue that's going to hold us together."

Meg picked up the next piece of silver and began polishing, grateful she had something to hold on to, something to think about other than the graphic details of the tragedy in Wade's life. "This house is special," she said. "It has meant a great deal to many people, but I'm not sure even Ashford House can accomplish what your son expects it to."

"I'M TELLING YOU Meggie, you should just get in your car and head back home."

For the first time in maybe ever, Jerry was actually taking one of Meg's problems seriously. In fact, later that afternoon when she'd finally had time to call him and explain what happened, she'd detected something almost like real concern in his voice. "I can't do that, Jerry," she said. "Aunt Amelia's counting on me. I've decided to hold the auction a week from Saturday, and I need to get every item catalogued, run ads in the papers, make flyers...."

"Meggie, you don't owe Aunt Amelia all this effort, especially if your life is in danger."

Meg twined the kitchen phone cord around her finger. "It's not as dramatic as all that, Jerry. Besides, I really do owe her. Aunt Amelia gave me this house, remember?"

"Yeah, I remember. A lot of good it's doing you now."

"And that's another reason I have to stay. I have to fight for my right to Ashford House and I can't do that if I run back to Orlando because of one little incident."

Even as Meg said the words, she realized she was growing tired of the constant struggle with Wade over Ashford House. For very different reasons, the house meant as much to him as it did to her, but if she left now, he would conclude that she was giving up her claim to the property. And she wasn't willing to do that.

"I'd be leaving the door wide open for Wade to press the legality of his lease-option contract," she explained to Jerry.

"I'm not so sure that you shouldn't just let the deputy have the place," Jerry said. "Take our twenty percent for doing the auction and call it quits."

"Call it quits?" Jerry definitely didn't understand her connection to Ashford House, and she couldn't blame him. While he'd enjoyed his summers at the house, he'd never truly experienced the place like Meg had. He'd never felt the comfort of its walls around him, protective, caring. He'd lived at Ashford House for weeks at a time, but he'd never really belonged here. Meg had. She always would. Even Wade Murdock, with the tragic circumstances that led him here, couldn't appreciate the house the way she did. He cared about the property, but he saw Ashford House through the eyes of a grown man. He saw potential. She saw it through the eyes of a woman growing up within its walls. She'd lived its past.

Jerry's voice brought her back to their conversation. "Well, one thing's for sure. You can't stay there alone. What if these burglars come back? You're definitely not taking Spencer back there this weekend."

Since when had Jerry become so paternal? Oh, yes. Since Mary Beth had become attached to Spence and Jerry had become attached to Mary Beth. "You don't have to worry," she said. "We won't exactly be alone."

"What do you mean? Who's with you?"

"The sheriff of Mount Esther came up with a solution to protect the house…and me, I guess."

"Oh yeah? What solution?"

"He suggested that Wade move in."

Normally Jerry would have made a snide comment about such a living condition being cozy or convenient, or some other such euphemism with a sexual connotation. But not this time. "The deputy's living there? Good grief, Meg, you claim the house is important to you. But why don't you just hand Wade the key?"

"He already has a key."

"Oh, that's nice."

"It's not like you think. He's here just as a precaution against further break-ins. He knows this arrangement doesn't give him any more claim to Ashford House than he already believes he has."

"So, it's just the two of you sitting in front of the fireplace every night popping corn…"

"No. It's not just the two of us. Wade's father and daughter are also moving in."

Jerry whistled through his teeth. "I hope you know what you're doing. What's that old saying, 'Possession is nine-tenths…'"

"I look at it this way, Jerry. No one's going to possess Ashford House if vandals destroy it. I'm just trying to keep that from happening. Now tell me about the auction. How is merchandise coming in for this week's sale?"

"Mary Beth is an angel."

"So you've told me. And, by the way, does your angel know the true facts about Spence—that he has a mother who's coming to get him on Sunday?"

"You're sort of forcing my hand on this, Meg."

"Good. Tell her the truth. Now, what about the auction?"

Despite being told to set the record straight with Mary Beth, Jerry's voice brimmed with excitement. "You should see the stuff she brought in this morning. Name-brand power and garden tools. Top-of-the-line exercise equipment. Bicycles, women's jewelry, you know, the good stuff that doesn't turn your skin green."

Meg's suspicions were aroused once more. "Jerry, this just doesn't make sense. Where is she getting these things?"

"I told you. She runs this charity organization and people donate—"

"What people?"

"Lots of different people. Right now it's a couple of men who buy factory close-outs, returns, overruns, you know, the usual channels merchandise takes when it ends up at a place like an auction."

That was true enough. Over the years they'd gotten a lot of saleable goods through those exact avenues, and it was all perfectly legal. Still, she hoped Jerry wasn't being taken in by con artists or a pretty face. "But what do you know about these men?" she pressed.

"I haven't met them yet, but I will. They're dropping off the stuff at Mary Beth's place and taking fifty percent of whatever sells here. It's a win-win situation. We make twenty-five percent, which is decent. Mary Beth and her charity get twenty-five. I'm not having to work my butt off getting things to sell. The customers love the stuff and are getting great buys. What's not to like?"

"Oh, I don't know. Jail?"

He brushed off her comment with a throaty chuckle. "Don't be ridiculous, Meg. Nobody's going to jail. This is all clean merchandise. Good grief, the guys are giving it to a charity. What could be more honest?"

She supposed he was right if that were true. And besides, what could she do about the situation anyway? She was a five-hour drive away. She'd never met Mary Beth or her contacts, so she really couldn't judge. Like it or not, she'd just have to trust her brother. "Okay, Jerry, keep up the good work. I'll see you Sunday when I come to pick up Spence."

When she hung up the phone and walked into the parlor, Meg heard the rumble of a large vehicle. She strode to the front window and looked out. A moving truck was backing up to the house. "What's going on now?"

On the side panel of the van were the words, A Couple Of Guys And A Truck. No Job Too Small Or Too Large. The movers stopped at the base of the porch and the two advertised men got out. And the Mount Esther patrol car pulled up beside it.

Wade stepped out of the car and met the men at the steps. "It's all on the third floor," he said. "Go up the main staircase just inside the front door. At the end of the hall, you'll see another set of stairs to the attic."

They went inside and Wade remained behind with Meg.

"What have you done?" she asked.

"I arranged to have all evidence of the casino cleared out. Isn't that what you want?"

"Well, yes, but do we have the right to do that? After all, everything up there really belongs to Aunt Amelia."

"I'm just moving it to a storage facility. If Amelia wants it back, she can have it."

Meg truly doubted that Amelia even remembered the casino existed, and she knew her aunt would have no use for the crumbling old tables and stools left behind by Stewie decades ago.

"Besides," Wade added, "I saw the way Jenny kept glancing up those stairs the other day. I figure she'd have been in the attic by suppertime tonight and would be thinking of a way to introduce middle school kids to blackjack."

Meg nodded. "Yeah, and all we'd need is for Mount Esther parents to be calling us about their kids losing their allowance at Ashford House."

"Exactly." Wade headed for the front door. "Let's give the guys a hand. With four of us working, they'll be gone before Jen gets home from school."

They met the movers as the men were coming down the main staircase. Each one carried a pair of bar stools. In the bright daylight, the furniture looked even shabbier than it had in the attic. The chrome legs were pitted and scarred. The leather fabric on the seats was cracked and worn. And a sheen of dust coated everything.

When one of the movers saw Wade, he chuckled. "I can't believe what's up there." He looked at his buddy. "We've decided that we were born in Mount Esther about five decades too late. There must have been some wild parties in that room back in the day."

"And that picture!" the other one said.

Meg flinched.

"Looks like more than gambling might have been going on up there," the fellow added.

"Never mind about that," Wade said. "We'd like to keep the artwork in that room from becoming a headline in the local newspaper. Your job is to move the things, not to make any assumptions or spread any rumors about what you found. Remember, Mrs. Ashford still lives in Mount Esther and is respected by everyone here."

"Hey, no problem," the other man said. "It's not the strangest thing we've ever come across."

For the next hour, the three men emptied the attic of all visible traces of Stewart Ashford's bygone days. Meg used a broom to pull down the remaining cobwebs Wade had missed on his first cleaning, and sucked over half a century of dust into a vacuum cleaner. Before long, all that remained of the casino was the mural and Meg's very active visualization of what the room might have looked like in its heyday.

When the movers had gone downstairs with the last gaming table, Meg leaned against the door frame and released a sigh that seemed despondent even to her own ears. "Can't you just picture the way it must have been?" she said to Wade. She looked up at the crystal chandeliers that hadn't been lit in years. "When the ceiling lights sparkled on silver tokens and taffeta dresses? When the clatter of dice and spinning wheels and the slap of cards meant the difference between good luck and bad?"

Wade stood beside her, silent, thoughtful perhaps, drawing his own conclusions about glittering summer nights in Stewart Ashford's hideaway. "Yeah, I can picture it."

His lips curved upward in a little smile. "Your uncle must have been well connected," he said. "What he was doing here was illegal as hell. But it wouldn't surprise me if his best customers were the mayor of Mount Esther and the governor of the state, not to mention a number of Florida congressmen."

Meg knew it was true. Even when she was a little girl, before Stewart died, she remembered seeing dignitaries at Amelia's dining table. She walked into the now empty casino and paced slowly around the room, examining small cracks in the wood paneling, dents in the planked floor. "So, do you think there's money hidden up here?" she asked Wade. "Uncle Stewie must have made a tidy sum."

Wade scrubbed his hand down his face. "If there is, then I don't know why your aunt didn't uncover it and spend it. When I met her, she was in bad straits. She owed money to almost all the merchants in town."

Meg stopped pacing and stared at Wade. She didn't know her aunt's finances had been *this* disastrous. "She did?"

"Yep. She'd been buying on credit for a long time, and the store owners apparently didn't have the heart to turn her down. That's one of the reasons I agreed to the large down payment on the lease-option contract. She needed the money right then. She did pay some bills I guess, along with spending the majority of the money on the purchases you've seen."

This was a revelation. "So Amelia actually talked you into giving her the twenty thousand?"

Wade grinned a little sheepishly. "We sort of agreed on that amount. And you were right when you said I got a good buy on the house. Even though it needs a lot of work, I know I got a bargain. Still, twenty thousand was a big chunk of change to put down."

When you're only buying a house, Meg thought. But maybe it isn't too much when you're investing in the future and trying to erase bitter memories.

She resisted the urge to tell him that she knew about his past, that for a while this morning when Roone told her, she'd been shocked, angry, even felt some of his pain. But now wasn't the time. Maybe there never would be the perfect opportunity to tell him she knew. Maybe he didn't want her to know. Maybe he'd established enough of his new life that his tragic one was finally fading into some dark part of his mind. So instead she said, "I'm beginning to believe that my relatives were not the people I'd thought they were."

"Hey, everybody has a few skeletons in the closet…."

Laughter from the outer room interrupted him. The movers had returned. When Meg and Wade went out to meet them, they found the men staring at the mural.

"What do you want us to do with this?" one of them asked.

"Take it?" Wade said, looking at Meg for confirmation.

"We'll have to chop it up to get it out the door," the mover said. "Whoever painted it must have done it in parts elsewhere and then carried them up here and put them together." He illustrated his point by showing where four distinct panels of wood had been connected to make one whole painting.

"Just so you know, we'll never get it out of this room without wrecking it," he added.

"Do what you have to do," Wade said. He took Meg's arm and gestured toward the door. "I guess we don't have to stay and watch."

The older of the men instructed his helper to take his hammer from his tool belt. "Start whacking," he said.

With an expression of near glee on his face, the mover gripped the hammer tightly, raised his arm and prepared to swing. And all at once Meg sucked in her breath in something very like the terror she'd felt the night before. It was as if the hammer were aimed at her skull instead of the mural. "Stop!" she cried. "Don't do it."

The two workers stared at her. Wade tightened his hold on her arm. "What's wrong?"

Her voice shook. "I can't let them destroy it."

Wade moved aside, leaving the entrance to the attic free. "Thanks anyway," he said to the movers. "You guys can go. I'll come outside in a few minutes and pay you."

Exchanging confused looks, the men left and went down the stairs. When they were alone, Wade turned to Meg. "You want to tell me what's going on?"

"I don't know." Her voice cracked. "We've definitely done the right thing by clearing the attic. But now it's all gone, the mystery of this room, the games, the excitement that was here once, the past. It still existed in this house an hour ago and now it's gone." She walked over to the painting and studied it as if seeing it for the first time. In the past few moments it seemed to have lost its garish lewdness and become a testament to an unknown artist's imagination as well as a part of Ashford House history.

She released a long, trembling breath. "This painting is all that's left."

Wade came up behind her and put his hands on her shoulders. "Why, Miss Hamilton, I believe you're showing your romantic side."

She smiled even as she fought to hold back tears. "I guess I am." She pressed her fingers under her eyes and blinked hard at the painting. "It is romantic," she said. "Even sweetly so in a way."

His low laughter rumbled in her ear. "The mural is sweet now?"

"Yes. Those people caught in time, in a sublime setting, with nothing on their minds but the meadow, the sun…"

"And the anticipation of a certain obvious gratification," Wade added.

"Yes, that, too." She turned to look at him and found his gaze understanding and comforting. "It seemed a shame to destroy it."

"Then we won't. But since I have a teenaged daughter moving into the house, I suggest we turn it around and fasten it to the wall."

She smiled and looked at her watch. "Oh, definitely. It's almost three o'clock. We'd better nail it quickly."

"You got it," Wade said. "And only you and I, two movers, and one old guy who raises peacocks will know of its existence."

"An old guy who raises peacocks?"

"Yeah, and cuts out on his gasoline bill. He's a relic from your Uncle Stewie's past, and the one who told me about the mural. I'll take you out to meet him some day, but right now I've got some hammering to do."

WADE HAD REVERSED the painting and secured it to a wall in time to meet Jenny's bus and take her to pack her belongings for the stay at Amelia's. Roone had started a pot roast cooking in the oven and the smell of garlic and onion permeated the first floor and made Meg's mouth water. She had her doubts about this living arrangement, but she knew one of them wasn't about meals. Roone Murdock loved to cook, and, unlike Meg, he seemed blessed with considerable skill in that area.

Now that the house was back in order, at least as much order as could be expected with auction preparations underway, Meg concentrated on gathering family photos to take to her aunt. It wasn't easy to narrow the choices to just a few. Through the years, Amelia had collected many portraits, both formal and casual. In the end, Meg chose a picture of the three children, Gloria, Jerry and herself, in a rowboat on the Suwannee River. Jerry was just a boy, while Meg and Gloria were in their adolescent years, their smiles proof of the pure, innocent joy of a summer afternoon.

She also chose a photo of Amelia and Stewart on their wedding day and one taken of Amelia ten years ago when she was given an award from the Mount Esther Historical Society. This picture had always been a favorite of Meg's since her aunt, then eighty-two, was an elegant, graceful woman in an aqua suit adorned with a pink-and-white orchid corsage.

And last, she picked a portrait taken of Stewart on Smoky, his Arabian mare. Meg had been nine years old the day the picture had been shot, but she remembered when her uncle sat astride the beautiful gray horse in front of a photographer. She'd admired the photo many times over the years, and when she looked at it today, she found that her admiration had not faded even after learning the secrets of Stewart Ashford. In his black jodhpurs and charcoal-gray jacket, her uncle had been frozen in time through the camera lens as a dashing country gentleman both to the young girl who had idolized him and to the woman who was mystified by him now.

Meg tucked the photos into a canvas bag for the trip to Shady Grove and left the house. She stopped in the driveway before getting into her car and looked back at the old Victorian structure that was both the embodiment of her past and the fulfillment of her future. Not nearly as grand as it once had been, Ashford House still spoke to her heart.

She slowly shook her head at the dilemma she faced with Wade. The compassion she felt for him was deep and real. In truth, perhaps she was beginning to feel something even stronger than compassion. But it would break her heart to let him have her house. She might never be able to restore it to its previous glory but this home was always meant to be hers. Just as Stewart had conceived it and Amelia had safeguarded it, Meg was destined to keep it company in the years to come.

CHAPTER ELEVEN

ROONE MURDOCK'S pot roast was the tenderest and most flavorful Meg had ever tasted, but the dinner was a jittery affair. Wade tried hard to keep the conversation on a friendly, nonconfrontational level, but Jenny seemed determined to thwart his efforts. Apparently the close proximity to Lady Jay wasn't enough to compensate for the sudden move.

First she complained about not having enough drawer space for her clothes. Meg offered to have another bureau brought into her room. When the teenager remarked that she didn't have her own telephone, Wade promised to inquire about having an additional line installed the next day. But when she referred to Ashford House as the creepy haunted mansion, Wade scowled her into submission.

She was silent and sullen for the rest of the meal, prompting Meg to decide that tonight wasn't the appropriate time to announce that her ten-year-old son would be arriving in a few days. After she finished eating, Jenny said she was going to ride her horse.

"Fine," Wade said. "As soon as you rinse the dishes and put them in the dishwasher."

Jenny's lips turned down in a deliberate pout.

"I'll help," Meg offered, trying to keep the tenuous peace. "When I was growing up, my mother had one rule we all lived by. Whoever cooked the meal never touched a dirty dish." She pointed toward the front of the house and smiled at Roone. "There's a television in the parlor that has your name on it, and the remote control is on the coffee table."

"You don't have to tell me twice," Roone said and left the kitchen.

Wade carried his own plate to the sink and then his cell phone rang. "Wade Murdock," he said when he'd connected to the caller. He paused and then groaned. "Not again. Can't you just put the dog back inside the Arnolds' fence?" Another pause. "All right. I'm on my way."

He stuck the phone in his pocket, mumbled something about small-town sheriff departments and citizens having cell numbers, and picked up his car keys from the kitchen counter. "Looks like a rose bush trampler is loose over on Mulberry Lane. I'll be back as soon as I can." He pointed a finger at Jenny. "Make sure you buckle that cinch tight enough, young lady. And take it easy. No fancy stuff."

Jenny *tsked* as she put a plate in the dishwasher. "I know, Dad."

He jotted a number on a notepad, tore off the paper and handed it to Meg. "This is my phone number. But if it looks like anything's broken, call 911 first."

Jenny rolled her eyes. "Just go, okay?"

He went out the back door, but hollered on his way to the patrol car. "And do your homework!"

Meg released a long, shoulder-drooping sigh, her best portrayal of a teenager put upon by an obtuse parent. "I wonder which one of us he's talking to."

Jenny almost smiled. "You'd think I made a regular habit of bailing on my assignments."

"We're about done here," Meg said. "Why don't you start saddling up. If you don't mind, I'd like to come out and watch you ride."

It had been Meg's experience that no kid could pass up an audience. Spencer had been urging her to watch his feats ever since he'd first tackled his three-foot Little Tykes slide. Jenny tried to hide her pleasure behind a blasé look as she went out the door. "Sure. If you want."

Meg set the dial on the dishwasher and went to the telephone in the front hallway. Since she had a few minutes, she was finally going to make the phone call she'd promised to make the night before. Besides her own motives for calling Gloria, Meg knew it was past time to inform her cousin of the auction.

She sat down, took Amelia's address book from the small drawer in the phone bench, and looked up Gloria's number. Her cousin was home.

"Gloria, it's me, Meg."

"Oh, my God, Meggie! I haven't heard from you in ages. Is something wrong?"

It was a typical but somehow sad reaction from relatives who rarely stayed in touch. Something catastrophic had to have prompted the phone call. "You could say so. I'm at Aunt Amelia's." She explained about Amelia's condition.

Gloria asked a few questions and concluded with a resigned observation. "Well, Meggie, we knew you and I would have to face this some day."

You and I? Meg looked around at the myriad items in this room alone that still had to be catalogued for the auction but refrained from asking Gloria exactly what *she* was having to face. "I just thought you'd want to know, Gloria."

"Oh, absolutely. You know I'd come down and re-lieve you at the nursing home, but we're terribly busy at the store just now. The summer line has come in and Desiree's is swamped."

Meg had never seen the upscale women's clothing store on Michigan Avenue where Gloria worked. But she imagined "swamped" was an exaggeration for a store that catered to a specific upper-class clientele. "It's all right," she said. "I've got everything under control." *Right.* "Anyhow, Aunt Amelia has asked me to auction everything in the house and send you the proceeds."

Gloria's voice bubbled with excitement. "Wow. That's right. She told me I would someday get the con-tents of the house. How marvelous that she's taking this step now. I mean, why wait until—?"

Meg cut her off. "Exactly." She didn't tell Gloria that she'd advised Amelia to keep the money herself.

"Are you running the auction?" Gloria asked.

"Yes. It's a week from Saturday. I'll deduct our com-pany percentage and send you an accounting of the sale and a check for the rest."

There was a pause as if Gloria were deciding how to pose her next question. "Ah, Meggie, you know I trust you, but just out of curiosity, what is your take?"

"Twenty percent."

"My, isn't that a little high?"

"No, Gloria, actually it's very low. The standard rate in Florida is forty percent these days."

"Well, of course you would know." If she were still

skeptical, Gloria at least had the good sense to hide it. "You know me, Meggie. I don't have a head for numbers, so I'll just put my faith in you to do a good job." She lowered her voice. "You know how it is. We girls can always use a little extra cash."

Like for rent, electricity and food, Meg thought. "There's one more subject I'd like to discuss with you, Gloria," she said. "It concerns the house and property."

"I thought Amelia was giving you the house," she said. "You always cared more for it than I did anyway, and that's probably why."

Meg allowed herself to feel hopeful. "Four years ago, she gave me the property in a Quit Claim Deed. Did you know anything about that?"

"A what?"

"A deed. A special document that granted the house to me as a gift."

"Wasn't that generous?" Gloria said.

"Yes, but I need to find a copy to prove my ownership. Do you know where Aunt Amelia might have put it?"

"Why would I know about it? She didn't give it to me."

"No, but I just thought Amelia might have mentioned something to you…."

Meg heard the beep of a microwave in the background.

"I've got to go, Meggie. Sorry I can't help you with that quickie thing or whatever it was. It was great hearing from you. And give Aunt Amelia a kiss for me. Tell her thanks and I hope she feels better."

"Sure thing. Bye, Gloria."

Meg set the phone into the cradle and stared at the walls, the ceiling, the wood floor. Back where I started, she thought, trying to understand her aunt's pecu-

liar way of thinking. "I wonder which old plank that
deed might be hidden under."

MEG OBSERVED JENNY until dusk began to settle over the
property. She helped return the riding equipment to the
tack room and put the horse into a stall for the night.
Wade hadn't returned yet, and Roone apparently hadn't
stirred from his chair in front of the television.

"I guess I'd better do my homework now," Jenny
said. "Deputy Murdock will probably write me a ticket if I haven't gotten it done."

Meg didn't feel like going in the house. The sun was
a hazy golden orb sliding behind the old oak trees, and
seemed to set the Spanish moss aglow. The breeze from
the river was cool and fresh, and so Meg followed it,
down a twisting path to the edge of the Suwannee.
Sumac and wild ferns blanketed the river bank, their vibrant green color no doubt due to the special fertilizer
Wade deposited from the barn. Meg walked along the
edge of the river until she reached the end of Amelia's
property. She came to a spot she remembered well from
her childhood.

She climbed down a short embankment and sat on
an outcropping of boulders worn smooth and slick from
centuries of river water rising and falling with the whims
of seasons and storms. One of the many springs that fed
the Suwannee eddied just inches below her, and she
gave in to temptation and stripped her feet of sneakers
and socks, and dangled her toes in.

The cold water stung, but Meg met its challenge as
she had many times in the past, by letting loose with a
squeal of invincibility and lowering her feet even more

into the swirling depths. She knew her nerve endings would adjust to the chill and the discomfort would soon pass. This was the Suwannee River, eternal and unchanging, and humans had to adapt to its environment. Here the river ruled.

Within a minute Meg was kicking her feet in the air, sending droplets of pure clean water dancing upon the surface of the spring. She hugged herself tightly. And she rejoiced, freely and without restraint, as she had many years ago.

Despite darkness falling around her, Meg remained at the spring, putting off the trek back to the house. She lay back against the river grasses rising from the spring to the bank and stared at the stars. When she was younger she used to try to count them.

Creatures scurried in the brush above her head and somewhere in the near distance owls hooted and night birds called. Meg closed her eyes and listened to sounds that were so different from the night sounds of downtown Orlando. Minutes later she sat up, took a deep, refreshed breath, and then was startled to notice that she could no longer make out the details of the land across the river. The night around her wasn't just dark. The scant sliver of moon sat in a black-as-pitch sky that shrouded the landscape in unrecognizable shapes.

Meg scolded herself for not bringing a flashlight. She peered over the embankment and squinted into the distance hoping to see the outline of the barn or the high pitch of Ashford House's roof. "What have you done, Meggie?" she said to herself when she realized that the area around her was broken only by the soaring trunks of towering oak trees.

Deciding that inaction would get her nowhere, Meg reached for her shoes and socks. But before she could put them on, a beam of light sliced through the oaks and veered off in different directions, bouncing off branches and leaves. It was followed by a familiar voice. "Meg? Are you out here? Meg!"

This couldn't be happening. Despite her overwhelming relief at hearing his call, Meg couldn't let Wade think she wasn't able to take care of herself—again! He'd come to her rescue too many times as it was. She wasn't about to add stupidity to her list of weaknesses. Still, she didn't want him to wander around in the dark looking for her. So she waved her hand above the bank and hollered back to him. "Over here, Murdock!"

The light shone upon her arm, followed by the snap of twigs and the scurrying of some critter as Wade approached. Soon he stood above her and pointed the flashlight on her face. "What are you doing out here?" he asked. "We were all worried about you."

You weren't the only ones worried, she thought. "Oh, sorry. I didn't mean to alarm anyone. I used to come here all the time when I was a little girl. I know these woods like the back of my hand."

He gave her a skeptical look, one she was getting used to. "Yeah? Well, what about when it's so dark you can't even see your hand? Do you even have a flashlight?"

She shielded her eyes and squinted into his light. "Don't need one. I just told you…"

"Right." He cast the beam onto the water. "What's so special about this spot?"

She followed his light and watched the ripples swirl and sparkle. "It's a freshwater spring," she said. "The

Suwannee River has lots of them. Water bubbles up from an underground river deep in the earth's core, millions of gallons a day." She patted the rock, offering him a place beside her.

"You want me to come down there? Is it wet?"

"Just where my feet have been."

"I guess I can stand that. But first I'm calling the house." He punched a number into his cell phone and told Roone that he'd found Meg. Then he climbed down the embankment and sat next to her.

"Take your shoes off," she said.

"What?"

"Here, see?" She stuck her own feet back in the water and kicked vigorously, laughing when he ducked flying spray.

"That's cold. I'm not putting my feet in that freezing water."

"You'll get used to it." She flashed him a daring grin. "Are you chicken, Deputy?"

"No, I'm smart. And I'm from New York. We keep our feet out of the rivers up there."

She stared hard at him until he accepted her challenge. He yanked off his boots, rolled up his pant legs, and suspended his bare feet over the spring.

"Well, go on," Meg said.

"Don't rush me. I'll do it." He dunked his heels into the water and whistled through his teeth. "Ho! That's some kind of cold."

"You get used to it."

And, good sport that he was, he did get used to it. At least the bottoms of his feet did since that's about all that actually touched the water.

"So what happened with the dog and roses?" Meg finally asked him.

"It was a little more involved actually," he said. "Turns out the dog is a sensitive creature who jumps the fence in his backyard whenever he senses trouble in the family."

She gave him a perplexed look. "Trouble? What happened?"

"Mr. Arnold, a sixty-five-year-old recent retiree has too much time on his hands. Unfortunately it's time he doesn't know what to do with and he spends it picking on Mrs. Arnold. And in this case she pressed charges."

"Wow," Meg said. "Imagine an abuser in Mount Esther."

"Yeah, well he's not in Mount Esther tonight. He's in the county lockup. When I left him, he was blubbering like a baby and swearing he'll never touch demon gin again."

"And Mrs. Arnold?"

"She was with three neighbor ladies who were consoling her with tea and chocolate cake. And the dog was resting under the kitchen table." Wade smiled a little. "Mrs. Arnold really wasn't hurt. But I think a night in jail will straighten her husband out."

Wade drew one foot out of the water and wrapped his hands around his knee. "But enough about that. How is Amelia today?"

"I took some family pictures to her this afternoon, but she slept through my visit. The nurse said she's been sleeping more than usual lately."

There being nothing to say, Wade picked up the flashlight and aimed its beam around them until he settled the light on a tire hanging from a tree branch.

"I can't believe that's still there," Meg said. "Uncle Stewie made it for us. We used to swing out over the water."

Wade chuckled. "You crazy kids."

"We loved flying over the water and taking that deep breath of courage before…" She stopped when her thoughts filled of Spencer. And she realized she'd never mentioned him to Wade. She looked at him now and said, "There's something I have to tell you."

"Okay."

"I have a son."

"And a good-looking little fella he is, too."

"How do you know that?"

"Mrs. Ashford's pictures. They're not *all* of you."

Meg nodded and felt a twinge of guilt that she hadn't brought Spence to see Amelia often enough. "There's something you don't know," she said.

He raised his eyebrows in question.

"He's coming here. I'm going to pick him up on Sunday and bring him back. He'll stay here with me through the auction and until I wrap up the paperwork."

Wade's answer was simple and direct. "The more the merrier." Then he laughed. "In fact, that changes the dynamics around here to three guys and two girls. Those are my kind of odds."

She smiled. "Spencer's a good boy, but he's quiet and sometimes withdrawn. Things have been hard on him. I'm just telling you because this living arrangement might be difficult."

"For who?" Wade shrugged. "As I see it, Spencer's a kid. He's most likely going to act like one which means he probably isn't perfect. And one thing I know for sure is that when he grows up, he still won't be." He smiled at her. "We'll get along okay." He pointed in the direction of the tire swing. "Maybe I'll get my courage up and let him teach me to soar over the water like you used to."

Meg didn't admit that the suggestion pleased her, though it probably wouldn't have that effect on Spence.

"Which reminds me," Wade added. "Jenny said you watched her ride tonight. Thanks."

"No problem. I enjoyed it. She's a good rider, at least from my limited perspective. I hope she and Spencer get along."

Wade appeared thoughtful. "Let's see. A teenaged girl and a ten-year-old boy. It's a match made in heaven."

Meg smiled. "I know what you mean. I'm hoping Ashford House might bring Spence out of his shell a bit. I've always regretted that I didn't share more of this part of life with him."

Wade shifted slightly so his deep brown eyes focused intimately on hers. "I've been told that regrets are a waste of good energy," he said. "But most of us have them. I have a couple of really big whoppers that will probably never go away."

Meg knew he was talking about his wife's death. Instinctively she wrapped her hand around his wrist. "I guess regrets are a part of becoming an adult."

The flashlight lay in the grass above their heads, providing just enough glow for her to study his rugged, experience-scarred features, the fine lines around his eyes, the creases at the corners of his mouth. Wade Murdock's face had character that reflected his history. "So, Deputy," she said, "what are your regrets today?"

His gaze remained locked with hers, warm and intensely personal. After a moment, his eyes sparkled with humor. "That's an easy one. I regret that it's Tuesday."

She smiled. "What do you mean by that?"

"It's been three whole days and I'm sorry that I never finished what I started on Saturday."

She nearly asked what that was. But then she knew without asking, and her smile faded. She was grateful for the night shadows that cloaked the flush she felt on her cheeks. Three whole days had gone by, and he'd been having the same thoughts she had—the same regrets as it turned out, the same longings. He was talking about the kiss that never happened.

Her lips parted, but no words came. She was certain he could hear the beating of her heart. Just like the water churning from hidden sources at their feet, Meg's heartbeat surged through her bloodstream and pounded in her ears. She felt dizzy, as giddy as the waters in the center of the spring. She licked her lips, subconsciously preparing them to accept what Wade offered. "Wade, I don't know if we should…"

Stupid words. She didn't mean them.

"I am going to kiss you, Meg," he said, giving her fair warning, in a soft yet masterful way that stole her breath.

He took her in his arms and pressed his lips to hers. His kiss was hard, insistent, a bit awkward for both of them. But that first clumsy touch was soon erased by the full onslaught of his eager mouth. He kissed her completely. His lips grew soft and sensuous and hers became pliant, accepting. When his tongue invaded her mouth, her inhibitions faded as her senses took over. It had been so long. This felt so good.

When Wade ended the kiss, he wrapped his hand around the back of her head so her face nestled into the warm, vaguely spice-scented crook of his neck. He teased the hair at her temple with his breath.

"Thank you for showing me your favorite spot, Meg," he whispered.

She clung to him until continuing to do so would have demanded more from each of them than they were prepared to give. When she withdrew, the world intruded upon them, bringing with it an uncertain future. "I wonder if you'll thank me tomorrow when we have to face…"

"I think we should let tomorrow take care of itself," he said. He picked up her shoes and handed them to her, and then put his boots on. When he offered his hand, she took it, and with his light guiding the way, they walked back toward Ashford House.

ROONE TURNED DOWN the television volume when Wade came into the parlor a few minutes later. "So tell me about the doggone caper you had tonight," he said.

Wade explained about the Arnolds and his decision to send the husband to the county jail for the night. As he spoke, Meg hurried through the room, waved quickly to Roone and climbed the stairs without a backward glance.

"What's gotten into her?" Roone asked. "She looks like she's seen a ghost."

"Nothing so bad as that I hope," Wade said. "I think she may have lost her way out there in the woods, but was reluctant to admit it."

Roone stared at his son. His eyes narrowed with suspicion and he rubbed his fingers along the shadow of his beard. "Looks like more than that to me. She's all flushed like something scared the daylights out of her." When a pleasing thought occurred to him, he added, "Maybe she's given up on her claim to the house. Might as well. She never found the deed, if there ever was one."

"No, that's not it," Wade assured him.

"Well, if she's not ready to buckle under, then the only other thing I can think of that gets a woman all flustered like that is…" He frowned. "No. When you were out in that woods together, you two didn't…" He shook his head. "Of course not. You wouldn't…"

Wade had been about to sit down and talk to his dad a while, but thought better of it now. He picked up a magazine from the top of a stack on the coffee table and headed for the stairs. "None of your business," he said. "I'm going to bed."

"I hope you didn't do anything foolish," Roone warned. "Because if you did, you're heading for trouble that's a lot worse than any dog-catching caper in town tonight. Don't forget you've got twenty thousand dollars at stake."

"I'm not forgetting anything," Wade said. "I'm just tired, that's all."

"I hope that's what it is, but I wonder." Roone picked up the TV remote. "Because, macho man, you're carrying a catalogue of flower arrangements up to your bedroom."

CHAPTER TWELVE

WADE CAME DOWNSTAIRS the next morning at 7:30. Roone was reading yesterday's newspaper and sipping coffee. Jenny had poured a mountain of Frosted Flakes into a bowl and was drowning it in milk.

"Hurry up. You'll miss your bus," Wade said.

"That's okay. You can drive me."

"No, I can't."

Roone lowered the paper and peered over the top at Wade. "Where are you off to?"

Wade looked down the length of his uniform and answered, "Gee, I don't know. Dressed in this getup, I figured I'd go parasailing on Panama City Beach."

Both of his family members stared at him as if he'd lost his mind, which wasn't far off the mark.

"Little touchy this morning, aren't you?" Roone said.

"I didn't sleep well." Of course that didn't excuse him from acting like a jerk.

"Well, apparently you're the only one who didn't. I haven't seen Meg yet this morning."

Wade poured himself a cup of coffee and pretended disinterest.

Jenny stopped crunching, and stared first at her father and then her grandfather. "What's going on?"

"Nothing!" both men said at once.

"To answer your question," Wade said with more civility this time, "I'm going over to Vera Arnold's to see if she'll consider dropping charges against Clifford. If so, I'll pick the guy up and bring him home, with a warning and the advice that he find something to do to occupy his time."

"You might suggest that he try training his dog," Roone said.

"Can I have some friends over Friday night for a sleepover?" Jenny asked.

"It's not a real good time, Jen," Wade said. "You should check with Meg anyway."

"Why?" Roone asked. "It's not *her* house."

"Yeah, Grandpa's right," Jenny said. "I shouldn't have to ask Meg."

"Well, you're going to," Wade said. "It's the polite thing to do." He stopped there, thinking he'd avoid a conversation that would only aggravate his already churning stomach.

Jenny's shoulders sagged with resignation. "And if she says yes?"

"Then…maybe. No boys at all. Three girls."

"Four girls."

Wade gave her a warning frown. "Don't push your luck, Jen."

He set down his mug, picked up his keys and cell phone and headed for the back door. He'd just made it down the porch steps when Jenny called to him.

He turned around. "What is it, Jen? We're both late."

"What's really going on with you?" she asked. "Are you, like, seriously mad at me? You haven't been this grumpy since…well, since Brooklyn and the stuff that happened there."

He sighed and looked down at the dirt. Jenny didn't bring up her mother's death often, so when she did, he had to address it. "Look honey, I'm sorry. I'm not mad at you, and I'm not grumpy, really." Well, maybe he was, but how was he going to tell his thirteen-year-old daughter that his foul mood had more to do with his hormones than anything else at the moment?

"It's her, isn't it?" Jenny said. "Meg? She's making you miserable."

"No!" That much he knew for sure. Meg was making him a little crazy, but certainly not miserable. "I've just got a lot on my mind," he said. "This house, the job I'm still adjusting to…" He smiled. "…trying to figure out my baby daughter who's suddenly older and wiser and wearing little bitty things."

"It's not that I don't like Meg," she said, completely discounting his litany of excuses. "She's okay I guess, but I don't want you jumping into something you may not be ready for."

Was this his daughter giving him advice as if their roles had suddenly become reversed? "Pumpkin, I'm not jumping into anything." He thought about last night at the spring, about the kiss and his disturbingly male reaction to it. "In fact," he added, "I'm not even getting my feet wet."

"Well, good," she said. "Because some men need more time after something like what happened to us." She gave him an earnest assessment with her mother's eyes. "You're kind of a slow-mover, Dad. And that's probably good. I don't want you to get hurt."

He kissed the top of her head. "Thanks, Jen. But I'm fine. Really." He turned her around and walked her up the steps to the back door. "And you're still late." He shot a warning look through the door at Roone, and said, "Behave yourself."

As he walked to the patrol car, he heard Jenny grumble, "I'm never really sure who he's talking to."

"Both of us, I guess," her grandfather said.

LATER THAT MORNING, Wade dropped Clifford Arnold at his house after securing the man's solemn pledge to keep his temper under control and take up a hobby. Then Wade stopped at the Quick Mart to get a cup of coffee. As he was paying, he noticed a flyer stuck to the back of the cash register. It advertised the auction at the house on the following Saturday beginning at ten o'clock in the morning.

Fast work, Wade thought, knowing Meg must have delivered the flyer this morning.

Harvey Crockett nodded toward the poster. "Guess that auction's about the biggest thing to happen around here in a long time," he said.

"I suppose so," Wade said.

"I heard folks talking about it even before that lady brought the flyer in this morning. A lot of people think they might end up with more than just one of Miz Ashford's treasures."

Having slid a five-dollar bill across the counter, Wade still waited for his change. "Really? Like what?"

"Money. I understand there could be a good bit of cash hid in that house. Folks'll be bidding up the prices of anything that looks like it might hold cash."

"Oh, great. That's just the rumor I *don't* want to hear started around this town. It's that kind of talk that resulted in Ashford House being broken into the other night." He wiggled his fingers with impatience. "My change, Harv."

The clerk counted out bills and handed them to Wade. "I don't think it's a rumor. I remember Stewart Ashford. Once he got up in years I think the old fella was just nutty enough to leave money squirreled away in Mason jars."

"Think it if you like, Harvey, but don't go getting everybody in town believing that they might strike it rich. Miss Hamilton just wants a smooth-running auction without a lot of complications about hidden treasure."

"You don't have to worry about me," Harvey said. "You know I just mind my own business. Live and let live, I always say."

That's not how you reacted when you wanted Newt Bonner strung up for running out on a twenty-dollar gas bill, Wade thought. But, wisely, he said, "Okay, I appreciate that."

Wade left the Quick Mart, got in his car and headed toward the town hall where he shared a two-desk office with Bert Hollinger. They didn't need much more space than that since Mount Esther didn't have its own jail cell. All the desperate criminals like Clifford Arnold were taken to the county seat to do time. Wade intended to complete his report on the Arnold incident and then check the traffic flow out on the highway for a couple of hours. He was passing River Real Estate just as Betty Lamb came out the front door. She flagged him to the curb and Wade rolled down his window. "Something wrong, Betty?"

She leaned on the door frame and stuck her head in the patrol car. "Good morning, handsome. I was just coming to see you." She held up a manila folder. "I have your Right to Purchase Agreement here. All you have to do is sign it. Once you do, Mrs. Ashford will have thirty days to vacate the property, your mortgage will kick in and all this nonsense about a deed will be a thing of the past."

"You're sure it's nonsense?" Wade asked again.

Betty nodded. "Just to be sure, and because I know what a stickler you are, I did a recheck through county records. No deed for that property was ever filed."

"That doesn't mean Mrs. Ashford's lawyer didn't prepare it. It might have gotten lost at county records."

She shook her head with impatience. "Look, Wade, you've got to stop borrowing trouble and think about your investment." She stepped back and shoved the folder through the window at him. "Sign this so we can finalize the sale of the house."

Logically Wade knew she was right. He could put an end to this ownership debate once and for all by signing his name. But morally, he couldn't bring himself to do it. He'd given his word to Mrs. Ashford, and he couldn't kick her out of her house even if it was generally assumed that she was never coming back. Feeling mostly like an idiot for sticking to principles that might bite him in the butt, he said, "I can't sign it now, Betty. I don't have time."

She heaved a sigh of frustration. "Wade, how long does it take to scribble your signature on a piece of paper?"

"It's not that," he said. "I don't have time to read it now. I'm running late."

"Read it?" Betty drummed her fingernails on the top of the car door. "You know, Wade, I hate to sound self-serving about this whole situation, but my commission on this sale doesn't come into effect until you sign the Right to Purchase Agreement. I'm sitting on a few thousand dollars that I could be happily spending."

"I know," Wade said. "But you prepared this contract knowing I wasn't going to force Mrs. Ashford out of her house."

"Right. But that's before I knew there might be a complication."

"So you admit there might be one?"

"No! I'm just doing all I can to prevent the possibility."

Wade did feel some sympathy for the Realtor. After all, Betty had put a lot of time into this deal knowing her commission wouldn't come for a while. She'd been creative in her negotiations and come up with a contract that seemed equally fair to both Wade and Mrs. Ashford. It wasn't her fault that Meg Hamilton showed up with her own claim to the property. "I'll stop by the office later," he finally said. "I'll look over the agreement then."

"When later?" Betty said. "Today?"

"Maybe. Soon."

She backed away from the car. "I'll hold you to that."

He drove off down the street and pulled into a parking place in front of the town hall. Before getting out of the car, he thought about the predicament he was in with Meg. "Basically, Murdock, you're a moron, a thirty-nine-year-old moron to be exact," he said to himself. "You acted like some two-bit Romeo last night, and then you suffered the consequences like a high-school kid experiencing his first crush." And bit everybody's head off at breakfast, he added to himself.

It had been a long, torturous night. Wade hadn't been able to stop thinking about Meg and where the kiss might have led if they hadn't been sitting on granite boulders freezing their toes off in sixty-degree water. His body had reacted to the fantasy for hours. He wasn't a moonlight and poetry kind of guy. He was straightforward, sensible. And yet all night he'd fancied himself courting Meg almost as if he were one of those cavaliers in Stewart Ashford's attic painting.

He squirmed a little on the car seat, relieving some of the discomfort coiling right now between his legs. He stretched his arms, rotated his neck muscles and looked out the side window.

That was a mistake.

There she was, sitting next to the town hall, smack in the middle of the sunny corner window of the Print-Smart Shop. Wade watched Meg as her hands flew expertly over a computer keyboard. Her auburn hair was tied up in a bundle of curls on top of her head, leaving her slender neck exposed. She chewed on her bottom lip, deep in concentration.

There was no kidding himself. Meg Hamilton looked every bit as desirable with her hands on a keyboard as she did in the moonlight over a Suwannee River spring.

He got out of the car and forced his mind to the job he came to complete. He had to write up a report on Clifford Arnold's night in jail. And he couldn't do that if he kept staring in the window of the PrintSmart Shop.

He yanked open the door to the town hall and walked inside. He had to focus on his family and the new start he had promised them. He didn't think he could handle getting involved with another woman and the possibility of losing her. "Is it really worth the risk?" he said aloud. "Especially with *this* woman?"

When he noticed heads turning in his direction, he clamped his mouth shut. *You don't even know if Meg Hamilton is interested in you. Right now she thinks you're the biggest problem she's got in her life.* He smiled to himself and suddenly walked with a bit more confidence. *Though she did seem to like kissing you.*

BY WEDNESDAY AFTERNOON Meg had posted auction flyers in two dozen locations in Mount Esther, sent more than fifty announcements to antique dealers and furniture stores in the tri-county area, and placed three classified newspaper ads. At each stop, the people she contacted were enthusiastic about the auction.

"I've always wanted to see inside that big old house," the lady at the dry cleaners told her.

A young man at the hardware store mentioned that his grandfather had spoken of fast times at the Ashford place, and he would definitely be at the auction.

After hearing several comments like these, Meg was certain there would be a big crowd spilling over the lawn and into the first floor of Ashford House for the event. And Gloria would be happy with the check she received a few days later.

At four o'clock, Meg finally took a glass of iced tea onto the veranda, put her feet up, and dialed her home telephone number on her cell phone.

"Hi, Mom," Spence said. "How's it going?"

"Really well, honey. So, you only have two more days of school. I can't wait to see you on Sunday."

"Yeah, me, too."

"I think you're going to like it up here," she said. "We have a lot of work to do to get ready for Aunt Amelia's auction, but we'll have some fun, too."

"Uncle Jerry says I'll be living with a policeman."

"Actually he's a deputy. That's what policemen are called up here, and yes, he's staying for a while."

"Why is he living in Aunt Amelia's house?"

What should have been a simple answer wasn't, and Meg paused for a moment to consider how to respond. She'd told Spencer that they would someday own Ashford House and maybe live there, and she didn't want to try to explain the complicated circumstances surrounding the deputy's claim. And she couldn't tell her son that Wade was staying to deter burglars. Finally she said, "He's a friend of Aunt Amelia's, a very nice man, and he helps her with some of the chores. He has a daughter—"

"You mean a girl's living there, too?"

"Yes, and the deputy's father, who—"

"Oh, great. I thought it would just be the two of us."

Spencer hadn't been to Ashford House in so long, perhaps he had forgotten how huge the place was. Meg tried to allay his concerns by pointing out the size of the house. "There are twelve rooms, remember? We'll have plenty of our own space."

He was quiet for a moment, and Meg didn't press him. Finally he said, "You know, Mom, Uncle Jerry isn't too happy that you're coming to get me."

And suddenly you don't seem too happy either, Meg

thought. "Spencer, I know you have fun with Uncle Jerry, and he cares for you a great deal, but you also know that one of the reasons he's not pleased I'm coming on Sunday is that he'll have to tell Mary Beth the truth about you and me."

"She's here now," Spencer said. "He's going to tell her tonight. We've sort of got a plan worked out."

Meg's maternal instincts went on alert again. "Spencer, you know how I feel about lying."

"I'm not going to lie, Mom. And Uncle Jerry's just telling a little lie, but he really likes her. He says guys do some crazy things when women are involved."

Meg sighed. Apparently her son was learning a dangerous lesson that, in matters of the heart, the end justified the means. She didn't need another man in his life setting a bad example. His father had already done that. Dave hadn't left his son a darn thing when he walked out—not even a trait the boy could think back on and admire. He just left him sad and feeling that he'd done something to make his dad go away. And now Meg had to worry that Jerry was becoming another poor role model for her son.

Meg hated the miles that separated her and Spence, miles that she could only breach with words, not hugs. "Honey, Uncle Jerry never should have let Mary Beth believe that you didn't live with your mother," she said. "That's the thing about lies. They build on each other until they're out of control. Now Uncle Jerry has to tell yet another lie so it didn't look like he was lying in the first place."

"I guess it wasn't a good thing to do," he admitted.

"No, it wasn't. You have a mother who loves you very

much. And she can't wait until Sunday. Enjoy your last two days of school. Is Mrs. Johnson having a party on Friday?"

"I guess so," he said without enthusiasm. "But it's out on the playground, and it's hot. I figured I'd just bring my Game Boy to school. Mrs. Johnson said it's okay."

Once again Spencer put himself on the fringe of life where he didn't have to risk being hurt or ignored. Meg's heart ached for him. "We're going to have a wonderful summer," she said, and she wished it were true for both of them.

MARY BETH SAT on the sofa in Meg's living room and looked up at Jerry. "So he's talking to her right now?"

"Yeah," Jerry said. "My sister called just a few minutes before you got here. I wasn't really surprised." Jerry walked from the sofa to the window and looked out on the street. He needed a few seconds to formulate the words in his mind. "Meg's not a bad person," he said turning back to Mary Beth. "She loves Spencer. She just goes through these difficult periods in her life when she needs a little time to find herself again."

Mary Beth nodded. "I guess I'm happy for Spencer," she said, "but I still don't see how your sister could have left him."

Jerry gave her a little half grin. "It's not as if Meg left him with an ogre or anything."

"Oh, no, I didn't mean that. You obviously love Spencer and he feels the same about you. You're a wonderful uncle."

He sat down next to her. "I try."

"How do you feel about Meg coming to get Spencer? About her taking him from Orlando? Will she be responsible?"

Jerry took Mary Beth's hand in both of his. "I'm sure she will. Spencer will be fine. Besides, he knows how to reach me if he has to."

Jerry rested his elbow on the back of the sofa. "You've been a big help to me with Spence," he said. "But I wouldn't mind having a little time alone with you."

She smiled at him, parting her full pink lips, and lowering her eyelids until her lashes lay delicately against her pale skin. She was the most perfectly put-together female Jerry had ever seen. Maybe she wasn't the type he'd always gone out with. But Mary Beth was definitely the woman he wanted. He'd been content for a while to wait for her to realize she had feelings for him, to recognize that they could share more than an interest in Spencer and a profitable business relationship. But a man could only stand so much.

He lowered his arm to her shoulders and wrapped his hand around her arm. She didn't pull away. That was good. He slipped a finger under her chin and turned her face toward his. "Mary Beth? I think it's time we notched up our relationship to something more personal, don't you?"

She raised her eyes and stared intently at him. He swallowed, forced himself to breathe. He'd said the wrong thing.

And then she grinned. "Frankly, Jerry, I don't know what you've been waiting for. There could be advantages to being alone."

Dumbfounded, he stared back at her. He threaded his fingers through the golden curls tumbling over her shoulders and grasped the nape of her neck. That was all it took. She came to him, all soft and yielding and ready. He kissed her warm mouth and tasted her with his tongue. And she kissed him back with equal enthusiasm.

Until they both heard the subtle rasp of someone clearing his throat.

With a groan, Jerry pushed Mary Beth away. "Spencer! Come in," he said.

He came through the doorway and sat on the floor.

"How'd it go with your mother?" Jerry asked in a husky voice.

"It went great."

"Then you're okay about going away with her?" Mary Beth asked.

"Sure." Then, responding to Jerry's subtle glare, he added, "My mom's fine now. She had some time to herself, and she's really anxious to see me."

"That's wonderful," Mary Beth said. "But we'll miss you here."

"Oh, boy will we," Jerry said. He glanced at Mary Beth whose luscious lips were still moist from their kiss. "About what time will your mom get here on Sunday?" he asked.

MEG PUSHED Mr. Cuddles away from her chest and rolled over to grab her wristwatch. She pressed the tab that lighted the digital display. 11:35. "What's the use," she grumbled and threw off the covers. She couldn't sleep despite being exhausted and despite accomplishing nearly all her goals. It had been a difficult day. She'd had trouble concentrating especially when she'd been typing auction advertisements she'd eventually mailed to shopkeepers. The store where she'd used the computer was right next to Mount Esther's town hall, and when Meg had seen Wade's car in the parking lot, she'd spent more time watching the vehicle than the monitor.

And now it was late and she hadn't seen Wade all day. He'd called and talked to Roone, telling him that he was going to stake out the environmental preserve outside of town. Somebody had been dumping old tires on the protected property, and Bert and he were taking turns watching the site.

Meg put on her robe and went downstairs. Maybe a glass of milk and a couple of cookies would at least make her inner clock think it was bedtime. After winding through the dining room where Amelia's unwrapped purchases now sat on top of the table, she heaved her shoulder against the swinging door. It met an immovable object on the other side at the same time a loud *ooomph!* sounded from the kitchen.

Cringing at the damage she might have inflicted, and praying she hadn't knocked Roone on his backside, Meg gently pushed the door with the flat of her hand. But it was Wade's startled expression she saw when she stepped into the room. She bunched the yoke of her robe into her fist, and emitted a most unladylike squawk.

Wade rubbed his shoulder with one hand while balancing a plate holding a half-empty glass and a piece of pie swimming in a pool of milk.

Meg stifled a giggle. "You're home."

"Yep. And trying to recover from your sneak attack." He set the plate down on a counter and frowned at the door. "Tell you what. I'll be Curly and you be Moe."

As she breezed by him she picked up his plate. "I'll get you another piece. Sit down."

He did and she cut two more slices, one for him and one for herself. She brought two glasses of milk to the table and sat across from him. "Did you catch the tire dumper?"

"Sure did. A fella with a wheel and hubcap store in the next county. I guess he couldn't dirty his own territory so he chose to pollute the environment of Mount Esther." He took a large bite of pie and talked around it. "I questioned him about the break-in here, by the way. He didn't do it."

"So, what did you do with him?"

"Bert took him to the county lockup. He'll see a judge in the morning and probably be out by noon. But I don't think he'll bring any more tires to Mount Esther. And if Bert has his way, he'll be spending the next four Saturdays picking up garbage along the pedestrian catwalks to the limestone caves in the preserve."

"What a pity," Meg said. "He'll miss the auction."

Wade smirked. "I'm sure he would have been a big bidder." He took a swallow of milk and said, "Did you make the pie?"

"Almost," she said. "I bought it."

"Okay, then, I can tell you. It's not very good."

"Do you want some leftover lasagna? Your father made enough for an army."

Wade chewed on the last bite of the not-so-good pie. "I'll pass. I had a sub earlier." He leaned back in his chair and gave her an odd, indecipherable grin. "Mostly I just want to look at you."

Meg wished she had a huge glass of ice cubes she

could pour down the front of her robe. It was the only thing she could think of to combat the sudden burst of heat infusing every inch of her body. She'd never been very good at flirtatious comebacks. "Oh, well…" She stood up and carried his plate to the sink.

"And that was a stupid thing for me to say," he said. "Truthful but stupid."

She turned around, leaned against the counter. "Under the circumstances, probably."

His gaze passed from her mussed-up hair to her fuzzy slippers. "But you're cute, Meg," he said. "I like looking at you."

He stood up and came toward her. Every muscle in her body tensed at the same time she thought she might melt to the floor like a warm puddle of butter.

"And I liked kissing you," he said. "I thought you should know that."

"Okay. Thanks."

He reached up and ran his hand down her hair, her cheek, her jawline. She stood rigidly, her chest rising and falling with each effort to keep from panting.

He rubbed his thumb over her bottom lip. "Damn. I want to do it again."

He leaned closer. She placed the flat of her hand on his chest. "Wade, don't. We shouldn't get involved this way. Not when there are so many problems. This house. Our kids might not get along. Your dad resents me." *Your past.*

She was saying the words, knowing they were true, but wanting to take them all back. It had been so long since a man made her feel like she had last night at the spring. But this was not the right time nor was this the right man.

"I think our kids will get along fine," Wade said. "And Pop will adjust to whatever he has to. But if all this stuff bothers you, I don't like it, but I understand." He took a step back from her. "But if I can't kiss you, I'm going to bed. Because it doesn't make much sense for a man to stand in the kitchen with a sexy woman in her nightie and talk about tires and garbage dumps."

He walked away from her and left the kitchen without looking back. And Meg stared down at her large, comfy robe that was just fine on cold lonely nights in Orlando, but seemed terribly frumpy right now. Then she sighed and looked at the swinging door that had just closed on a man who'd had the wonderful grace to call her a sexy woman in a nightie.

CHAPTER THIRTEEN

THE NEXT THREE DAYS PASSED in a flurry of activity for Meg. The phone rang constantly at Ashford House with people asking about the auction. Between taking calls, she continued organizing Amelia's belongings, and with Roone's help, she carried pieces from the attic to be included in the sale.

She also made time each day to visit her aunt at Shady Grove. Amelia's mental capacities seemed to be declining rapidly now. There were still moments when she recognized Meg, and during those times, Meg asked her about the deed. When Amelia could not give her a definite answer, Meg didn't press her.

Wade concentrated his refurbishing efforts on the interior of the house, taking down old rotted wainscoting, resealing windows, and patching cracked wall boards. On Saturday morning Meg remarked that he was fixing the house as if he were convinced that it would be his.

He'd smiled at her as he dipped his trowel in plaster. "I *am* convinced. Almost as convinced as I am that you're never going to stop looking for the deed." Then he'd taken her hand, pulled up a desk chair and urged her to sit. "But since one of us is probably going to end up with this house, I think we should discuss a few things."

"Like what?"

"Like sanding the kitchen cupboards before I paint them. Is it all right with you if I get started on that project?"

"Sure," she'd said with a devilish grin. "But just don't choose the color yet. I might not like it."

Late Saturday night, the house was quiet. Wade was patrolling. Roone was watching television. Jenny was sound asleep recovering from the slumber party she'd had the night before. Meg went out on the veranda, sat in the cushiony softness of an old padded wicker chair, and put her feet on the porch rail. Light from the parlor filtered through Amelia's lacy curtains and turned the veranda's maple floorboards a burnished gold.

After a few moments she noticed for the first time that a few of the spindles looked different from the rest. They were newer, sturdier, and lacked a coat of paint. She realized that Wade must have replaced them some time ago, probably before she arrived, and she smiled at his efforts.

And then her smile faded because the skill and pride Wade put into each project around the house touched a chord of sadness inside her. He had done so much to make this house his. His mark was in nearly every room now, in the screen he repaired in her bedroom, in the new plaster in the parlor, the more efficient plumbing in the bathrooms.

If she had to lose Ashford House, Meg knew the home would thrive under Wade's guardianship. Perhaps he truly believed that this house was healing him, and for that reason he would protect and preserve it in the years ahead. Certainly he'd made himself a part of Ashford House history in the weeks he'd been in Mount Esther. Still, Meg had been a part of that history since the day she was born, and her ties to the house couldn't be discounted because of a little hard work and twenty thousand dollars.

Headlights appeared at the beginning of the lane, and Meg recognized the sound of Wade's patrol car. She was as accustomed to the purr of the engine as she was to the whine of his drill, or the hiss of sandpaper as he caressed a rough piece of wood. Or his mock-stern warning to teenaged girls who celebrated the start of summer by playing music too loud on a Friday night.

Wade's sounds were becoming as familiar to her as were the features of his face, the gestures that spoke his thoughts when words did not. She stood up and grasped the veranda post as the car pulled to the house. Wade got out, arched his back and released the deep, contented sigh of a man who had come home. And it was that sound more than any other that unsettled Meg because it seeped into her heart and made her know that deep down, despite her best efforts, she'd started to imagine what it would be like if Wade were coming home to her.

MEG ARRIVED at her home in Orlando just after noon on Sunday. Spencer ran out to her car the minute she pulled in the driveway, and she pulled him to her in a huge bear hug. After a week, she relished the feel of his arms around her waist, his cheek against her chest.

And she admitted to herself that Spence had fared quite well under his uncle's supervision. Despite the fact that Jerry used his nephew to attract a new girlfriend, Spencer had obviously been well-cared for.

"Thanks, Jerry," she said to her brother when she went into the house to get Spencer's bags. "I really appreciate you looking after Spence all this time."

"Hey, no problem," Jerry said with a rare guilty grin. "Even if you did criticize some of my child-rearing techniques."

"With good reason," Meg said as she moved Spence's suitcase and backpack to the front door. Next she went to her desk to check the mail that had arrived in her absence. Flipping through a stack of bills, she put the most urgent ones in her purse. "By the way, where is Mary Beth today? I thought I'd get to meet this ideal of womanly charms."

"It's Sunday," he explained. "The busiest day for her charity operation. She's sorry she couldn't be here to meet you."

"I'm sorry, too," Meg said.

"Anyhow, before you leave for Mount Esther, I want you to come by the auction house. You can see some of the merchandise Mary Beth has been bringing in."

The suggestion was a good one for a couple of reasons. Maybe Meg could put her mind at ease about the origin of this merchandise, and she could skim over the paperwork from the last two auctions. "Okay, but let's hurry. It's a five-hour trip and the day's not getting any longer."

They loaded Spence's things in Meg's car and Jerry followed her to the auction house in his car. He took her to the storage room in back of the office and unlocked the door. Then he stepped back so she could look inside. "See? What did I tell you. We have all this stuff for next week already."

Meg was impressed. She perused tools, lawn equipment and electronics whose cumulative retail value amounted to several thousand dollars. "Nice stuff," she said to a beaming Jerry. "Did you say the men donating these things to Mary Beth's charity had more?"

"That's what she tells me. I suppose they'll run out eventually, but for now working with her is making my job much easier." He caught her eye over the top of Spencer's head. "Among other, equally as pleasant advantages."

"So you've told me." Meg investigated a computer tower, noting that it was a late model. "This is nice. I wish we could bid on this for the auction." And then the metal plate on the back of the unit grabbed her attention and she crouched down to examine it. "Jerry, what's this?"

He peered down at the computer. "You talking about the serial number?"

"Exactly," she said, tapping the plate with a fingernail. "The number's been scratched so it's unreadable."

Jerry waved off her concern. "Oh, that. The men told Mary Beth not to worry if she couldn't find serial numbers on all the items. He said the companies that wholesaled these things obliterated the numbers so people trying to make a dishonest buck couldn't get away with returning them to retail outlets for a full refund."

"Wouldn't the companies have a record of the serial numbers of items they sold at a discounted price so they could be cross-checked if someone tried to return the computer? They wouldn't need to scratch the numbers off everything."

A flash of anger lit Jerry's eyes. "Meg, stop looking for trouble where there isn't any. I've just explained this to you. Besides, I have the name of the guy who brings this stuff in if there's ever a problem—which there won't be. The flow of merchandise in this country revolves around guys just like Mr. Horton who have the contacts to get excess merchandise and channel it into retail operations like ours."

She recited aloud the brand names on some of the boxes in the storage room. "So you think these respected companies called Mr. Horton to pick up their excess?"

"I certainly do. And we were lucky when Mary Beth offered the opportunity for us to benefit from his connections." He frowned at her worried expression. "For Pete's sake, Meg, can't you just appreciate our good fortune for once and quit looking for the dark cloud behind the silver lining?"

He looked like she'd just dumped buckets of water on his one-man parade, and Meg chastised herself for her usual, and sometimes unwarranted suspicions where Jerry was concerned. "You're probably right," she said and almost convinced herself that it made sense for the manufacturers to obscure the serial numbers to keep these discounted things from showing up in a regular retail market.

"Of course I'm right."

Spencer had wandered to the exit and was waiting impatiently. "Mom, let's go. I'm hungry and you promised we'd stop at McDonald's."

Meg stood up and followed Jerry out of the storeroom. "See what you've done? Turned my son into a junk-food addict. And while I'm thinking of it, you might as well throw out the turkey meat loaf I left in the refrigerator nine days ago. It must be green by now."

He turned around and grinned. "It was green two days ago. Spence drew the short straw and got rid of it."

"HOW MUCH FARTHER?" Spencer asked just before slurping the rest of his root beer from the bottom of the cup. They'd stopped about an hour ago for gas and dinner, and Spence had polished off an order of chicken fingers, a large order of fries and a candy bar. Meg was definitely going to filter vegetables back into his vitamin-deficient system starting tomorrow.

She exited the highway and turned onto the county road that led to Mount Esther. "About twenty minutes," she said. "It's been a few years since you've been here, but do you recognize any of this scenery?"

He glanced out the window without really looking. "Nope. Can I play my Game Boy the rest of the way?"

Meg sighed. "Sure." She couldn't blame him for passing the time with game cartridges. Into her tenth hour of driving in one day, Meg wished she, too, had something to stare at besides asphalt. She'd caught up on all of Spencer's news the first hour until she could tell he was bored with relating every little detail of his week with his uncle. After he pulled some comic books out of his backpack, she'd had nothing to do but dwell on the conclusions she'd drawn in the little time she'd been home.

She hadn't been able to stop thinking about the merchandise Mary Beth brought to the auction. Everything she'd seen was clean, new, expensive, and too good to be true. Something just didn't add up. She wished she'd had the opportunity to meet the men who were supplying Colonial Auction with the goods, or at least meet Mary Beth.

"Quit worrying," Jerry had advised one last time when she'd gotten into her car to head back to Mount Esther. "You've got enough on your mind without inventing more problems." He'd gleefully repeated the auction profits from the past two weeks. "Trust me on this, Meggie. Think about the bottom line, and stop letting your imagination run wild."

It had been good advice, and Meg wished she'd been able to follow it. But even now as she was approaching Mount Esther, and a host of other more pressing problems, she couldn't get Colonial Auction out of her mind. Her livelihood depended on its continued operation and reputation, now and in the future. And that was especially true if she lost Ashford House.

The old home popped into her mind as it had so many times during the last few hours. And so did the man who was living there. Wade Murdock was her biggest problem, and now, her most frustrating fantasy. His supportive presence had become a constant in her life, and she decided that perhaps he could be some help to her with regard to Colonial Auction. She would mention her concerns to him and see what conclusions he might draw based on his law experience. Maybe Jerry was right and there was nothing to worry about.

"We're here," she said to Spencer as she pulled into the property.

He turned off the Game Boy, stared into the trees lining the drive and said, "Pull over."

"Why? What's wrong?"

"I've got to ask you some things."

"Now? Spence, you've had hours to ask me questions."

"I know, but I forgot to. And now I have to ask them."

She stopped in the middle of the lane. "Okay, what's bothering you?"

"Is the deputy nice?"

"Of course he's nice."

"Is he allowed to boss me around?"

Meg smiled to herself. "Well, since bossing you around is my biggest responsibility, and I haven't been able to do that in over a week, the deputy will have to knock me out of the way to have a chance at you."

Spencer frowned. "Mom, I'm serious."

"Okay. Wade Murdock is a sensible man. He's an adult and you aren't. So if you were about to do something that in his mind were dangerous, foolish, or morally wrong, then, yes, I suppose he could advise you against doing it and you should listen and react appropriately. Does that answer your question?"

"Yes. You're selling me out. What about the girl? What if I don't like her?"

Meg flexed her fingers on the steering wheel. She wished Spencer had brought up these matters hours ago so they could have thoroughly discussed them, instead of asking them now when they were halfway up the drive to Ashford House.

"Since you're asking that question," she began, "it seems to me that you are already prepared to not like Jenny. If that turns out to be the case, then I would suggest that you avoid each other. It's a big house, and that shouldn't be a problem. But before taking such evasive action, I would also suggest that you try to like her."

He nodded, apparently accepting that advice. "One more thing. Will Aunt Amelia know me?"

"She might. But she probably won't." Meg put her

hand on Spencer's arm. "But she has remembered you since I've been here and she asked about you. And I put a picture of you by her bed."

"Okay." He looked out the front windshield, tightened his features into a mask of determination, and said, "Let's go then."

She resumed driving. "It's going to be all right, Spence. You'll see."

As if he'd been waiting for her, Wade came out on the porch when she pulled up. He leaned against a post and crossed one ankle over the other. His hair, streaked with copper in the veranda light, curled over his collar and lay in tousled waves on his forehead. His smile was warm and natural, and he was as beautiful a sight as Meg had ever associated with Ashford House. In faded worn jeans and a short-sleeved plaid shirt he looked utterly male and totally at ease. He seemed to belong right where he was, as if he were meant to be standing there to welcome her back.

An intense sexual longing, a feeling so alien to the last years of Meg's life, jolted her so that for a moment all she could do was sit behind the wheel and simply stare at the man on the porch. Her reaction to seeing him again terrified her because of its effect on her mind and body. She had to put any domestic thoughts of her and Wade out of her head. Yes, he'd kissed her, even said that he wanted to again, but he was a man with a family and a past. She was a woman with responsibilities. And even though they claimed to share Ashford House to protect it, truly they were both here because neither wanted to give it up.

"Is that him?" Spencer asked.

Meg's answer came out on a wistful breath of air. "That's him, all right."

He came down the steps and reached the car in a few long strides. He opened Spencer's door and stuck his hand inside. "I'm Wade Murdock and I'm pleased to meet you."

Spence shook his hand though the look on his face was guarded as he climbed from the car.

"You got a lot of gear?" Wade asked.

Spence grabbed his Game Boy and backpack from the floor of the front seat and then opened the rear door and pulled out his duffel bag. "Yeah. A couple of bags and some stuff in the trunk."

"I'll take that one." Wade slung the bag over his shoulder. "You can help your mother with the rest."

Meg had unlocked the trunk and waited for Spencer to retrieve his small suitcase. When she noticed that Wade watched her over the raised lid, she let her gaze linger on his face.

"Long drive?" he finally said.

She slammed the trunk lid and came around the car. "Too long for one day."

"Dad's got stew on the stove."

Meg had only ordered an ice cream when they'd stopped, and Wade's announcement made her realize she was starved. "Remind me to do something nice for that man," she said. "Whatever he wants."

Wade touched her arm and began walking with her to the house. When Spencer ran ahead of them, he leaned over and whispered in her ear. "In that case, next time *I'll* make the stew."

The bones in Meg's legs felt as though they were

melting inch by inch. Surely it was fatigue, she told her-self. When they entered the house, Jenny was standing in the foyer and Spencer had rooted himself to the floor about five feet from her. He backed up when Meg came up behind him. "This is Wade's daughter," she said. "Jenny."

"Hi."

Jenny crossed her arms and assumed an I'm-not-re-ally-interested slouch. "Hi. You can ride my horse if you want."

Meg sensed she'd been coached to say that as a wel-coming line.

Spencer shrugged. "I don't want to."

Meg nudged him from behind, reminding him of his manners.

"…but thanks anyway." He turned to look at her. "Where's my room?"

"Upstairs, turn right, third door."

He tore up the stairs, his backpack clomping behind him on every step. Jenny went into the parlor and sat down in front of the television with Roone.

"Where's the boy?" Roone called over his shoulder.

"He's escaped unharmed," Wade answered.

Meg dropped her purse and keys on the hall stand. "That went well," she said.

"Hey, things can only get better." He followed her in-to the kitchen, pulled out a chair for her, and placed a bowl of stew and thick slice of bread on the table.

After taking a few bites, Meg thought of her brother and Colonial Auction. "Wade, there's something I'd like to ask you," she began. "It's kind of a legal issue."

"Sure, but I have something to tell you, and maybe I should go first."

She stared up at him, instinctively ready for bad news. "Oh? What is it?"

"Someone called for you today. Her name is Gloria. She said to tell you she was flying down, and would be here on Wednesday."

Meg dropped her fork on the side of the bowl. Oh, great. Gloria. In a few days there would be six of them living in Ashford House and Meg couldn't imagine a more diverse group of people. Suddenly this grand old house with twelve rooms was beginning to feel like a closet.

"Is something wrong?" Wade asked.

"No. Yes. I don't know."

"What did you want to tell me?"

"It can wait until tomorrow." She didn't want to think about Colonial Auction any more today. She didn't want to think about Gloria arriving in three days. She just wanted to enjoy Roone's stew and the man who'd served it to her.

MEG WAS UP EARLY the next morning, though she hadn't beat Wade. A rinsed coffee mug and a wrinkled newspaper were the only signs that he had awakened and left the house. Refusing to admit she was disappointed she wouldn't be sharing breakfast with him, Meg told herself she was lucky to have a few minutes of peace and quiet to start the day.

She decided to let Spencer sleep as late as he wanted. And since Jenny was a teenager enjoying the first of summer vacation, there was no guessing when she might come downstairs. The hum of a television was the only artificial noise that disturbed the solitude. Roone was obviously watching the news in his bedroom above the kitchen.

Meg had just finished her own coffee and a bowl of oatmeal when the doorbell rang. She went to the foyer and opened the screen door to a woman in a tan business suit. Her dark hair was impeccably groomed into a neat French twist. Completing the professional demeanor, she carried a briefcase and flashed a practiced smile at Meg. After handing Meg a business card, she said, "Hi. Is Wade Murdock home?"

Meg glanced at the card. The woman's name was Betty and she was from River Real Estate. Of course Meg had heard of her. She was the agent who'd put together the deal to sell Amelia's house to Wade. "No, I'm sorry. He's left already this morning," she said.

"Well, shoot. I came by early hoping to catch him. That man is as slippery as a Minnesota sidewalk in February." She smiled again. "I'm originally from Minnesota."

"Oh."

"You must be Mrs. Ashford's niece."

"That's right."

"Everybody in town is talking about you," Betty said. "I imagine you'll have a big crowd at the auction."

"I hope so. I want to do the best I can for my aunt."

"Of course you do." Betty's smile turned a bit cunning. "And make a little bundle for yourself as well."

Meg refrained from responding as she wanted to. "Is there a message I can give Wade for you?"

Betty appeared to consider her answer for a moment. "As a matter of fact, there is. Tell him I came by this morning with his Right to Purchase Agreement. I really need him to sign the dang thing so we can proceed with the paperwork on the house. I'm sure you both want this matter settled."

Meg didn't have a comprehensive understanding of real estate, but the term *right to purchase* obviously meant trouble for her. And Betty's calculated announcement was a warning.

"I don't want to get in the middle of this spat you're having with Wade," Betty continued, "but he could conclude the purchase by dashing off his signature on the bottom of the agreement I have in my briefcase. Why he's procrastinating is beyond my comprehension. He claims he wants this house so badly. Well, he could have it, free and clear in thirty days, if he'd only sign his name and get the ball rolling."

Meg stared at the briefcase as if it contained the demise of everything she'd counted on. In fact, it did. And this overly confident agent knew it. She started to close the door, indicating that her conversation with Betty was over. "I'll tell him you came by," she said.

"Thanks. Tell him to stop at the office. Or at least call. If I don't hear from him, I'm only going to keep bugging him. And I'll eventually find him even if I have to fake a robbery or something to get his attention." Betty smiled again and breezed down the steps. As she opened her car door, she called up to Meg, "Have a nice day."

Fat chance! Meg went back through the house to the kitchen. As she washed the few breakfast dishes, she replayed Betty's visit in her head. Wade could end this drama and own Ashford House with one signature? Since she still hadn't found the deed, Meg felt her last hope of owning Ashford House slip away. But, then, she wondered. If Wade could so easily press his claim, why hadn't he?

CHAPTER FOURTEEN

IT HAD BEEN an interesting day starting with an early-morning car chase with a fifteen-year-old kid from Lake City who'd topped a hundred miles an hour on the high-way. Wade joined the county sheriff's department in trying to stop the kid before he killed himself or some-one else. Road spikes had finally done the job with no injuries.

The afternoon had progressed to a report of petty theft. Wade got the call that a camper had been broken into at the Tree Spring Campground. He successfully closed the book on the case when he caught the home-less guy who'd taken a CD player and portable televi-sion from a northerner's RV.

Now, as he pulled up the Ashford House drive, all Wade could think about was how nice it would be to sit on the front porch of the house that might someday be his. He was climbing the steps, his arms loaded with un-usual purchases he'd made on the way home, when he was struck with the realization that the scenario in his mind would be even better if he were sitting there with Meg—the woman determined to snatch that porch out from under him.

He smiled at the irony of his thoughts as he walked

through the house with the intention of finding her. Leaning his new equipment against a wall in the dining room, he went into the kitchen where he saw Meg. She was removing stacks of green dishes from a high cupboard. Her tempting bottom was covered in the scantiest amount of denim, and a tank top showed off her slender arms and the curve of a breast. Wade came up behind her, resisting the urge to put his hands on her hips and said, "Hey, you could use some help."

She squealed, spun around and grabbed the edge of the counter to steady herself. "For heaven's sake, Wade, you scared me half to death."

Her top gaped open, revealing a generous amount of cleavage, and Wade's throat went dry. "That wasn't my intention," he finally croaked. "I just came in for a glass of water."

"Well, since you're here, and since you offered..." She pointed to a stack of at least a dozen bowls. "You can put these in the box on the table."

He did as she asked and she handed him a stack of cups which he also put in the box. "What are these?" he asked. "They look old."

"They are old. They're made by a company called Fire King and were distributed in boxes of detergent. My aunt collected them, probably fifty years ago."

Wade stared at the mountains of green dishes he was going to have to cart to the table. "Amelia used a lot of detergent in those days."

Meg laughed. "She's always been very tidy."

"How are you going to sell them?"

"Altogether to the highest bidder. We won't have time to break up the set into smaller numbers. Besides they should bring a couple of hundred dollars as a group."

She stretched her arms to get a load from the top shelf. The tank top strained until a slash of white skin at the base of her spine was revealed. Wade swallowed hard. "Why don't you take a break?" he suggested. "Come out on the porch and have a drink with me."

She looked over her shoulder. "Can't. There's too much to do. The auction's this Saturday you know."

He buried his disappointment behind carting more dishes. "Why haven't you gotten the kids to help?" he asked.

"They did, for a while."

Wade pulled another box from under the table and began filling it. "Where are they now?"

"Jenny's at a friend's house—the girl with the swimming pool. Spencer's in his room playing video games."

"And Pop?"

"I'm right here," Roone said, coming into the kitchen. "And I've been turning people away from this house all day."

Wade narrowed his eyes at him. "What do you mean by that?"

"It's a madhouse around here. Folks coming by wanting to see the merchandise before the sale."

Wade thought of the break-in which occurred one week ago, and assumed his deputy persona. "People? What people?"

"Just curiosity seekers," Meg said.

"Yeah. Curious about the money that's supposedly hidden here," Wade said.

"Maybe." Since the cupboard was now empty, Meg

climbed down off the chair. "Frankly, I don't think there is any money." She put her hands on her hips and stared at Wade. "Remember, I've been all over this house looking for…things. And I haven't found so much as a quarter."

He knew she was referring to her search for the deed. And she had looked thoroughly. If there were money hidden in Ashford House, she would have found it.

"You had a visitor this morning," she said. "Betty from River Real Estate."

Wade wasn't surprised. Betty had left several messages for him at the office. "I'll catch up with her later."

"Wade, she said you haven't signed some sort of agreement that would insure your purchase of Ashford House."

At the refrigerator, Roone pointedly cleared his throat before pouring himself a glass of iced tea.

"Betty never should have told you that," Wade said.

"Why haven't you signed it?"

"I haven't had time." It was the excuse he used most often, so he used it again with Meg.

She didn't believe it any more than Betty did. "You're too busy to sign a document?"

"Today I am. I've got big plans." Dodging the issue of the Right to Purchase Agreement, he went to the swinging door, stuck his hand inside the dining room and grasped the items he'd bought. Enjoying the surprised look on Meg's face, he stood a pair of fishing poles against the pantry door and set a new tackle box beside them.

"You're going fishing?" she asked.

"Yep. Me and Spencer."

Meg's eyes rounded with amusement. "Spencer told you he wants to fish?"

"No, but I bet I can get him to."

Having carried his tea across the kitchen, Roone snickered from the back door. "You're not gonna tell the boy that he has a chance to learn from an experienced angler, are you?"

"No, I'll be honest," Wade said. He'd just managed to squeeze in a half-hour fishing lesson from the guy who owned the Mount Esther Bait Shop. The basics didn't seem all that difficult even for a guy who'd never baited a hook before. "Pop, I left a bucket of live shiners out on the front porch. Would you get it and take it out back?"

"Live shiners, eh?" Roone echoed. Wade knew his father, a native of New York City, too, had never fished either, and didn't know a minnow from a marlin.

"I'll get your shiners, son," Roone said. "In fact, I'll go on down to the river and wait for you. I wouldn't miss this fishing expedition for the world."

Meg was watching Wade intently, a sly smile curving her lips. "And I can't wait to see how you get my son away from his video games and down to the river. I'm all for it, you understand. I just don't think it can be done."

A crazy dare popped into Wade's mind and he blurted it out without thinking of the consequences. "I'll challenge you to an even more interesting outcome, Miss Hamilton. I'll bet I can get your son to the river in the next ten minutes, and you to the river later tonight, say just about dark."

Her jaw dropped and just the softest little squawk came out of her mouth. "M…me?" she finally said.

"Yes, ma'am. If you want the answer to that ques-

tion about Betty Lamb, that's where I'll be giving it."
He pushed on the door to go get Spencer. "And wear a
bathing suit. We might just try swinging on a tire."

He didn't look back at her. His skin was scalding, and
he knew if he looked at her she'd read his bluster in his
face. Wade Murdock wasn't a flirt. And he was about
as cool a guy as any old fogey passing his hours on a
park bench—lately anyway. But here he was, flirting
like a Hollywood hunk with Meg. And it was absolutely
terrifying. She probably wouldn't come. She probably
shouldn't come. He probably shouldn't have asked her.
But the door was open now, and he'd just have to wait
to see if she came through it. And what he would do with
her if she did.

AT FIRST WADE DIDN'T KNOW if Spencer agreed to come
fishing because he was truly interested in the activity or
because he was too polite to turn down the invitation.
But after a few minutes of watching the kid plod along
the pathway to the river, Wade had figured it out.

"You know, I saw that look on your face when we
walked by your mom in the kitchen."

Spence looked up, for the first time taking his eyes
off the wild shrubs and twigs that might send out armies
of insects, snakes, or other creatures to attack his sneakers. "What look?"

"The one like this was Tombstone and you were on
your way to the gallows."

"Huh?"

Wade came up with a more appropriate ten-year-old
example. "Like you were at an all-girl party."

"Oh. I've just never fished before."

"And you think I have?"

Spencer stopped plodding, pushed his glasses up his nose, and stared at Wade. "Well, I hope you have. One of us better know what he's doing."

Wade shook his head. "Sorry. This is the blind leading the blind."

"How about your father? You said he was going to meet us at the river. He must know how to fish."

"Nope. No help there."

The Suwannee came into view through a thick copse of oak and pine trees, and Wade announced, "Well, there she is, Spencer."

With a blasé shrug, the boy acknowledged what was in front of them. "It's a river."

"Right, and it's chock-full of fish just waiting for us to catch them."

"If you say so."

"Hey, look over there." Wade pointed to a giant tree whose leafy branches were shading a sleeping Roone Murdock.

The kid half chuckled. "Looks like he's not going to catch anything."

"Unless that's poison ivy he's sitting in. I suggest we set our gear down right here so his snoring doesn't chase away the fish."

Spencer set down the rod he'd been assigned to carry. Wade put the other rod and the tackle box next to the bait bucket Roone had carried down. He stretched his arms over his head and then placed his fists on his hips. "Nice afternoon for fishing, isn't it?"

"Yeah, I guess so."

"The guy at the bait house where I bought all this

stuff rigged the rods for me." He picked one up and examined it, showing the various parts to Spencer. "We've got our reel and line, our bobber, and a hook tested for one- to five-pounders."

"So now what do we do?" At last Spencer seemed a little intrigued by the adventure. "Do we wait for the fish to jump out of there and grab the hook?"

"Naw, that'd be too easy. Now, we get one of these…" Wade put his hand in the bait bucket and scooped the bottom for a minnow. Several slipped through his fingers, but he finally pulled out one wriggling, silvery creature. He picked up the hook from the first rod and slipped the point into the tail of the minnow. Then he handed the rod to Spencer. "You want to cast out?"

"Sure, why not?"

Following the bait store manager's instructions, Wade showed Spence how to open the bail, hold the line against the reel with his index finger, and whip the tip of the rod over the water. Spence lifted his finger when Wade told him to, and with a satisfying hiss, the line let out, and the hook and minnow sailed into the current.

"Nice cast," Wade said, hoping he'd do as well.

Spencer smiled.

An hour later, the minnows were all gone, and Roone had wakened and tried his luck. In that time, Spence had caught four fish. Wade had caught three. Roone had cursed a good bit. Once the men proclaimed that the specimens were no doubt the finest ever snagged in these parts, they tossed the catch back into the river and watched them swim off downstream.

"So what do you think, Spence?" Wade asked as they

gathered up the equipment and headed back to the house. "Want to try again tomorrow?"

"I suppose," he said. "It wasn't all that bad."

Wade smiled at Roone over the top of the boy's head. "I'm glad to hear you say that, because your mother bet me a dollar that you wouldn't like this. And I can really use the money."

The kid snorted out a sound that might have been stifled laughter and ran ahead, this time not seeming to care where his sneakers hit the dirt. And Wade thought about later that night, the second time today he would go to the river.

MEG SCOWLED over her shoulder at Mr. Cuddles who was lying on her pillow not paying the slightest bit of attention. "A bathing suit!" She resumed scrunching and fluffing her hair in front of the mirror until the freshly washed auburn waves fell to her shoulders in something resembling an actual style. "I didn't bring a bathing suit from Orlando. And anyhow, has Wade forgotten how cold the water is?"

She angled sideways in front of the glass, sucked in her stomach and checked the fit of her jeans, though she'd worn this particular pair at least a hundred times. At the last moment before leaving her room, she unfastened the top button of her blouse. Her necklace, a simple heart pendant Spencer had given her for Christmas, hung just at the top of her breastbone, its garnet stones glistening against her skin.

She thrust her shoulders back, giving her posture a last-minute boost, and started to walk away from the mirror. But something in her reflection made her stop and take another look. She leaned close to the glass, scrutinized her features, and decided that she almost looked like someone else entirely. Her face glowed. Her eyes sparkled, her lips, with a light touch of coral, had a lipstick-model fullness. She looked sexy. And it had been a long time since Meg had thought of herself in those terms. A long time since she'd cared.

From her bedroom window, she'd seen Wade leave the house ten minutes before. She didn't know what he'd told his family, but she'd told Spencer she was going for a walk and would be back shortly. He hadn't objected to staying with Roone and Jenny, probably because he was still floating on a fisherman's high from hauling in the biggest catch that afternoon. And Meg had picked up the latest Harry Potter movie from the video store. She peeked in at the three people whose eyes were glued to the TV screen and then ducked out the rear door. Very soon she would be at the river, dusk would be falling, and she might be kissing Wade Murdock again. Unless, of course, she did the sensible thing and maintained control of her emotions.

He was leaning against a pine tree, his arms crossed over his chest. When he saw her approach, he gave her a smile that was warm and welcoming, and something decidedly more intimate as if he'd saved that smile just for her. Her gaze flowed from his short-sleeved white shirt to his black denim-clad legs. "Where's your suit?" she teased.

The grin widened and was reflected in his dark eyes. "I was caught up in the moment when I said that. It's only June. I might consider jumping in when the temperature hits mid-August. Still, I was hoping you'd wear one."

She stopped in front of him and gave him a challenging stare. "I think we should concentrate on why you invited me here."

"I absolutely agree." He wrapped his hands around her arms and pulled her to him. His mouth covered hers for a sweet, lingering kiss that left her dizzy with surprise because it wasn't so sweet as to be a show of affection between friends. Oh, no. It was much more than that. It was a promise.

"What was that for?" she asked, when she'd found the breath to speak.

"To get it out of the way. If I hadn't done that, I wouldn't have been able to think about anything else." The corner of his mouth curled upward. "As it is, even now that I've done it, I don't think I'm out of the woods."

She stepped away from him, noting with a mixture of relief and disappointment that he stayed by the tree. "Wade, we came here to discuss Betty Lamb and her visit this morning."

"Maybe you did," he said. "I just used that as an excuse." He pushed away from the pine and stood with his legs wide, his unabashedly appreciative gaze firmly fixed on her. "That's quite a kid you've got," he said.

"Thanks, and you've changed the subject." She stared at the curvature of his lips, imagining them fitting so well with hers just a moment ago. After giving herself a mental shake, she said, "I want to know, Wade. Why haven't you signed the Right to Purchase Agreement Betty told me about?"

"Okay, I'll tell you." He led her to a fallen log where they both sat. "There are a couple of reasons."

"And the first one is?"

"I promised your aunt I wouldn't give her an ulti-matum. If I sign Betty's papers, I'm effectively kicking Mrs. Ashford out and breaking my word to her."

Meg nodded. It was a noble explanation, but not real-ly the one she'd hoped to hear. "And reason number two?"

"I decided to wait until after the auction. I figured if you were ever going to find the deed, it would be while you're going through Mrs. Ashford's things."

She stared at the spring swirling below them. "I don't think I'm going to find it, Wade. And neither do you."

"I suppose you still could, and I want to be fair, Meg. I told you before…I don't want to rob you of your house. I'll admit that didn't matter so much the first day you showed up here. But it does now."

"And if I never prove the house is mine?"

"Then I'll own it," he said matter-of-factly. "I've paid for it. I've put my heart and soul into it."

She turned to look at him and found his deep brown eyes were as earnest as she'd ever seen them.

"I want this house, Meg," he said.

"I know you do."

"If you find the deed, then we'll sit down together, maybe with a lawyer if we have to, and try to work something out. But if you don't find it, and if your aunt isn't coming back, I'm sure as hell not going to let someone else have this place."

Meg couldn't imagine strangers living in Ashford House, especially now that she no longer considered Wade a stranger. He was right. He'd entered into a con-tract that made the house his, and she wanted him liv-ing in it if she couldn't. And he was trying to be just.

She took a deep breath, tried to smile. "So, I've got until the weekend to find that stupid deed," she said.

"Something like that."

She ran her hands down the length of her jeans and started to rise. "Then I guess I'd better go back and keep looking."

He placed his palm on her thigh. "No. Don't go. I want you to stay." He stopped her with the pressure of his hand, and she sat down again, her shoulder touching his.

"I wish this house didn't stand between us," he said. "I wish I didn't care so much about how this will all end up. When I bought Ashford House, I thought I was buying it from a little old lady who couldn't keep it up any longer. Hell, Meg, I even told myself I was doing her a favor. But now…someone is going to get hurt, and that's not what I wanted."

He lifted her hand and held it in both of his. "You've changed everything, Meg. And frankly, I don't know what to do about it."

"You've managed to throw a curve into my future, too, Wade. But you'll do what you have to do, what's best for you and your family."

"But that's not what's best for you."

"No. But I'll go home to Orlando and pick up where I left off." Again she tried to smile, but it was no use. "I'll be fine. Don't worry about me."

He clasped her hand to his chest over a firm, strong heartbeat. "You told me once that you'd never been able to count on the men in your life. And now I'm just one more in a line of men that let you down."

If he only knew, despite his claim to her house, he

was becoming the one man she *could* depend on. Struggling to keep her voice even, she said, "Wade, you can't let me down because you don't owe me anything. My brother does, perhaps. My husband definitely did. And Uncle Stewie, well, he obviously lived his life the way he wanted to, and though I'm learning that he wasn't who I thought he was, I can't blame him for that. But you don't owe me, Wade. The only person who deserves your best is Jenny. And you're a good father."

He acknowledged the compliment with a nod. "Maybe I just want to make things right with you, Meg." He bit his bottom lip, looked away from her for a moment and then returned a steady gaze. "I've got these feelings for you. I never expected to have them. Hell, I never expected to have them for any woman again."

Meg could see his deep emotional connection to his wife in the veil that suddenly clouded his eyes. She worried that he was transferring his guilt over Brenda's death to his guilt over owning Ashford House. It didn't make sense of course, but Wade Murdock was an honorable man, and honorable men carried guilt on their consciences until the burdens nearly broke them.

"Maybe you just want to make up for what you see as past mistakes," she said. "But you can't do it, Wade. What happened in one chapter of a lifetime is history. It can't be changed or amended by what we do in this one."

He released her hand, stared out over the water, and spoke his wife's name for the first time. "Brenda was my life," he said. "We began dating when we were juniors in high school. Once I started going with her, there was never anyone else. And she died so suddenly, so violently, I never had the chance to say goodbye. I probably hadn't even told her I loved her in days, maybe weeks."

She placed her hand on his thigh and let it rest there. "She knew, Wade."

"You're the only woman besides Brenda that I've kissed in more than twenty years. And I'm liking all these feelings again. Maybe I shouldn't, but I am."

She understood exactly what he was experiencing.

"In fact," he continued with a little smile, "I'm thinking about kissing you so much that you've become a major roadblock in my dream of home ownership."

She gave his leg a playful slap. "Then I think we should stop the kissing so you can go back to stealing my house with a clear conscience."

He laughed, a rich and throaty exhalation of relief. Then he placed his hands on each side of her face. "That's not going to happen, Meggie, not if I have my way."

He pressed his lips to hers, a mere whisper of a kiss, then sat back so he could see into her eyes. "You've made me come alive. You've made me think about things that were buried so deep I never thought I'd experience them again. I want to be with you, talk to you, argue with you. I want to touch you like this and make love to you."

He massaged her temples with the pads of his thumbs as his lips came down to claim hers with insistent nips and nibbles. When he drew away, she kept her eyes closed, not wanting to relinquish the feelings swelling inside her. His hands felt so strong, so sure cradling her face. His voice teased her as his warm breath caressed her skin. "But maybe we ought to have a date first."

He curled his leg between her thighs so his knee

pressed against that part of her where warmth was beginning to flow to every cell. She opened her eyes, tried to take a deep breath, but it hitched, only half filling her lungs. "Isn't this a date?" she whispered. "You invited me here and I came. And somewhere back at Ashford House a father is probably waiting with a porch light on."

He coiled his fingers into her hair and drew her closer. "Okay," he said hoarsely. "This qualifies." This time his kiss was a thorough invasion of her mouth and her senses. When he finished, she felt herself go limp in his arms. He pressed his lips to her jaw, her cheeks, her eyelids. So gentle, so complete, he left no part of her face untouched. Her hands clenched his shoulders as she arched her neck, giving him license to continue his delicious exploration.

It was as if every moment of the last two years had been leading to this one night. All the sacrificing, all the denial of her desires had been for this meeting with this man.

His hand flattened on her chest over the garnet heart, then covered one breast. He released the buttons on her blouse and drew the fabric down both shoulders. His knuckles grazed her flesh with the rough yet silken touch of a working man's hand. Her nipple grew taut, aching. She took a deep, trembling breath and thrust her breast upward to fill his palm.

And then the night and the river called her back. Cool air fanned her face and the exposed skin of her chest and cleared her mind of the reckless passion flowing through her. The sound of the water at their feet quieted the hum of desire in her head and reminded her that this was a little bit crazy. It was dangerous. And potentially more devastating than the loss of a house. He'd just been telling her about his wife, the woman who had been his life, the woman he'd lost.

She shook her head. He stilled his hand. "What's wrong?" he asked.

She stammered, sought the right words. "This, what we're doing here. We shouldn't."

"You want me to stop?"

Yes. No! "Yes."

"All right." His voice was low, husky. He turned away from her and stared into the inky darkness. "I'm sorry, Meg. It was too fast."

And wrong. All at once Meg saw clearly what was happening. Wade was reaching for her because in two years he'd never let himself reach for anyone else. For so long he'd been a man trapped by his guilt and his anguish. She was the first woman who'd helped him break down the walls of his emotional isolation. He was heady with the freedom, the sensations of coming up for air. He was grateful. That's all it was. Meg was his liberator, the woman who would satisfy his passion, dull his pain and then move on as she'd sworn to. And maybe at last Wade would be free of the past. Free to choose someone else.

The only problem was, she was falling in love with him.

CHAPTER FIFTEEN

"WHAT DO YOU MEAN she's stopped eating?" Meg's question was addressed to the nurse monitoring Amelia's vital signs. But her attention was focused on her aunt's pale face. "What's happening? She's so still."

The nurse put a comforting hand on Meg's shoulder. "She hasn't eaten a bite in two days, Meg."

"Two days? You've brought her food, haven't you?"

"Of course. She's had trays delivered for every meal. And each time they've been picked up without the food being touched. Today I tried to coax Miz Ashford into taking a little. But it was no use."

The tone of the nurse's voice was one of resignation. Meg couldn't believe that a medical professional could be so callous. "If my aunt doesn't eat, she'll die. Of course there's use."

"Honey, Miz Ashford doesn't want to eat, and she doesn't want us to force feed her."

Meg reached for an IV tube which had been inserted in her aunt's vein some time in the last twenty-four hours. "What about this? You can put nutrients in here until she gets better."

"You don't understand, Meg," the nurse said patiently. "Your aunt has a living will. Her wishes are clearly stated with regard to her care."

"A living will? I didn't know that. Does the will say that this slow starvation is what my aunt wants?"

The nurse pulled up a chair and sat beside Meg. "We are doing exactly what Miz Ashford requested. Most of our patients have living wills just like your aunt's," she explained. "Most of them state that if there is no medical probability of recovery, then the patient should be allowed to die naturally, and life-prolonging procedures should be withheld. These patients have chosen not to prolong the process of dying."

Though she understood the principles behind a living will, now that she was faced with the near certainty of losing Amelia, Meg didn't want to accept the concept of a medical facility withholding life-saving methods. "Why wouldn't anyone want to forestall death?" she asked.

"It's Miz Ashford's time, honey," the nurse said. "This is the way she wants it."

Meg stroked Amelia's hand. It felt cool and dry. "Is she in any pain?"

"No, of course not. That's what the IV is for. We're administering all her usual medications, plus ones that will make her comfortable."

The raspy words that came from Meg's mouth next sounded as if they'd come from another person, one who'd gone without water for days. "How long…?"

"It's hard to say. She still drifts in and out of consciousness, though her alert stages are fewer and of shorter duration." The nurse stood up, walked toward the exit. "Probably a few days." At the door she gave Meg one last smile of encouragement. "You press the buzzer if you need me."

Meg nodded. "I'm going to stay for a little while."

The room was eerily quiet. There was no hum of conversation from the Game Show Network. Family pictures still sat on Amelia's bedside table, but her gentle voice didn't murmur loving words to the faces. Only the persistent bleep of machines broke the stillness of the antiseptic air.

"What a stupid expression," Meg said aloud to combat the hysteria lingering at the edge of her mind. "A *living* will. As if it had anything to do with living at all." She brushed hair from her aunt's forehead. "Living is what I associate with you," she whispered. "Not dying."

Her aunt made a little sound. It almost seemed like a sigh of contentment, acceptance. Meg smiled down at her. "You're right, dear. Enough talk about sad things. Let me tell you what's been happening at Ashford House.

"Gloria is coming tomorrow," she said. "Isn't that a lovely surprise? She'll insist on coming to see you, of course. And Wade has started painting the parlor. It's a pale shade of yellow. Spencer is helping him, but I think he makes more of a mess than anything else. But Wade is so patient. And Jenny has her own telephone, and she and Spence are tolerating each other a little more every day."

She stopped, reflecting on what she'd said. It felt good to talk to someone, to sort out her feelings, even if that person couldn't hear or didn't understand. Maybe it was enough for Meg to know that the person lying in the bed would care deeply about what she was saying, as she always had. "And Wade," she began again. "I can see why you sold Ashford House to him, although it left me in something of a pickle. But he's a good man. I have these terribly confused feelings about him...."

"And then there's that Quit Claim Deed you told me you made out, the one giving the house to me. I haven't found it yet, and I'm running out of places to look." Amelia's hand lay on her chest and Meg covered it with her own. "That brings me to the auction. Interest in the sale is growing every day. People in town seem to think Uncle Stewie hid money somewhere in the house. Isn't that silly? Of course he didn't. You would have known."

One slim finger flexed under Meg's palm. Thinking it was only her imagination, Meg nevertheless gave the hand a squeeze. The same finger curled, pressing a small, brittle knuckle into Meg's skin. Meg looked at her aunt's face. Her lips curved slightly and then moved.

"Aunt Amelia?" Meg leaned over the bed. "Are you trying to say something?"

A sound like a whisper came from Amelia's mouth. When Meg placed her ear next to her aunt's lips, a warm breath tickled her skin.

"Margaret, dear…"

Meg held her breath, remained perfectly still, desperate to hear and understand. "I'm here."

"That money…where there's smoke…"

Five words that seemed to have come from somewhere deep in the recesses of Amelia's mind. Meg waited for more, but felt only the shallow, soft exhalations of her aunt's breathing.

She sat up and stroked her hand down the side of Amelia's face. Then she turned off the overhead light and left the room.

"WELL, WILL YOU LOOK at this place! I'd forgotten how rambling this old house is!" Gloria dropped her suitcase in the middle of the foyer and scanned the room from the decorative punched ceiling to the wide staircase which disappeared into the second floor. Then she administered a quick hug to Meg.

"And look at you," she said. "You haven't changed in ten years." She tugged a strand of Meg's hair. "Though I expected to see you still in pigtails."

Meg couldn't say the same about Gloria. Careful not to let her jaw drop in shock, she purposely avoided staring at the burgundy highlights streaking Gloria's cropped blond hair. But then she realized she was gaping at a pair of bright floral ankle-length pants and pink patent-leather sandals.

"I guess the years have changed me," Gloria said, forcing her amply-gelled locks into little spikes. "Contrasting highlights are the rage in Chicago these days. I have to keep up with the styles because of my position in the shop."

"It's nice," Meg offered, deciding that grazing for meals must also be the rage. Once a pudgy, pink-cheeked teenager, Gloria was now porcelain-pale and rail-thin with that can't-pinch-an-inch-of-fat toning that only comes from a personal trainer.

Gloria strode into the parlor, her heels clicking on the hardwood floor. She wandered the room, stopping at tables Meg had set up to hold items for the auction. Pausing at a stack of old board games, she said, "Doesn't this bring back memories? I always beat you at Scrabble, Meg."

"Hey, Mom, whose car is that outside?" Spencer skidded to a stop inside the doorway.

Gloria went over to him and clasped his chin in her hand. "This is Spencer?"

He tried to nod despite the tight hold.

"This is your cousin Gloria," Meg said. "I told you she was coming for a visit."

"I haven't seen you since you were a year old," Gloria said. She turned his face to the side. "You look just like your handsome father. Doesn't he look like David, Meg?"

"Not at all," Meg snapped, resenting the reference to her jerk of an ex-husband. "He looks like my side of the family."

Gloria released Spencer and grudgingly admitted there was something of a resemblance to Meg's father. "So which room should I take?"

Meg gave directions to the only empty bedroom in Ashford House with the apology that Gloria wouldn't be able to put her clothes in the bureau. "I've cleaned out all the drawers in preparation for the auction," she explained. "Most of the furniture will be sold, and we're just using a few pieces to get by."

"No problem," Gloria said. "I don't mind living out of my suitcase for a few days. It just means more money for…us, right, Meggie?"

"Yes, I suppose."

When she returned to the foyer to retrieve her bag, Wade came through the front door. He was in his uniform and had his hat tucked under one arm. He saw Gloria and gave her a quick once-over glance. It was nothing like the thorough perusal Gloria gave back.

"Gloria, this is Wade Murdock," Meg said. "He's living here for a while. Wade, this is my cousin, the one who called the other day."

Gloria's lips curled up in a blatantly sensual grin. "So you're the fella I talked to on Sunday? I wondered why a man answered." She darted a look at Meg. "You didn't tell me you were under house arrest, Meggie. Whatever did you do?"

Meg bristled. "We had a little problem here," she said. "Wade's staying to help us out."

"Whatever the problem, it's a wonderful solution," Gloria said, her eyes simmering with sexual interest.

"Yes, it is," Meg quickly agreed. "He's staying here and so are his father and his thirteen-year-old daughter."

Unfazed, Gloria picked up her suitcase and headed for the stairs. She stopped on the first rise and looked back at Wade. "I'll look forward to getting to know you, Sheriff," she said.

"It's Deputy, but thanks for the promotion."

"You won't have any trouble recognizing your room," Meg said. "It's the one with the safari decorations. You'll notice the zebra-striped satin comforter and chimpanzee footstool. Aunt Amelia just recently purchased them."

"Wow. Who would have thought she had such cutting-edge taste?"

As soon as Gloria disappeared, Wade raised his eyebrows in amusement. "You and that lady come from the same family?"

Next to Gloria, Meg felt she might as well be wearing a Woolworths housedress and bandana. "Shocker, isn't it?"

"Kinda."

"To you and me both." She grasped Spencer's shoulders and turned him toward the kitchen. "Come on, you two. I've got roast beef and cheese sandwiches made. I suppose I should offer lunch to Gloria, too. I think I have a couple of carrot sticks that will fill her up."

Gloria spent the next hour rummaging through every room on the first floor. She told Meg she was getting back in touch with those golden days of their youth. Meg wasn't fooled. She knew Gloria was examining every little trinket and mentally calculating her eighty percent of the auction profits.

After securing Wade's promise to fish later, Spencer finished his sandwich and ran off. Wade lingered in the kitchen.

"Don't you have to go back out?" Meg asked when it became obvious that he was in no hurry to leave.

"Eventually," he said. "But I remembered that you wanted to ask me about a legal matter. I guess I kind of sidetracked the discussion on Sunday night by telling you about your cousin calling. And then Monday I steered the conversation in another direction again when we met down at the river and we…" He paused, looked down at the table as if he were studying the watermelon design in the old placemats. Was Wade Murdock embarrassed?

Meg finished the sentence for him as she rinsed the dishes. "We talked about Betty Lamb and the Right to Purchase Agreement instead."

He gave her a direct stare. "*You* talked about the Agreement. I kept trying to kiss you."

No, he wasn't embarrassed. His straightforward reference to the other night unnerved her, but Meg concentrated on her concerns about Colonial Auction. She hadn't forgotten that storeroom of new merchandise Jerry had showed her. She dried her hands and sat across the table from Wade. "Since we're not at the river now and not likely to repeat past performances…"

He slapped his hand over his heart. "You really know how to wound me, Meg."

She smiled, warmed by the thought that Wade wanted to pick up where they left off.

Jenny popped in the back door, preventing Meg from responding. "Hi, Dad. Mrs. Jenkins just dropped me off from the mall. Want to watch me ride?"

"Give me twenty minutes, Jen."

She grabbed a peach from a wicker basket in the center of the table and took a bite. "Who's that lady with the weird hair on the front porch? She's looking everything over like she's checking for cooties."

"That's my cousin," Meg said. "And I guarantee you she's not interested in cooties."

"Oh." Jenny left through the back door with a promise to ready her tack.

After she'd gone, Wade sat back in his chair, crossed his hands over his abdomen and smiled. "Listen to that, Meg. What we have right now is silence. I suggest you take advantage of it."

And she did. She told him about Mary Beth and her work with the charity, and Mr. Horton and the recent flow of brand-name merchandise into Colonial Auction. She explained how auctions generally operated but admitted that this good fortune, though plausible, had her concerned.

She told him about her trip to the auction warehouse on Sunday and how she'd seen the merchandise for herself as well as the obliterated serial numbers. She also repeated Jerry's explanation, which really could be logical.

And with each detail she watched Wade's face, looking for some sign, a twitch of an eye, a subtle downturn of his lips which could be interpreted as bad news. He simply sat quite still and listened to her story. And Meg began to believe that her fears were unfounded.

"You don't seem too worried about this," she said when she'd revealed everything, including Jerry's infatuation with Mary Beth.

Wade sat up straight in his chair and threaded his fingers together on the table. "Did you meet this Mary Beth?"

"No. But I've heard enough about her to know that she's not the type Jerry usually goes for. At first I thought that was a good thing. Most of Jerry's love interests aren't exactly the type of women you'd take home to mother. What do you think? Could she be giving him a line?"

Wade shrugged. "Not necessarily." He scrubbed his hand over the nape of his neck. "But I am a bit suspicious. Something crossed my desk a few weeks ago…"

Meg's nerves prickled with alarm. "What? Something bad?"

"If I remember it correctly, then, yes, it could be. I didn't pay much attention to it at the time because the notice specifically referred to auction houses, pawnshops, wholesale operations, and we don't have any businesses like that in Mount Esther."

"What did it say?"

"That there has been a barrage of thefts in the southeast, Florida, Georgia, Alabama, some other states as well. Freight trucks have been hijacked, distribution warehouses targeted, probably with the help of insiders. At any rate, a lot of merchandise has gone missing. The point of the memo was that law enforcement officials should be on the lookout for new goods that could show up at unconventional retail operations."

Meg blinked hard. "Like an auction."

"Yes, like an auction. In fact, now that I think about it, it's the perfect scenario. Merchandise comes in during the week, right?"

"Yes."

"Then it's all sold in one night, dispersed over a wide segment of the population, and, I would assume, without detailed receipts."

"The only receipts demanded of an auction house by the Department of Regulation are little cardboard cut-outs, copies of the sale which we give to customers after they pay. The merchandise they bought is written on one line with very little description."

The implication of such lenient record-keeping was suddenly appalling to Meg. Now that she thought about it, an auction house could be the perfect route for stolen goods. "Sometimes we don't write anything on a receipt more detailed than 'computer keyboard' or 'weed eater.'"

"Do you specify whether merchandise is new or used?" Wade asked.

"Hardly ever. It's not important since nothing sold at an auction is guaranteed. You've heard the expression, 'as is, where is'?"

He nodded.

"That means everything is sold without guarantee and the buyer is totally responsible for what he's bidding on. Of course we try to give an accurate description of each item we sell. We point out defects, but it's still 'buyer beware.'"

Wade tapped his index finger on the tabletop. "So merchandise is sold, it's picked up the same night, it can't be brought back. Transaction closed."

"Pretty much," Meg said.

"And anyone who brings merchandise in to be sold gets payment without ever coming face-to-face with a buyer? And the merchandise is virtually untraceable once it goes out the door."

"Not exactly. We keep records of who our consignees are as well as bidding numbers and records of who was at the sale…assuming these people give us accurate personal information."

"But there are no signatures required, no verification of consignees' or bidders' identities?"

"No."

Wade gave her a sympathetic smile. "No offense, Meg, but an auction is a fence's dream, like pawnshops used to be before new state regulations clamped down on them."

She clenched her hands tightly on the tabletop to stop them from trembling. "But problems rarely happen. We've never had stolen merchandise at Colonial Auction that I know of. Almost everything we sell is used and comes from someone's home, just like the auction I'm having for Aunt Amelia's things. We never have to worry about verifying ownership."

He cocked his head to the side and raised his eyebrows at her. "Till now maybe."

"Right. Till now." She gave him a pleading look. "What am I going to do? If these things are stolen, my brother could end up in jail."

Wade smiled, a comforting but most inappropriate gesture to Meg's sudden panic. Her business was at stake. Her brother could be a criminal.

"Let me track down that memo first. If I have my

facts straight then we'll follow up on this." He reached across the table and patted her hand. "Your brother doesn't have a record, does he?"

"Not unless you count parking tickets from leaving our truck in front of condo walkways."

"That doesn't count. He's never associated with known criminals? Never been caught stealing?"

"No, of course not."

"Then stop worrying. He's only sold this stuff at two auctions, right?" He stood up. "I'll spend a few minutes with Jenny and then go back to the office. I'll look up the report and call you."

Meg rose just after he did and came around the table. Telling Wade had been the right thing to do. Once again he had come through for her. "Thanks, Wade. I don't know what I'd do…"

She paused, aware that what she was about to say reflected a truth she wasn't ready to accept, or admit.

He stared at her, waiting. "Do you want to finish that thought, Meg?"

"Maybe some other time."

The kitchen door swung open and Gloria sailed in. She headed for the refrigerator, stopping long enough to give Wade a seductive little grin. "Well, howdy, Sheriff. Is everybody abiding by the law today in Mount Esther?"

"It's Deputy," he reminded her again. "And yes, so far."

She took a bottle of water and unscrewed the cap. "Maybe I'm just the girl to change that." With her gaze firmly fixed on Wade, she took a long swallow of water. "What do people do around here after the sun goes down?" she asked.

"I don't know about everybody else," he said, "but I paint, plaster, and put wood filler in mouse holes."

She shook her head, her spiky blond hair refusing to move. "Nope, not my thing. But when I was driving into town today, I did see this place on the outskirts. They advertise live music. Have you been to McGruder's Tavern?"

"Once or twice," he admitted.

"Good. What do you say we go there tonight and kick back?"

Wade looked at Meg as if the decision were hers. "If you want to go, then fine," she said.

He shrugged. "I guess there's no harm. Bert's doing downtown duty tonight, and Pop will be here to maintain peace between the kids. What time you girls want to go?"

"Oh, I won't be going," Meg said. "I have too much to do, and I was planning on going back to Shady Grove to be with Aunt Amelia." She gave Gloria a pointed look. "Don't you want to go with me?"

"I really should…." Gloria said. "But, heck, tomorrow's soon enough." She passed a glance Meg's way, and added, "Don't tell her I got in town today, Meggie, okay?"

"Fine." At least she wouldn't really have to tell that lie. Amelia wasn't exactly watching a calendar these days.

Wade looked as if he'd been sucker-punched. "You're not going?" he said to Meg.

"No."

"I'll be ready at seven," Gloria said as she left the kitchen. "See you then."

Wade looked at Meg a few more seconds as if expecting her to explain herself. When she didn't, he set his hat on his head, crushed the brim down low on his fore-head and strode from the room.

Later that night, after Meg returned from Shady Grove and Wade and Gloria had left for McGruder's, Meg spread auction supplies on the cleared kitchen table in front of Jenny and Spencer. She handed Jenny a black marker and a stack of blank index cards. "Go ahead and number the cards from 1 to 100. These will be our bidders' cards, so write nice and big so I can read the numbers from several yards away."

She gave Spence blank sheets of paper, a pen and a ruler, and told him to draw straight lines across each page and write the words, *Name, Address and Phone Number* on the top. Without the forms she'd saved on her computer at Colonial Auction, she'd have to use these hand-written sign-in sheets to record bidders' information.

Jenny numbered a few cards and then set down the marker and scowled at Meg. "You should have had Dad and Gloria do this," she said.

Surprised at the girl's sudden outburst, Meg said, "Why? Is this such a hard job?"

"No, but it would have kept them from going out on a date together."

Spencer dropped his pen. He didn't seem to notice when it rolled to the floor. "It's not a date, is it Mom? They didn't go on a date."

"I don't know what else you'd call it," Jenny answered with the authority of a woman who knew all about dating. "They got dressed up, they left together. I'll bet he pays her way in."

"I don't think they charge to get into McGruder's," Meg said, knowing it was a lame way to avoid the real issue. Maybe the trip to McGruder's hadn't started out as a date, but it could quickly become one if Gloria had her way.

"See, they don't charge, so it's not a date," Spencer said to Jenny. "Wade wouldn't go on a date with *her*."

"You better hope that's right," Jenny warned. "Gloria is the last person I'd want to see with my dad." She focused a defiant glare at Meg. "I'd rather pick you over her, so you'd better do something to keep them apart."

"Wow," Meg said. "Thanks for that ringing vote of confidence. Now start writing numbers."

CHAPTER SIXTEEN

THURSDAY STARTED OUT miserably. By eight o'clock Meg had gotten a disheartening medical report about Amelia. And she faced the rest of the day with a million details on her mind, all of which needed to be addressed before Saturday's auction. To make matters worse, she'd lain awake until well past midnight when she'd finally heard the front door open and close and Gloria giggling all the way up the stairs.

Then, she missed seeing Wade this morning, which meant she wouldn't get any insight on "the date" from him, not that she'd have the nerve to ask him about it. And there was no guessing when Gloria might stumble downstairs to gloat over the evening.

Deciding the best thing to do was to immerse herself in auction preparations, Meg began polishing Amelia's furniture to a glossy shine. But even that chore didn't stop her from imagining what Wade and Gloria had done the night before or from analyzing her past relationship with her cousin. While Gloria slept off the effects of her night at McGruder's, Meg looked back on her childhood at Ashford House with a new and profound understanding of those carefree days. The truth was, they had not been nearly as carefree as her faulty memory had led her to believe.

Adjusting to the clear, levelheaded view from adulthood, Meg now remembered that those times when she and Gloria were together, quarrels and petty jealousies had often sent the two strong-willed girls to separate bedrooms for the night without speaking. It had been Amelia's diplomatic skills that had mediated the problems the next morning and brought harmony to the house again.

"Well, Amelia's not here now," Meg said as she applied polish to an old cup ring on the top of an end table and wiped furiously. "And even if she were, no amount of sweet talk could negotiate a peace this time."

Meg truly tried to make Gloria the target for her anger. She told herself that Gloria could have asked if Meg minded if she went out with Wade. She could have asked if Meg had an interest in him.

"Did Gloria care enough to even ask how I felt?" Meg said aloud. "Did she think beyond her own selfish interests for once? No. In typical Gloria fashion, just like always, she saw what she wanted and went after it."

Unfortunately Meg's attempts to make Gloria the bad guy made no sense. Not this time. She plopped down in an old chintz chair and dropped her polishing materials to the floor. Reason had suddenly prevailed, and Meg shook her head and turned her frustration where it rightfully belonged—on herself.

"Snap out of it, Meggie," she said. "You've got no claim on Wade. You could have gone out with them last night, but you didn't, so why blame Gloria for taking advantage of the situation?" She sat forward, dangling her hands between her knees. "Still she could have asked if I minded."

"Who didn't ask?"

The question from the staircase was delivered in Gloria's sleep-husky voice. "And didn't ask what?"

Meg jumped up from the chair. "Oh, you're up."

Gloria stepped lightly off the bottom step. "Don't remind me. Your son's video game in the next room sounds like the real Indy 500." Her fingers pressed to her temples, she said, "Where's the aspirin?"

Meg followed her into the kitchen. She couldn't help pointing out the obvious. "It's nearly 10:30."

Gloria made a beeline for the cupboards. "And that's important because…?"

"Maybe you shouldn't have stayed out so late."

Gloria slammed a succession of cupboard doors after finding each one empty. "The aspirin, Meg. Or have you catalogued it to be sold in the auction?"

Meg retrieved the bottle from the pantry, took out two capsules and deposited them on the table.

Gloria sat in a chair, swallowed the pills without water and lay her head on her crossed arms. After a moment she looked up at Meg with red-rimmed eyes. "Correct me if I'm misreading you, but is something wrong?"

Meg slammed a glass of water on the table even though she knew Gloria didn't require it. Liquid sloshed over the side and soaked the sleeve of Gloria's bathrobe. "Why would something be wrong?"

"Oh, I don't know. Because you're you."

"What's that supposed to mean?" Meg asked the question even though she knew the answer. She had always been the righteously indignant one. Gloria had always been the free spirit who didn't give a damn.

Gloria released a long, dramatic sigh, raised her head with a wince of her colorless lips, and said, "Okay, let's have it. What did I do this time?"

Meg leaned against the counter and clamped her arms over her chest. She simply couldn't ignore all the old resentment that welled up inside her. "You like playing the martyr, don't you?"

"No more than you like playing the judge, Meg. It's been that way since we were kids. I screw up. You tell me how. And Aunt Amelia makes us kiss and make up." She buried her face in her arms again and groaned. "Only Amelia's not here, and I feel like crap, so let's cut to the chase and get this over with."

Knowing her anger was misplaced, Meg sighed heavily. Gloria was truly miserable, and Meg didn't have a reason to scold her for something that was just Gloria being herself. Besides, what had she done that was so unforgivable? All their lives, Gloria had acted on impulses that Meg denied herself because she overanalyzed them or they scared her to death. Now that she thought about it, she wasn't angry at Gloria. She was jealous of her.

Meg sat down at the end of the table nearest her cousin and gently placed her hand on Gloria's arm. "You didn't do anything, Gloria. I'm the one who screwed up this time."

Gloria raised her eyes. "Really?" A skeptical but slightly victorious grin curled her lips. "What did you do?"

"I stayed home last night while you and Wade went out. And I'm mad at myself for that and for blaming you."

Gloria reached for the glass of water and took a sip. Then she sat up straight. "You like the guy, don't you?"

"I don't know. I shouldn't."

"Why not? He's definitely decent-looking. Tall, law-abiding. Just your type, cuz. And he's wild about you."

"He is?"

"Oh, yeah. When he wasn't saying how we ought to be getting home, he was talking about you." Gloria frowned and gulped the rest of the water. "To tell you the truth, Meggie, he's something of a drag in my opinion, but I can see where you'd like him." She stood up and grabbed a box of cereal off the top of the refrigerator. "So, have you two had sex?"

"What? No!"

She found a plastic bowl on the counter and filled it with corn flakes. Meg got a little satisfaction from not telling her it was Mr. Cuddles's food dish.

"So why haven't you?" Gloria said. "Had sex, I mean."

"We have issues, Gloria."

"Oh, this house thing?" Obviously Wade had told her about the problem. "Big deal."

Big deal? "Yes, it is, but that's not all. There's his wife who died. I don't know if he's come to terms with losing her. And I think his feelings for me have more to do with gratitude than anything else. I'm the first woman…" She stopped talking and stared at her cousin, while she tried to decide how to end that sentence.

Gloria poured milk in the bowl and took a bite of cereal. While she chewed, her overly critical gaze made Meg squirm. Then she said, "You're an idiot."

Meg slammed the flat of her hand on the table. "Well, thanks for that!"

"Sorry, but you're just like you were way back when. Remember the old soapbox derby car that boy from down the road had? All us kids jumped in two at a time and tore down the hill, screaming our lungs out. But not you, Meg. Remember when we were teenagers and how everybody sneaked out at night and TP'd houses all over Mount Esther? But not you, Meg. Remember those guys from that little town west of here and the night they brought beer? We went down to the river and drank and roasted marshmallows. But not you, Meg. Remember?"

"You've made your point."

"Right, and this could end up just like back then with you and I arguing and yelling at each other till we're hoarse. But we're older now and should know better. Now I'll just say what's on my mind and go back upstairs where I plan to be until at least late this afternoon."

Meg didn't even try to cut Gloria off. Nothing stopped her once she got up a good head of steam.

"Take a chance, Meg. Quit thinking so damned much and *do* something. The guy likes you. You obviously like him. So stop worrying about consequences all the time and let the poor man take you to bed."

"But what about all the problems?" Even as she asked the question, Meg knew the answer. At least she knew what Gloria's answer would be.

"You mean this old house?" When Meg nodded, Gloria held up two fingers and used them to illustrate her point. "What do you want, Meg? The man or the house? I'll tell you this much. If you get the house, you'll probably lose the man. But if you get the man, you just might get both."

What Gloria was suggesting was ridiculous, and Meg told her so. "You're saying I should sleep with him to get the house?"

"Of course not, because it might not work. I'm telling you to sleep with him because you want to. Ashford House might just be a bonus." She blew out an impatient breath and gestured at all the kitchen collectibles Meg had spread over Amelia's counters. "Look, Meg, you might know a lot about all this old stuff, but I know about men. When a guy's been celibate for two years like Wade, and finally chooses you over every other woman he's encountered in all that time, he's serious. Give the guy a break, and yourself one at the same time." She shook her head, a sign of her pathetic appraisal of Meg. "For some reason, you've spent your life telling yourself you don't deserve the happiness other people take for granted."

Meg was too astounded to speak. Was that true? Had she done that? After a moment, she got up, poured herself a glass of water, and faced Gloria. "Let's assume you're right."

"I am right."

"Okay, but think about this. I can't have sex in this house. Not with Spence and Jenny and Roone…"

Gloria dismissed her with an abrupt wave of her hand. "You're hopeless, Meggie. In the first place, I don't care where you have sex, but this house is as good as anyplace. It's huge. If you can't find a secluded spot, you're not looking. Especially when I'm offering to take those two kids to the movies tonight."

Meg swallowed. "You are?"

"Yeah, but only once. And it's up to you to avoid Gramps. Think about it. I'm going back to bed."

Gloria left the room just as the phone rang. Meg picked it up and barely managed to say, "Hello."

"Hi, Meg. It's Wade. Can you come down to the office? I've got some information on that theft ring."

WADE'S VOICE ON the telephone had been serious, almost somber. For sure he had bad news to tell her, probably one more disaster in an endless parade of them. Her aunt was dying. She knew that now and had to accept that it was Amelia's wish. She was going to lose Ashford House. There was little hope of finding the deed. And now her brother might be in serious trouble with the law and the future of Colonial Auction House could be in jeopardy.

And Meg couldn't erase feelings of resentment with regard to their business. Why did she always have to bear the burden of her brother's lack of responsibility? She thought again about Gloria's suggestion that she grab a little happiness for herself and forget all her problems for a while. Could she do that? Did she deserve such happiness? Did Wade even think of her that way anymore? And, the most important question—was a one-night fling with Wade what she wanted, even if that's all it turned out to be?

She pulled into a parking space at town hall and got out of the car. She knew the answer, and it was yes.

Just thinking about what lay ahead in the next few minutes and maybe later that night, Meg was trembling when she entered Wade's office. This first encounter had her nerves crackling with dread. The one to come later that evening had her blood heating with anticipation Both were terrifying.

Wade looked up from a stack of papers when she came in. "Oh, Meg, good, you're here." Amazingly he looked at ease, even in this environment of clipboards, file cabinets, and computers. With his sleeves rolled up, his hair comfortably mussed, he appeared as relaxed in the office as he did on the porch of Ashford House. Maybe this was a good sign.

Meg took the chair he offered but remained silent, not trusting herself to speak.

He opened a folder on his desk. "It's all here," he said. "I got a faxed report this morning from the Jacksonville PD where the investigation originated."

"So there is a theft ring?" she said.

He nodded. "'Fraid so. It's pretty much as I told you yesterday. It involves stealing from freight lines and warehouses and then dumping the stuff at an assortment of irregular fence operations."

"Like Colonial Auction," she said, her voice tense with anxiety.

"It appears so."

She put her face in her hands. "Oh, God, I knew it. Jerry's going to jail." And then when an equally horrible outcome occurred to her, she added, "Maybe I am, too."

"Nobody's going to jail," Wade said. "At least not if Jerry cooperates now. He didn't knowingly sell stolen merchandise, did he?"

She shook her head.

"He acted in accordance with Florida State statutes regarding auction houses?"

"Yes, I'm sure he did."

"And he had no reason to suspect that the charity was involved in criminal activity?"

"No."

Wade shrugged, and the tightness in Meg's chest

eased. "I think law enforcement officials will regard your brother as a victim, not a conspirator," Wade said. "Maybe an inept, careless victim, but a victim nonetheless. I've seen lots of cases like this, and the poor guys who get caught with the merchandise usually just get a warning to be a little more conscientious from now on."

Meg placed the flat of her hand over her chest where her heart still hadn't returned to a normal beat. "Oh, Wade, thank you."

"I'll talk to the cops in Orlando and fill them in on what's been going on."

"And I'll call Jerry right now and tell him not to sell any more of that stuff."

Wade held up a finger. "I don't think I'd do that."

"What? Why not?"

"There's one other possible problem," Wade said. "According to the fax I got, the guys who handle the stolen merchandise don't always work alone."

"Well, then, who…?" Meg paused when the answer suddenly came to her. "Oh, no. Mary Beth?"

"A young, female accomplice has been reported in a couple of instances," he said.

Meg closed her eyes, tried to imagine her brother's reaction when he heard the news. "Poor Jerry."

"When is he likely to see the guys who've been bringing the merchandise in?"

"Probably Monday. That's when we make consignment checks available. I think he told me the men come by the auction in the morning and pick up their percentage."

"Then unless I miss my guess, that's the procedure I think the Orlando police will want him to follow. They don't want the perpetrators alerted because of a change in routine. I have a hunch your brother will be told to run a few of the items through the sale as he has been doing so Horton will be in on Monday as usual to pick up the check." He smiled. "And that's when he'll find a little surprise, like an FBI agent and a couple of Orlando's finest."

Meg wished the news weren't so damaging. Maybe Jerry wouldn't be facing a jail sentence, but he'd still very likely panic. This situation might be more than he could handle, especially now that he'd have to consider that Mary Beth was involved with the criminals. He might even insist that Meg come home, but of course she couldn't, not with Amelia's auction just two days away. And she couldn't even provide moral support on Monday when Horton came to pick up his check. She'd still be doing the accounting from the Mount Esther sale.

Concern etched Wade's features as he leaned forward. "Meg, what's wrong? I just told you that everything should be okay with your brother."

"You don't know Jerry. He's not a take-charge person and I don't know how he'll react to this news."

"Maybe you should give him more credit. He's a big boy, isn't he?"

Meg only grimaced.

"You probably should call him soon and let him know what's happening," Wade suggested. "Once I get in touch with Orlando PD, I figure the cops will be at your place pretty quick. They'll advise him what to do."

The police at Colonial Auction? Jerry never even dealt with customers coming in with complaints. He always sent them to Meg. And now he was going to face a police investigation?

Wade reached over the desk and touched her arm. "He'll be all right, Meg."

She nodded, resigned to putting Jerry in charge of this latest dilemma. Wade was right. Jerry was a big boy. He'd made a mistake and he would have to face the consequences. Then maybe she could turn her thoughts to her own goals, especially the one she'd set for that night. Time was running out, and she had to put a plan in motion to insure that she and Wade would be alone. She took a deep breath and initiated the first of the details that would result in a night she hoped she'd never forget.

"What time will you be home this evening?" she said.

Wade frowned. "I don't know. When will your cousin *not* be there?"

Meg held back a chuckle. "You didn't get along well with Gloria?"

"Let's just say I'll never forgive you for bowing out on that little excursion to McGruder's last night."

"Actually Gloria is taking both kids to a movie tonight."

His eyebrows arched in surprise. "No kidding? Maybe they can keep up with her. And maybe you can think of a way to make up for your traitorous behavior."

She stood. "Maybe I can. Maybe I already have."

She headed for the door before he could see the incriminating pink stain she knew had colored her cheeks. Jerry would just have to take care of himself. For once Meg was leading her own life, and it was getting pretty darned exciting.

"Seven o'clock, Meg. I'll be there at seven," he called after her.

CHAPTER SEVENTEEN

SOMEHOW MEG had managed to get everything done that afternoon. She'd shopped for a new dress at a little country boutique and purchased gourmet goodies at the market.

She'd called Jerry and explained what Wade had found out and warned him that the Orlando police would be following up. She'd advised, calmed and encouraged him and discovered to her surprise that he handled the news better than she'd expected. And when she told him that Mary Beth might be involved in the thefts, he even managed his broken heart with a stalwart determination to do the right thing. Still, he'd seemed genuinely relieved when she assured him that mistakes happen and of course she forgave him for having a trusting nature that got him into trouble.

And now she was determined to get the residents of Ashford House out of her way.

"Wow, this is the best supper ever, Mom." Spencer shoveled another spoonful of macaroni onto his plate and then asked if there were more chicken nuggets. Meg plucked a half dozen from Amelia's deep fat fryer, patted them on a paper towel to soak up the grease and brought them to the table.

Spencer blew on one and took a crunchy bite. "The best part is, there's no vegetables."

"Don't get used to this," she said. "We're back to meat and potatoes tomorrow night." She smiled. "Maybe even Brussels sprouts."

He popped another nugget in his mouth. "You'd never be that mean. So why are you being so nice tonight?"

Gloria darted a knowing glance Meg's way as she chewed on her salad. "Yeah, Meg, why? It isn't like you to sacrifice vitamins for flavor."

Meg glanced at the clock on the wall. It said six. Wade would arrive in an hour, and she wanted to be ready. "No reason," she said. "I just remembered you guys were going to a movie, and I wanted to prepare something quick and easy. I know you don't want to be late…." She gave Gloria a withering glance. "You want to be there for the previews, don't you?"

"Right," her cousin said. "We wouldn't want to miss those. So what did you two decide on for our big night at the Mount Esther Twin-plex? The horror flick or the animated bunny story?"

Jenny rolled her eyes. "I'm not going to any cartoon."

"Me neither," Spencer agreed.

"Great. You two agree for once. Horror movie it is. Let's go get our underwear scared off." Gloria carried her bowl to the sink and flashed a grin over her shoulder at Meg. "By the way, where's Gramps tonight?"

"Playing poker with the clerk from the Quick Mart and some of his buddies," Meg answered. "Sometimes fate just plays into your hand."

"Okay, then." She hustled the kids out of the kitchen. "Don't wait up, Mom. We might get real crazy and go for ice cream later."

"Have fun." Meg began rinsing the dishes. The minute she heard Gloria's car head down the drive to the road, she tossed the wet dish towel into the sink and left the plates soaking. Then she carried items from the refrigerator to the table and took one of Amelia's sterling silver platters from the china cupboard. The plate would be sold on Saturday, but tonight it would contribute one last sparkle of elegance to the romantic history of Ashford House.

She arranged meats, cheese and garnishes on the platter. At the last minute, she would add the lush globe grapes and ripe Greek olives. A loaf of crusty French bread, a jar of gourmet mustard, and a chilled bottle of Chardonnay would add the finishing touches to her picnic.

Satisfied with the preparations, Meg slid the platter into the refrigerator and dashed upstairs to take a shower. She didn't want the food, or even the secluded nook she'd chosen, to be the most seductive component of the night's activities. When she stepped under the warm spray, pinpoints of water sluiced over her shoulders, and her nerves tingled deliciously. Running her hands over her slick body, she imagined what Wade's hands would feel like when he caressed the same spots later.

A simple shower became the prelude for what was to come. Truly, nearly everything she'd done since leaving Wade's office, even the mundane chores which had become routine the last two weeks, had seemed part of an erotic pathway leading to a destination that both thrilled and terrified her. But what if Wade didn't react as she hoped he would?

She stepped out of the shower, patted her skin dry and

applied lotion to her legs. No, she wouldn't let thoughts of failure dissuade her now. She'd been too long waiting for the touch of the right man. Even if she only had this one night, it would be worth it because Wade had made her delight in being a woman getting ready for a man again.

THE HOUSE LOOKED DIFFERENT as Wade drove to the front entrance a little after seven o'clock. Quieter, more snug in its protective nest of oaks and sweetbay trees. Cozy and secluded with the curtains drawn but rippling gently in the evening breeze. The lights on the veranda were golden in the first shadows of dusk. He stepped out of the car and admired the fanciful angled lines of the old structure, the clean lacework of the porch trim that he'd brought back to life, the rich primary colors of the stained glass in the turret windows.

She really is a fine old house, he thought as he climbed the steps to the door. But tonight she looked even better than usual, and he knew why. Meg was inside and earlier, in his office, she'd been mysterious, alluring. He hadn't become such a dunce with women that he couldn't recognize when one was coming on to him. It had been a long time since he'd responded in an overtly physical way to a seductive suggestion, but when Meg had scurried out of his office with her cheeks flaming pink, he'd reacted instantly. It had been a good half hour before he'd been able to concentrate on his reports and even make that call to the Orlando PD.

All day he'd thought about coming home to Meg and fantasizing about what the evening might bring. It was the first time in over two years he could walk into a house, even when his daughter and his father were there, and not feel lonely. He opened the door and stepped inside. He was tense but energized, even a little nervous, but not lonely.

And not alone.

There she was, waiting for him, standing under the foyer light. She wore a dress. It was frothy, soft and pale, and flowed about her in the breeze through the front door. The material outlined her slim legs and rippled over her shoulders, baring her arms. Her hair was a loose tumble of auburn waves. She was like a flower in a mist, delicate and wondrous. Wade smiled because he wasn't a poet and yet those words had come to him. And, too, he smiled because she did.

"You look nice," he said, a pitifully insufficient observation from a man who'd just thought of himself as a poet.

"Thanks. Are you hungry?"

Oh, he was, though he hadn't thought of food since coming in the door. "Sure."

"I've made a little supper. Do you want to get changed first?"

"That'd be good. I think I'll take a quick shower."

"Meet me in twenty minutes?"

He nodded and went upstairs to his room. He was ready in fifteen minutes, freshly shaved and dressed in jeans and a soft denim shirt. He raked his fingers through his hair and went into the hallway expecting to go to the first floor and find Meg in the kitchen.

Instead, she was sitting on the top step and turned when she heard his footsteps. "That was fast."

"I guess I'm hungrier than I thought."

She held out her hand. He grasped it and helped her rise from the stairs. Then she gently tugged him toward the steps to the attic.

"We're going upstairs?" he asked.

"That's right. I've got a little surprise planned for dinner."

He willingly followed her up the narrow staircase to the third floor. She stepped aside at the opening to the attic storeroom, and he preceded her inside. And he was definitely surprised. Nothing was as he remembered. He knew most of the contents of the attic had been transferred to the lower floors for the auction, but obviously not everything had been carried down. Meg had used the remaining items to transform the once drab, dusty chamber into a sort of wonderland.

Darkness had fallen outside, and here in the attic candles were the only illumination. They were everywhere. On the floor, the windowsills, flickering in the glass of the turret. Exotic scents wafted on the breeze. Ropes of tiny lights twinkled around the ceiling. Since it was June, Wade figured Meg must have uncovered Christmas lights among Amelia's belongings.

And right in the middle of the room was a bed, probably the old one that had covered Stewart Ashford's mural for decades. Only now the rusty springs were gone and only the mattress remained. It was covered in cream-colored sheets and topped with a comfortably faded quilt. And serving as a headboard was the infamous painting itself. The robust nudes, zealous courtiers and mischievous cherubs seemed revitalized as if they understood what Wade was feeling, what this setting represented.

Meg slid her hand into the crook of his elbow. "It's not too much, is it?"

He covered her hand with his and felt her pulse, sure and strong in her wrist. "Only if you're teasing me, Meg, because I can guarantee you that I'm having the same thoughts as those old boys up there on the wall."

She leaned close to him and he breathed in the citrus scent of her hair.

"I'm not teasing you, Wade." Her breasts brushed his arm. She lifted her face to his. "I'm tired of longing, Wade. I don't want to be a still figure on the canvas of my own life. I want to feel alive again, and I want to feel that way with you."

Everything was suddenly perfect, better than he could have imagined. The woman, the attic room in this crazy old house, the yearning in his heart, the time. He knew he wanted Meg, wanted the loneliness and the loss to end with his arms wrapped around her.

He scooped Meg into his arms and carried her to the bed. She was light in his embrace yet her arms around his neck felt strong, her body eager. She nibbled on his ear as he lowered her to the mattress and then she gently turned his face to hers for a kiss that nearly shattered him with its tenderness.

He took his time undressing her, exposing first her shoulders. He kissed her neck, the hollow of her collarbone. He reached around her and found the zipper to her dress. It lowered with a subtle hiss, and he peeled the fabric away from her chest. She wore nothing underneath, and he explored one round, plump breast. He circled the nipple with his thumb and finger until it raised and puckered.

And he kissed her deeply and completely, probing the warmth of her mouth with his tongue, sliding the tip behind her teeth and down the insides of her cheeks. He sucked her bottom lip into his mouth and nipped it with tiny bites until she writhed under him. When she arched her hips, he slid the dress over her thighs and down her legs where the fabric puddled at their feet.

She fumbled with the buttons on his shirt, her small fingers working in a passionate frenzy. "I can't seem to do this right," she said breathlessly.

He stilled her hand. "Here, let me." He shed the shirt in seconds. Her hand spread over his chest and she began a slow seductive journey with her fingertips down his breastbone to the top of his jeans. He covered her hand and said, "I'll get it."

"No, I will." The button popped free, the zipper slid down. She worked his jeans and underwear over his hips and, with her feet, slid them down his legs. He kicked the clothing over the side of the mattress. She reached for him, wrapped her fingers around his penis. He groaned. She laughed softly. "I think I'm starting to get the hang of this."

Oh, yes. She was.

EVERY PART OF HER REACHED up and out to him. Every cell, every nerve ending, every inch of her skin craved what he offered so freely and so generously. Just as she'd imagined, Wade was a skilled, sensitive lover. His hands caressed while his lips teased and challenged. One moment he cradled her breasts as if they were made of porcelain. The next, his rough working man's hands chafed them with a delicious ache that jolted through her like tiny electric shocks.

Her pulse raced when he cupped her between her legs and rubbed her over her panties. She reveled in his touch with a primitive abandonment that left her heady with powers she'd forgotten she possessed. When his mouth closed around her nipple she hissed through her teeth. He suckled and licked the tip until her entire world was a mindless explosion of senses. He laughed, a throaty, deep-bellied sound that said he was as aware of his own powers as she was of hers. They were together on earth at this moment to please, to tease, to satisfy. And when his lips traced a warm, moist pathway down her belly, she nearly forgot to breathe.

When, at long last, he slipped her panties over her hips and down her legs and straddled her, she was wet and ready, her body telling her she needed his to complete her. He was swollen and throbbing when he entered her. She gripped his shoulders, arched her back and drew him in deeper and deeper with each thrust. The last vision she had was of the stars outside the turret windows. She closed her eyes and let them burst inside her mind.

They stayed in the attic two more hours, eating, talking, laughing and making love once more. And as the glorious minutes passed, Meg admitted to herself that she cared for Wade as she'd never thought she could. With every touch and whispered endearment, she was more ready to trust him and believe in his goodness and his honor. He'd made her want to give herself to a man again physically and emotionally. He'd made her confident and hopeful as she hadn't been in many years—perhaps ever.

When headlights speared through the rippled panes of the old colored glass, she moaned, "They're back." Wade sighed with acceptance of the inevitable and helped her gather their dishes and take them to the kitchen. They were in the foyer when Spencer came through the door.

"Wow, Mom, the movie was way cool," he said.

"It was okay, I guess," Jenny said, coming in behind him. "It held my interest in spite of being infantile."

Spencer snorted his opinion of her attempt at sophistication. "You screamed all the way through it."

"I only did that because it's what you expected me to do." She glanced back at him as she went into the parlor and picked up the television remote. "Remember, you promised you'd at least sit on Lady Jay tomorrow."

"I know and I will."

He trotted off toward the kitchen, leaving Wade and Meg with Gloria. "I hope you two found something interesting to do," Gloria said. "Because you don't know what you missed by staying home." She followed Spencer out of the foyer but called over her shoulder, "And Meggie, I don't have any idea how to get chocolate ice cream out of a T-shirt, so that's your job."

When they were alone, Wade kissed Meg's temple. "Welcome back to reality," he said.

ON FRIDAY everyone's attention was focused on the auction which would begin at ten o'clock the next morning. Meg allowed prospective customers to enter the house and inspect the items which would be up for bid. While keeping one eye on the visitors, she meticulously double checked each detail related to the sale until she was certain the auction would proceed without a hitch.

Later that afternoon, having finally persuaded her cousin to visit Amelia, she and Gloria drove to Shady Grove. Amelia did not acknowledge their presence, nor did she mention the strange message she'd whispered before when Meg told her the rumors about money being hidden somewhere at Ashford House. In fact, Meg discovered that her aunt had not stirred in more than twenty-four hours. Her nurse calmly and soothingly explained that Amelia's death was imminent.

"She seems so peaceful," Gloria remarked as they drove back to the house. That simple observation brought a sense of acceptance which Meg had been resisting. It was true. Amelia was at peace.

At eight o'clock Saturday morning, the grounds of Ashford House began filling with the vehicles of people who wanted to participate in the auction. By the start, the crowd of over a hundred people consisted of serious antique and collectible buyers, as well as folks who had known Amelia and Stewart for years and hoped to walk away from the sale with some trinket that would keep the Ashfords' memories alive.

Everyone had a job to do. Spencer and Gloria sat on the porch and registered bidders. Jenny tagged items as they were sold by writing the bidders' numbers on stickers which she affixed to each piece. Having taken the day off work, Wade, along with his father, held up each item as it was described by Meg from her perch on a kitchen stepstool she'd selected as a temporary auctioneer's podium.

The sale progressed from the parlor to the dining room and the front veranda until Amelia's possessions, even those bizarre things she'd purchased from catalogues, belonged to someone else. Even the lawn furniture and garden tools were auctioned off.

Meg successfully maintained her focus as the things she'd grown familiar with over the years became someone else's property. Some time during her preparations for the sale she'd begun to think of Amelia's belongings as merely extensions of the woman she loved, expressions of the person Amelia had been as a young woman, as well as the slightly odd woman she'd become in her declining years. But Meg now knew her memories of her aunt would live in her heart forever.

The sale lasted just over three hours, and was a huge success. Especially for Gloria, who tallied the final results and realized that she would be receiving eighty percent of twenty-two thousand, three hundred and twelve dollars. Colonial Auction, thanks to Meg's efforts, would see an increase in its bank account of over four thousand.

Once the bidders had left and most of the sold merchandise had been removed by the new owners, Wade went to the Quick Mart and bought sodas and beer and sandwiches. While everyone relaxed and talked about the most unusual moments of the sale, Meg's cell phone rang. The caller was Nadine Harkwell, the administrator from Shady Grove. She informed Meg that Amelia Ashford had passed away fifteen minutes ago.

WADE WALKED Meg to her car. "Let me go with you," he said. "I don't know what help I can be, but at least I'm an arm you can lean on."

She smiled up at him. "Thanks, but it's not necessary. I know what has to be done." And she did. Since having to face Amelia's mortality, Meg had recalled the times in her aunt's life when she'd talked about her death.

"Just put me in a pretty box and bury me next to Stewie," she'd said one night when she and Meg were sitting on the front porch and death had seemed a most remote possibility.

Meg had promised.

"And nothing fancy," Amelia had added. "Ashes to ashes is what I believe in. I don't want people blubbering over me or staring at some lacy old frock that makes me look like an old woman."

When she arrived at Shady Grove, Meg was informed that Amelia's body had been moved to a waiting area in a building at the rear of the main facility. Meg steeled herself to say a final goodbye.

She touched her aunt's still warm cheek and pressed a kiss to her forehead. And when she left the room to meet with the representative she'd called from the Mount Esther Funeral Home, Meg knew she'd crossed a bridge of her own life. She'd said goodbye to a part of her childhood that was gone forever because the one person who'd shared it so sweetly and so intimately had started a new journey without her.

IT WAS NEARLY DARK when Meg returned to Ashford House on Saturday evening. All arrangements had been made. Amelia's ashes would be interred at a simple graveside ceremony on Tuesday morning. Meg had actually been spared most of the decisions with regard to her aunt's final rest. Amelia had filled out the necessary paperwork with the funeral home several years before, and her wishes were clearly recorded. Strangely, Amelia had had the foresight to complete a document which declared her intentions with regard to her death, and yet she'd neglected to send Meg a copy of the deed to her house or even to inform her niece of its whereabouts.

But at least now Meg didn't regard that document as her insurance for a secure life. She now saw Wade as an integral part of her happiness. She loved him. He completed the part of her that had been a vacuum for the past years. She hoped that maybe now she could have what had been missing in her life—the sense of family she'd lost when David left her, the house that had been her safe haven, the future she'd come to believe would always be just out of reach. True, he hadn't asked to share her future, but maybe...just the idea made her tremble with delight...maybe he would.

She thought of Wade, Spencer, Jenny and Roone as she pulled into the drive of Ashford House. They could make a life together and create new memories to leave to their grandchildren of joyous times, warm nights, abiding love. Wade wouldn't let her down. He was strong, protective, honorable.

She had just started up the lane when she saw headlights of a car approaching from the house. Meg guided her car to the fringe of the lane and got out. Betty Lamb leaned out her window and waved. "Hi, Meg," she said. "I just heard about your aunt. I'm so sorry."

Meg forced a smile. "Thanks."

"I guess you'll be going back to Orlando now that the sale's over," she added. "There's nothing to keep you here."

Meg struggled to control her temper. "I haven't made definite plans yet," she said though she knew she would have to return to Orlando once a financial accounting of the auction had been completed. She still had obligations to Colonial Auction and Jerry. Through a haze of exhaustion that had suddenly overwhelmed her, Meg realized that Betty was still talking.

"...technically you have thirty days to vacate the property, but as Wade and I just discussed, you probably won't take that long."

Meg gave her head a shake, and forced her mind to focus. "What?"

She picked up a document from the seat beside her. "The Right to Purchase Agreement. Wade just signed it. He'd only been waiting until Mrs. Ashford wasn't a factor in his decision so he could officially make the house his. So, as I said, there's really no reason for you to stay. Your obligation to this old place is finally over."

Meg tried to make sense of Betty's words. Wade had signed the agreement? Ashford House was his? There was no reason for her to stay? Her head swam. He'd only been waiting for Amelia to die to press his claim?

Betty reached a hand out the window, her attempt at a comforting gesture. "Are you okay?"

Meg ran back to her car. She was only faintly aware of Betty calling out her ridiculous hope that Meg would have a good evening.

She leaned her forehead against the steering wheel and struggled to draw a breath through the tightness in her chest. She'd held back her tears when she saw her aunt for the last time at Shady Grove. But they fell freely now. That night at the spring when she'd questioned Wade about the agreement, he'd promised her he wouldn't break his word to Amelia. He'd said he would wait until after the auction to press his claim. Well, he had waited—a few short hours. And now, with the auction barely over, with Amelia gone for what seemed the blink of an eye, he'd already signed the papers which forced Meg out of Ashford House. It was obviously what he'd intended to do all along.

CHAPTER EIGHTEEN

ON MONDAY MORNING, Jerry was at Colonial Auction a half hour early for the first time ever. Of course he'd never fallen asleep the night before, so getting up had been no real feat. Despite having to face the consequences of his gullibility today, he was anxious to get the proceedings over with. In fact, he was wired. He hadn't even needed a second cup of coffee.

Shortly before the auction officially opened for business, four plainclothes police officers arrived from Orlando PD along with one investigator from the FBI. Two of the cops stayed outside in an unmarked car. The other three gave final instructions to Jerry and informed him that they would be wandering around the building pretending interest in merchandise.

Mary Beth arrived at 8:30, when she usually did on Monday mornings. "Hi, sweetie," she said, coming into the office and giving him a strawberry-flavored kiss. "Did you get all your paperwork done last night?"

Ha! Paperwork. Jerry had never kept books for the auction, but that was the excuse he'd given Mary Beth last night for not spending time with her. He'd said he wanted to surprise Meg with an up-to-date set of records when she returned to Orlando. It had been a good excuse. Mary Beth hadn't questioned him. The funny thing was, Jerry actually had spent the long evening hours entering credits and debits. It had been a way to keep his mind off what was to come the next morning.

"Yep. All finished," he said and stared at her with a longing he hoped she wouldn't interpret as his way of saying goodbye. The phrase "too good to be true" popped into his mind for the hundredth time. Mary Beth had seemed a perfectly packaged combination of beauty, sweetness and seduction. But he knew now it had all been a facade. She matched the description given him by the Orlando PD to a tee. And today she was going down—both as a criminal and as Jerry's ideal.

She perched on the edge of his desk and looked out to the public area. "You have customers already this morning?" she asked.

Jerry watched the cops dig through a couple of boxes of old books. "They're collectors," he said. "They come in every once in a while to hunt for first editions."

"Oh." She stood up and straightened the pens in a ceramic mug on his desk. "How's Spence?"

All at once Jerry didn't like her mentioning his nephew. True, she'd been good to the kid. She even acted as if she really liked him, but Jerry now figured she'd just done that to earn Jerry's trust. She'd believed that Spence was his responsibility and knew he cared about him. What better way to gain someone's confidence than through the people he loved? Mary Beth was good at her job.

"He's fine."

She glanced into the auction hall and tapped him on the shoulder. "They're here." She pointed to Mr. Horton and the fellow he always brought with him. Jerry realized that he'd never even gotten the other man's name. "Let's give them their check," she said. "They'll be so pleased."

Jerry picked up a check he'd faked and followed her out. Yeah, right. They were going to be overjoyed. One of the cops looked over at him and Jerry validated the identities of the two men with a discreet nod.

And then everything happened in a matter of maybe sixty seconds. Mr. Horton accepted the check. The two cops and the agent surrounded him and his buddy. One of the officers uttered a few crisp, legal-sounding words while his partner restrained the crooks with handcuffs.

And Mary Beth headed for the back entrance and her escape.

She didn't get far. An officer had positioned himself at the rear door, and within seconds he brought her back into the auction. She, too, wore cuffs.

Jerry steeled himself to look her directly in the eyes. He expected to see hatred, anger, disappointment, perhaps fear. What he found was acceptance, maybe even relief. She stared at him for a long time until finally her lips curved slightly and she said, "Sorry, Jerry. It was fun while it lasted. I guess I should have known that one con artist can't fool another con artist."

"What are you talking about?" he said. "I'm not like you."

She looked him right in the eye and said, "Oh, yes, you are. You lied about your nephew to get me to like you. You used him, and I used you."

For a moment, Jerry could only stare at her. "How did you figure that out?" he finally said.

"Oh, come on, Jer, I know when somebody's lying to me—most of the time. I knew the day we went to Disney World that Spencer had a good relationship with his mother. Good grief, he kept bringing her up in all our conversations."

It was true, and at the time Jerry had warned Spence to cool it with the references to Meg. "Still, you and I, we're not the same," he insisted again.

"Only because what you did isn't a crime."

"But I really liked you."

Her eyes glistened for a moment. He thought she might be going to cry. Of course he wouldn't believe they were real tears.

"That's another way we're similar," she said. "I liked you, too. And Spence. That part wasn't a lie." The officer led her toward the door. "I don't think I'll be locked up too long," she added. "Maybe when I get out…"

Jerry was glad she'd gone through the door. Damn. Even after all she'd done, he wasn't at all sure how he would have responded to her implied invitation.

EARLY TUESDAY Jenny came downstairs dressed for Amelia's memorial service in a black skirt and gray sweater.

"Did you see Meg?" Wade asked.

"She said she'd be down in a minute," Jenny answered. "As soon as she gets Spencer's tie on straight."

She went into the parlor and sat on one of the chairs Wade had brought over from his rental place so this house wouldn't be completely empty. He knew he could have gone back now that the auction was over and Amelia's belongings had been removed. No money had been found, and even those people who once believed it existed had to admit that the rumors were unfounded.

But he hadn't wanted to leave. Meg was grieving for Amelia and he thought his presence would help her to cope with her loss. He hadn't imagined that she would seclude herself in her room for most of the last forty-eight hours. It wasn't healthy, and it wasn't like her. Since she'd returned from Shady Grove and gone upstairs without speaking to anyone, the only time Wade had seen her was Sunday when she briefly came out on the porch to tell Gloria goodbye.

If he hadn't heard from the children that she appeared occasionally to work on the auction records, he might have broken her door down by now. As it was, he knocked periodically, and respected her wish that she just needed time alone. After all, he'd gone through the grieving process himself, and he knew that people reacted differently to loss. If it hadn't been for Jenny needing him after Brenda's death, Wade might not have spoken a civil word to anyone for weeks.

Still he wished she would come to him and share her feelings. He only wanted to help. Besides her son and Wade's little family, she had no one here to lean on. Even her brother couldn't attend the memorial since he had to deal with the Horton arrest.

With just a few minutes to spare before the service, Meg and Spencer finally came down the stairs. She looked drawn and tired. Her eyes were a lifeless, dusky blue. Her skin, which normally glowed with coppery health, was eggshell white against the black turtleneck of her sweater. She had really taken her aunt's death hard.

Wade met them at the bottom of the stairs and offered his hand. She curled her fingers around the newel post and stared into the distance.

He let his hand fall to his side. "Are you all right?"

She looked at him then, but her gaze was void of all emotion. "Yes, I just want to get this over with."

"Okay. I can fit us all in the patrol car."

She didn't argue, just walked ahead of him and out the door. When he suggested she sit in the front, she declined, offering the seat to Roone while she slid into the back seat with the children.

He leaned into the window to speak to her. "You know, Meg, when we get back, we need to talk."

Her gaze snapped to his and he saw something in her eyes he couldn't interpret. Sadness, yes, but even more—a deep profound anguish that surpassed grief. When she didn't speak he walked around the car and got in. Later, he'd have to find a way to reach her.

On the way to the cemetery, Spencer and Jenny sniped at each other as they usually did, only now their banter had grown more sibling-like. Meg never reprimanded them. Wade glanced in the rearview mirror occasionally to catch glimpses of her face. She sat rigidly, staring straight ahead, her features as still as a stone carving.

The service was short. A minister spoke of Amelia Ashford's many virtues and her contributions to the community. Friends offered condolences to Meg. She accepted their kindnesses with detached grace. Only when the etched bronze urn was lowered in the ground did she shed the first silent tear.

When the last people were leaving the grave site,

Wade walked to the car and waited for Meg there, giving her a few minutes alone with her thoughts. He hoped the service had provided her with the closure she needed to say goodbye to Amelia. While he waited, he saw a woman approach her. She gave Meg an envelope. Then the two women sat on folding chairs next to the grave and Meg took out the contents.

"THESE PAPERS WERE in my aunt's nightstand?" Meg said to Amelia's nurse.

"That's right. One of the cleaning crew was clearing out Miz Ashford's belongings, and he came across these papers. I thought you might want them."

Meg slipped several official-looking records from the envelope and placed them on her lap. Her mind spun. Was it possible that the deed she'd been looking for had been in Amelia's nightstand at Shady Grove all along? Her hand trembled as she picked up the first document. It was Stewart Ashford's death certificate. Beneath it were a number of papers related to the house—the satisfaction of a lien, a verification of the purchase of additional property in 1968. And last, a document enclosed in a blue legal cover. Meg lifted the stiff sheet and read the words, *Quit Claim Deed* at the top of the first page.

With her hand over her rapidly beating heart, she skimmed the sheet. She saw her name and Amelia's and the address of Ashford House. With deliberate care, without reading further, she pressed the cover over the document again. She took a few deep breaths and hoped her voice didn't reflect the torrent of emotions swirling inside her. "Mrs. Williams," she said to the nurse, "do you have the name of a local attorney?"

"The one we use at Shady Grove is Walter Erdman. He handles the affairs of most of our residents."

The nurse gave Meg the lawyer's address, expressed her sentiments once more at Amelia's passing, and went to her car. Meg stood, surprised to find her legs capable of holding her. She walked to the patrol car and slipped into the back seat again. What was she going to do now that she'd found the document? Surely it would negate Wade's claim to the house. She could have it back. She could own Ashford House free and clear.

"Is everything okay?" Wade asked.

"Yes, fine. But I need to run an errand as soon as we get back. Can I leave Spence at the house?"

"Of course."

The return to Ashford House seemed to take hours instead of a few minutes. Meg glanced at Wade's face in the rearview mirror. Since she hadn't seen him much in the past couple of days, she hadn't realized how the recent events had affected him. His eyes were pink-rimmed from lack of sleep. There were tiny lines around his mouth. He had hardly known Amelia, so she doubted those physical signs of distress were due to a lingering grief over her death.

Was he suffering because of his deception with regard to the house? Was he feeling guilty for proceeding so quickly with his plans? Did he even know that Meg was aware of his furtive dealings with Betty Lamb and that his deception had torn Meg apart, both because she would lose Ashford House and because she had lost faith in him? He'd told her once that he didn't want anyone to get hurt. Had those been just meaningless words?

Or had he believed her when she'd responded that if

his claim to Ashford House prevailed, she would go back to Orlando, and she would be fine. Ironically those had been just words. She knew that now, but if Wade believed them, then her casual attitude about her possible loss took away his guilt today. Meg wished she could take those words back, that she'd never said them. *She would be fine.* Meg doubted she would ever be fine again because that foolish statement had left Wade free to pursue his own goals without regret.

Meg had to ask Wade these questions. She would never fully accept the choice he'd made unless she heard his motives, judged his reaction. But she couldn't confront him now. Her grief was too fresh, the hurt too deep, her ability to comprehend too tenuous. She couldn't bear any more heartache, especially if she were forced to accept that Wade was not the man she'd believed him to be. So, right now, her next step was to discover if her claim to Amelia's property was real.

When they arrived back at Ashford House, Meg went to her car without going inside and set off for the attorney's office. What would she do if Mr. Erdman told her that her deed to the property took precedence over Wade's contract? She would confront Wade then. She would tell him straight out that she'd found the deed and was taking possession of what had always been rightfully hers. And he would either prove himself to be the fair-minded man she'd thought him to be or she would learn that she could never trust her instincts again. As Meg pulled in front of the attorney's business, she was trembling, not so much about discovering the truth about Ashford House as about discovering the truth about Wade.

The receptionist in the law office informed Meg that Mr. Erdman was in and would be available to see her for a short appointment in a few minutes. Meg sat by a window and waited.

She drummed her fingers on the envelope, picked up a magazine only to discard it after flipping through the pages without reading any words. She stood up, paced the small room and returned to her chair. Minutes dragged, leaving her too much time to think, to dread, to contemplate facing the tough decisions that lay ahead.

And then, suddenly, as if a bolt of divine inspiration interceded, everything changed. Meg began to look at her situation with a new clarity, a judgment unclouded by feelings of betrayal. She uttered a deep sigh, thrust back her head and stared at the ceiling. She'd come to the totally unexpected conclusion that she couldn't bring herself to resent Wade. The truth was, she hated herself for what she was about to do.

She tried to reason with her conscience. "Get over it, Meg," she said to herself. "You've won. You have the deed. All you have to do is verify its authenticity and the house will be yours."

So why was she so miserable?

But she knew. After thirty minutes of waiting, she realized she couldn't go through with her plan to take the house away from Wade and his family. Yes, he'd hurt her by not telling her he was going to sign the papers, but he'd really done nothing wrong. In fact he'd only done what he'd said he would do all along. The problem hadn't been Wade's deception. The problem had been her own illusions about having a future with him.

Meg made an excuse to the receptionist about why

she wouldn't be keeping her appointment and left the office. She crossed the street to the park where the strawberry festival had been held and sat on a bench under a century-old banyan tree. In the cool shade of the giant tree, she collected her thoughts.

Yes, she had known the pleasures of the house long before Wade had. But Amelia was gone, and buried with her this morning was much of the joy of Meg's past in Ashford House. In the last few months, Wade had put his heart and soul into making the old place his. With each swing of his hammer or stroke of a paintbrush, he'd left his mark on Stewart's legacy and made it his own. Meg would never be able to improve the house as he could. Plus, he'd bought the house in good faith, according to a fair contract, by giving and keeping his word that Amelia wouldn't have to leave.

And Meg had to consider her aunt's wishes. True, at one time, she had wanted Meg to have the house. But most recently she had chosen to sell it to Wade. This had been her decision as she faced the end of her life. Perhaps she had wrestled with this choice more than Meg knew. Or perhaps she had signed the contract only while her mind was failing her. But either way, what right did Meg have to alter the course of her aunt's final objective?

She rose from the bench and walked back to her car. Her decision was made. She and Spencer would leave Mount Esther tonight and go back to the life she had before she got the call from Shady Grove urging her to Amelia's bedside. Ashford House would enter a new phase, with new possibilities under the guardianship of a man who cared about it as much as Meg had. She wasn't the same woman she had been then—her life had changed dramatically. But she wouldn't carry any regrets with her about the choices she'd made. She had loved Wade Murdock, and she was grateful that he had reacquainted her with the possibilities of a life she had long ignored.

Meg's past was filled with cherished memories. And if Wade Murdock had to become another one, then she would accept that. She had to. Right was right.

"WHAT DO YOU MEAN we're going home?" Spencer scowled as he threw his clothes into his duffel bag. "I can't go home now. I promised Wade I'd help paint the cabinet doors in the kitchen. He said we were just waiting for you to choose the color."

She tried to ignore the choking sensation in the back of her throat, but still her voice trembled when she answered him. "That won't happen now, Spence. We've got to go home. I still have a business to run, and Uncle Jerry needs us."

Out of the corner of her eye she saw Mr. Cuddles standing on the threshold of Spencer's room. "And I don't want any trouble from you either," she snapped at the cat.

Spencer jumped at the chance to have an ally. "Yeah, what about Mr. Cuddles? We can't just leave him."

"Jenny loves him," Meg said. "He'll be fine. He belongs here."

"So do we," Spencer pointed out. "This isn't fair. I've got plans with Wade. When are we coming back?"

Her patience was wearing thin because the answers were so painful. "I don't know. Just get ready, okay? I want to be gone before…"

She caught herself before she admitted that she was running out like a coward while Roone and Jenny were at the grocery store and Wade was working.

Spence yanked the zipper on his bag closed. "We have to say goodbye. You're not leaving without saying goodbye!"

She unplugged his game system and packed it in a box. "You can call or write a letter. Or e-mail Jenny. I want to be home before dark."

Spencer looked out the window where the shadows were already long. "It's almost dark now."

"I meant I want to be home before morning, or… I don't know what I meant. We just have to leave, now."

They carried their bags to the car a few minutes later. As Meg backed around to head down the drive, her headlights reflected on the front porch and the envelope she'd leaned against the wall. It was the last image she allowed herself of Ashford House as she veered the car toward the county road and drove away.

WADE ARRIVED HOME just before midnight. He hoped Meg would be awake and willing to talk to him. Maybe now that the service was over, she would have gotten a handle on her grief. He'd missed being with her and regretted that the few moments they'd had together since Amelia died had been strained and uncomfortable.

When he entered the house, Roone and Jenny were waiting. His father had a manila envelope in his hand. It looked like the one Meg had received at the cemetery. Wade immediately sensed something was wrong. He took off his hat and hung it over the newel post. "What's going on?"

"She's gone, Dad," Jenny said. "Without even saying goodbye."

"Who? Meg? Meg's gone? When? How long ago?" The questions popped out his mouth almost faster than his brain could form them.

"'Fraid so, son," Roone said. "Meg and the boy left. Cleared out their rooms and took off." He handed the envelope to Wade. "She left this for you, though."

"Why didn't you call me?"

"At first we thought maybe they'd gone somewhere close by," Jenny explained. "We didn't check their closets till later. And we just found the envelope a couple hours ago. By then Gramps thought we should just wait for you to come home."

Wade walked into the parlor and sat on one of the hard chairs the family was using temporarily. The room was eerily quiet. Wade didn't like it. He'd come to prefer the staccato of hurried footsteps, the constant demands on his time from the kids. Silence didn't become the old house.

He tore open the envelope and took out the contents, a document covered in legal blue binding. He lifted the flap and said, "It's the Quit Claim Deed. She found it."

Roone exhaled a deep breath. "Well, I'll be. If she found the dang thing, why'd she take off?"

Wade's first thought was that she might have gone back to Orlando to seek legal counsel, that she'd decided to go after the house with every legitimate arsenal she could muster. Would she do that? It certainly wasn't *his* plan to battle over ownership of the house, not now. Not after what he and Meg had meant to each other. But maybe that night in the attic hadn't meant as much to her as it had to him.

He flipped to the back cover where Meg had taped a note and read to himself.

Dear Wade,
As you can see, I found the deed. At first I didn't know what to do with it, but after careful deliberation, I have decided not to press my claim to Ashford House. That's why I have left you the only copy I know to exist of the document. The house is yours. I wish you and your family years of contentment. I know you will safeguard this treasure as you are the one person other than myself who holds this property in your heart.

Thank you for your many kindnesses, especially to my son who will always think of you fondly.
Sincerely,
Meg

He held the paper out to his father. Roone took it and read out loud. Jenny spoke the words Wade couldn't say.

"What kind of crap is that, Dad? I thought you two were, well, getting along pretty great."

He stared at the document and slowly shook his head. None of this made any sense. Why hadn't she fought for the house? Why had she left so abruptly without even saying goodbye? "So did I, pumpkin," Wade whispered. "So did I."

"What are you going to do?" Roone asked.

"I don't know." He folded the deed and stuck it in his shirt pocket. Maybe he should be grateful. Maybe he should tear the thing into shreds and count his blessings that every nail he'd pounded and every piece of molding he'd replaced was for the benefit of his family alone. That goal had fulfilled him before Meg showed up.

But who was he kidding? Once Meg had been in his life for forty-eight hours, once he'd seen that her determination to possess the house was as great as his, he'd started thinking of the house as *theirs*. Sure, he'd given her a hard time, but always, in his mind, as he'd fixed one thing or improved another, he'd asked himself if she would approve. He hadn't known how it all would end, but he certainly hadn't figured on her dropping Ashford House in his lap and running out. And now that he had a plan that should have made them both happy, she hadn't stuck around long enough for him to tell her about it.

"I guess I'll try to call her tomorrow," he said, since his father was waiting. "She must have gone back to Orlando to the auction business. I can try her there."

He headed for the stairs. Involuntarily his hand went to his breast pocket and the document. It had taken on a life of its own, a menacing presence that symbolized the end of what he'd hoped was to be a future for him and Meg. They'd been brought together by a house. How sadly ironic that the same house had, for a reason he didn't understand, torn them apart.

MEG ALMOST FELT LIKE an onlooker at her own business. She had assumed she would come back to Colonial Auction and still be the driving force behind its operation as she had been only a few weeks ago. She'd thought she would have to boost Jerry's self-esteem and help him cope with a broken heart. But it hadn't happened that way. Surprisingly, Jerry was handling the day-to-day operations of the auction with a competence and authority she'd never seen before.

"So what do you think of this new guy I've hired?" he asked Meg on Saturday morning.

"He's a good worker." The truth was, Meg wondered why they'd never taken the plunge before and added more help to the payroll. The old adage "you have to spend more to make more" was proving true for Colonial Auction.

"I was hoping to take some of the responsibility off your back when you got home," Jerry said. "Especially since we have you to thank for that addition to our bank account from Aunt Amelia's sale."

Meg winced inwardly as she always did when mention was made of her time in Mount Esther. She'd only been back a few days, and it still seemed as if her heart had been left behind.

"Besides," Jerry said, "I'll never forget that I almost single-handedly ruined what we'd built over the years."

She curled her hand over his arm. "Quit beating yourself up over this, Jer. I've told you it could have happened to anyone. Remember those con men had been working at building their business probably longer than we have, so they were darned good at it." She smiled and was relieved to see the tenseness in his facial muscles fade. "And you're certainly not the only Hamilton who's done something stupid in the name of love."

"Maybe so," he said with his irrepressible grin back in place, "but I think you should be fair. When it comes to stupidity, I've got one up on you. I never even checked out that phony charity of Mary Beth's."

Meg gave in. "Okay, you win." She followed him to the stage to put finishing touches on the merchandise for tonight's sale. It was an odd feeling, this sense that she wasn't really needed anymore, that Jerry could run the auction without her and probably even deserved the chance to try. If that happened, where would Meg fit in? She'd only felt she truly belonged one place in her life, and she'd given up Ashford House without a fight.

"So what about you and the Mount Esther cop?" Jerry asked while screwing a lightbulb into a floor lamp. "He's called here a couple times and left messages. Have you called him back?"

"No, not yet." She'd been thinking of Wade constantly since she returned to Orlando. She owed him a phone call, though she couldn't imagine what they would say to each other. She would call him tomorrow and tell him that she was fine, just as she'd predicted. If he did feel guilty about the way their relationship ended, she'd let him off the hook and assure him she didn't blame him for protecting his investment. Or for never saying he loved her.

But she wouldn't tell him that her love for him had been stronger than her instinct to fight him, that she was hurt because his feelings for her hadn't been strong enough for him to include her in his future.

Technically you have thirty days to vacate... Betty Lamb's words had been seared into Meg's mind.

If you win the man, maybe you'll win the house, too.... Gloria had been wrong on both counts. It wasn't the first time a man had let Meg down, but she was determined to protect herself from now on.

"So what really happened with you two?" Jerry

asked. "I can accept that it didn't work out with the guy, but I can't believe anything would have made you give up the house." He shook his head. "If only you'd found the deed."

Meg smiled. "Yes, if only. I guess it just wasn't meant to be."

HALFWAY THROUGH the Saturday night auction, Meg once again found herself with nothing to do, no place where she was needed. Thinking he was doing her a favor after her hectic weeks in Mount Esther, Jerry had hired a replacement auctioneer for the sale, giving Meg a chance to catch her breath—a nice gesture on her brother's part, but definitely not something Meg needed.

The auctioneer was quite good. He commanded the audience's attention and seemed to be getting good prices. It was while Meg was caught up in his chant and the enthusiasm of the crowd, that a man came up behind her. She wasn't aware of his presence until his voice, husky and soft, and achingly familiar, filtered through the noise in the auction hall and penetrated her consciousness.

"Excuse me," he said. "But I need some advice, and I think you're just the woman who can help me."

She froze. Her hands clenched at her sides. She stopped breathing. The only part of her that still seemed to be working was her heart, and it was beating overtime.

She didn't turn around. Instead she stared straight ahead, willing the voice to be his, half believing that if she faced the source, the face would be different, the man would be someone she didn't know.

"I'll try to help you if I can," she said. "What is it you need?"

"I'm buying a house," he said. "It's in a little town about five hours north of here…."

Her body became liquid as her blood warmed. Yet her skin tingled as if she were caught in a cold wind. "Yes?"

"I have to furnish the whole thing, top to bottom, two floors with six bedrooms, and an attic, too."

Her lips trembled. "My, it's quite a large place."

"It is. And the specific problem I'm having is that I'm trying to furnish it with a particular woman in mind. She's kind of an old-fashioned girl, a wonderful mother, sweet as they come, but stubborn." He leaned closer to her ear. His breath fanned her cheek. "A bit impulsive though. It seems she heard a nasty rumor about my less-than-honorable intentions and left suddenly, sticking me with this big house and not enough people to fill it."

"She did?" Meg gulped, dared to hope. "How was she to know the rumor was false?"

"By asking me."

"Oh. She meant to ask you, she was planning to, but…" Meg took a deep breath. "Maybe she feared the truth, spoken by someone she'd come to care for, would hurt too deeply."

His arm came around her. His hand, strong and capable, covered hers at her waist. "Maybe. But I would never hurt her. I love her."

"You do?" The question was barely a whisper, and Meg wondered if he'd even heard it.

"I do," he said.

"I don't think she knew that."

"That was my fault. For some reason it was difficult for me to say, but I promise to say it every day for the rest of my life, if only she'll come back."

Meg bit her bottom lip to hold back a gasp of shock and joy. "And you say you need furniture?"

"I do." He rested his chin on the top of her head and stared at the platform. "What do you think of that mahogany bedroom set the auctioneer is selling right now?"

Meg smiled. "I think she'd love it."

He raised his hand and bought the bedroom set. "I have to take it back in a horse trailer. But I've brought along a teenaged girl who's right now sweeping out most of the straw. There's a great kid out there helping her. I think you know him."

"I'm sure this woman you're talking about won't mind if a few pieces of straw get stuck in the drawers," Meg said.

He turned her around and she stared into his warm brown gaze. "I hope she won't mind if I've saddled myself with thirty years of debt and sort of included her as well."

When she laughed her confusion, he handed her a contract. "The mortgage is in my name, but the title is in both. It's the only way I would sign it." He smiled at her. "In fact, once Amelia's estate is settled, I wouldn't be surprised if you stand to benefit in some way from my payments. Ironic isn't it?"

She scanned the document, saw her name and his listed as owners. A joint title just as he'd said. "Why did you do this?"

"I figured we'd work something out. Bigger mergers than this one have proved successful. All we need is a little vision and a bit of teamwork."

His gesture was wonderful, kind, beyond her wildest

dreams, but she couldn't help pointing out one obvious fact. "But, Wade, you have the deed. The house already belongs to me...to us...without a mortgage."

He arched an eyebrow at her as he produced the blue-covered document from his back pocket. "There was a little problem with the deed, sweetheart." He opened it to the last page. "It seems your aunt never signed it. That's why it was never filed by her lawyer. I checked with an attorney. It's worthless, Meggie. But I thank you for it anyway."

She leaned her forehead against his solid chest. A low bubble of laughter began deep inside her and worked its way to her throat. It emerged as a full-bodied chortle. "Poor Aunt Amelia," she said. "The tricks her mind played on her in those last years."

He stroked the back of her head. "*Dear* Aunt Amelia, I would say. If it hadn't been for her creative decision-making, I wouldn't be here now to offer the perfect solution to our dilemma."

She looked at him, read the desire in his eyes and knew beyond any doubt that it was all for her. "And that is?"

"That we get married and simplify the title by combining our two names into one. I have no doubt that the marriage will work. The dang house will keep us together for the rest of our lives because it will take us that long to fix it."

She pressed her body against his and relished the feel of his arms around her. And then she tugged him outside away from the bright lights of the auction hall and kissed him in the shadows. When she was breathless with happiness, she looked up into his eyes and said, "It's a deal."

EPILOGUE

THE NEXT MORNING Wade and Meg left for Mount Esther with plans to return later for Meg's car and personal belongings. Jenny and Spencer sat in the back seat of the Mount Esther police pickup truck and squabbled and joked and eventually settled into a routine of video games and license-plate spotting.

When they exited the highway and headed down the county road toward Ashford House, Meg reflected on the turns her life had taken in the last few days. She had lost Amelia, and she thought she'd lost Ashford House and Wade. Yet, her broken dreams had been restored more completely than she'd ever dared hope.

She was leaving Colonial Auction in capable hands, and she planned to open an estate buying operation in Mount Esther. Jerry was happy for her and excited about the merchandise she planned to send from North Florida to Colonial Auction. The influx of items from the antique-rich section of the state would revitalize the auction and allow Meg to remain involved in its growth.

Spence was truly happy for the first time since his father left them. On the ride back to Mount Esther, he and Wade made plans that included home renovations, fishing, and video game challenges. Spence even agreed to serve as Lady Jay's groom for Jenny's upcoming horse shows.

With one exception, Meg's life was moving on a track to fulfillment, and the future of Ashford House seemed bright as well.

Sensing her distraction, Wade said, "You're not sorry about your decision, are you?"

She reached across the bucket seats and squeezed his hand. "Oh, no. I'm still having a hard time accepting that any person deserves all this happiness."

"Then why the frown?"

She confessed her one concern. "It's the money. There were so many people who believed Uncle Stewie hid a fortune on his property. I still can't figure out why we never found it." She paused. "When I mentioned the hidden money to my aunt, she said something puzzling."

"What was it?"

"She said, 'Where there's smoke…' That was it. Nothing more, but I know she was trying to give me some information about the money."

Wade rubbed his finger along his jaw. "I wonder what she meant."

"I think I know."

Meg turned to stare into the back of the pickup. Spencer sat forward and gripped the back of her seat.

"You know about the money, Spence?" she asked.

He looked at Jenny. "Remember that day we went exploring, Jen? Remember what we found?"

She nodded. "Right. The grave."

Wade speared her a look in the rearview mirror. "What grave?"

"The horse's," Spencer said. "Smoky's. It's behind the barn down by the river."

An icy shiver crept down Meg's spine. "Uncle Stewie's horse is buried in our backyard?"

"It's not that unusual, honey," Wade said. "Since I've been here I've heard stories about the locals burying pets in their yards. Apparently it's a common practice around here."

"But a horse?"

He shrugged. "It's not the only strange thing your uncle ever did."

She jostled his arm. Amelia's strange clue suddenly made sense. "Then that's where the money is. Smoky's grave. Hurry up, Wade. We've still got daylight. Let's find it."

Jenny and Spencer led them to Smoky's burial place. A small marker bore the animal's name and stood at the head of a mound of weed-covered earth. Wade and Roone began digging carefully so they wouldn't disturb the remains of Stewart's beloved mare. After a few minutes, Wade's shovel hit a solid object. Ten hands scratched at the earth, finally uncovering an old metal box whose lock had rusted away.

"Looks like we've found Stewart's treasure," Wade said.

Meg held her breath as he lifted the lid.

The stench of mold and mildew filled the air. Wade upended the box, dumping scraps of sodden paper and a pool of slimy liquid onto the ground. He scowled at the puddle and then looked at Meg.

"That's our treasure?" she said. And then she remembered. "The flood of 2002. Mr. Acres at the bank told me about it. It destroyed the files in the office of Amelia's attorney." She frowned down at the soupy mess. "And obviously our fortune as well."

Wade poked among the monetary scum with a stick. "Which might have amounted to a grand total of three or four hundred dollars from the looks of what's left," he said. "These are only fives and tens."

Meg gaped at the slop. "That's all Stewie saved from his ventures, his casino, his scams?"

Roone picked up a slippery piece and watched it disintegrate between his thumb and finger. Then he started laughing. "I wish these crazy old folks around here could see what all the fuss was about."

Wade's response was a slow-building chuckle. "If Uncle Stewie was saving for a rainy day, he sure as hell got one."

Meg joined them until all three adults had convulsed against a giant oak tree.

Spencer backed away. "What's the matter with them?"

"They're nuts if you ask me," Jenny said. "I sure would like to have three hundred bucks."

"Me, too."

The children walked back to the house shaking their heads. Meg fell into Wade's arms and felt the tremors of his laughter merge with hers. The mystery of Stewie's fortune was solved, and it was really very simple. The real treasure of Ashford House wasn't in greenbacks and never had been. The true value of Stewart and Amelia's legacy was its tradition, its lasting ties to the past, its faded glory destined for greatness once again.

As Wade's arms tightened around her, Meg knew

that it wouldn't have mattered if they'd discovered three hundred dollars or three hundred thousand. She had everything in life she'd ever wanted.

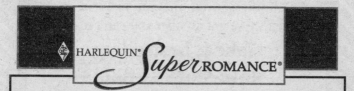

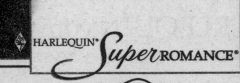

HARLEQUIN *Super*ROMANCE

On sale May 2005

With Child by Janice Kay Johnson
(SR #1273)

All was right in Mindy Fenton's world when she went to bed one night. But before it was over everything had changed—and not for the better. She was awakened by Brendan Quinn with the news that her husband had been shot and killed. Now Mindy is alone and pregnant…and Quinn is the only one she can turn to.

On sale June 2005

Pregnant Protector by Anne Marie Duquette
(SR #1283)

Lara Nelson is a good cop, which is why she and her partner—a German shepherd named Sadie—are assigned to protect a fellow officer whose life is in danger. But as Lara and Nick Cantello attempt to discover who wants Nick dead, attraction gets the better of judgment, and in nine months there will be someone else to consider.

On sale July 2005

The Pregnancy Test by Susan Gable
(SR #1285)

Sloan Thompson has good reason to worry about his daughter once she enters her "rebellious" phase. And that's before she tells him she's pregnant. Then he discovers his own actions have consequences. This about-to-be grandfather is also going to be a father again.

Available wherever Harlequin books are sold.